Excess Baggage

EXCESS BAGGAGE

A Novel

Tracy Lea Carnes

iUniverse, Inc.
New York Bloomington Shanghai

Excess Baggage

iUniverse books may be ordered through booksellers or by contacting:

iUniverse
1663 Liberty Drive
Bloomington, IN 47403
www.iuniverse.com
1-800-Authors (1-800-288-4677)

Because of the dynamic nature of the Internet, any Web addresses or links contained in this book may have changed since publication and may no longer be valid.

This is a work of fiction. All of the characters, names, incidents, organizations, and dialogue in this novel are either the products of the author's imagination or are used fictitiously.

Cover design by Steven Miramontz

ISBN: 978-0-595-47744-9

Printed in the United States of America

for my mom
who was, and still is, always there for me

Acknowledgments

Thanks first and foremost to Janet Brown for her encouragement that I could actually write a novel and for putting up with me during those weeks at the beach in Florida or at her retreat on the reservoir all through the writing of this novel— you're the best and I love ya; to Lew Hunter for persuading me to turn my screenplay pitch into a novel; to my writing teacher, the late Elizabeth Bowne, who made me "slash & gash" my way to succinct writing; to Cynthia Sample, Jerry Ratcliff & Pam Hulse, who gave me incredible support & valuable critique; to Mary Roberson, my best friend and cohort in crime, for keeping my grammar correct and my wit sharp; to my late father, who I miss very, very, very much; to my new friends at UOAA for their support, acceptance, and encouragement for me and my fellow ostomates to live life to its fullest and for their ongoing effort for IBD, Ulcerative Colitis, Crohn's Disease & Colon Cancer awareness; to Kurt Howse, Lea Desmarteau, Lisa Gallegos and to the rest of my friends and family for their love and constant support—I appreciate you all so much.

¹bag \bag *also* bāg\ *noun* Middle English *bagge,* from Old Norse *baggi,* 13th century
1: a usu. flexible container that may be closed for holding, storing, or carrying something: as **a: PURSE;** *especially* **: HANDBAG b:** a bag for game **c: SUITCASE 2:** something resembling a bag: as **a (1):** a pouched or pendulous bodily part or organ; *especially* **: UDDER (2):** a puffy or sagging protuberance of flabby skin **b:** a puffed-out sag or bulge in cloth **c:** a square white stuffed canvas bag used to mark a base in baseball **3:** the amount contained in a bag **4 a:** a quantity of game taken; *also* **:** the maximum legal quantity of game **b:** an assortment or collection especially of nonmaterial things <a *bag* of tricks> **5:** an unattractive woman **6:** something one likes or does regularly or well; *also* **:** one's characteristic way of doing things
—**in the bag 1: SURE, CERTAIN** <her nomination was *in the bag*>; *also* **:** assured of a successful conclusion **:** sewn up <have the game *in the bag*>

—Merriam-Webster Dictionary 2007

The Baglogue

Welcome to the Dart Comfort-Fit 9000 Stoma Support System, designed for optimal comfort and control. First, find the exact size of the stoma by measuring the diameter with the templates provided.

Second, remove the Dart Comfort-Fit 9000 wafer from its container and center the template around the small opening. Trace the cutout onto it.

I will remove the template from the box and place it over my two-week old stoma. I will stare at the staples which keep my insides and guts from falling out onto the Berber carpet.

"God."

I will touch the moist, pink small intestine that protrudes out of the right side of my belly, the stoma. I will place the template over the stoma. The hole will be too big for it. I will take three or four measurements with the template before I will find the right size. I will place the seven-eighths inch cutout onto the back of the wafer as instructed and trace the shape with a ballpoint pen. I will glance at my neglected nails and nervously cut the opening with my cuticle scissors.

Third, remove the Handy-Prep Skin Wipe from its sterile packaging and swab the area around the stoma. This will provide a protective barrier between you and any intestinal discharge which might penetrate the appliance.

I will gently swab the area around the hideous protrusion which is supposed to be my salvation. I will wince at the stinging sensation of the alcohol in the wipe's solution. I will discover that there is no feeling whatsoever between the stoma and my scar.

"I guess I won't be needing my bikini anymore." I will shake my head and stare at my reflection in contempt.

"Why, God? Why?" I will ask.

Fourth, apply a thin bead of Dart Stoma Paste approximately one half inch away from and around the opening of the wafer.

I will pick up the tube of paste, open it, and squeeze an awkward bead of the mixture around the cutout as if it were caulk. The tube will sputter and spray paste inside the opening and all over the marble counter top of the lavatory.

"Oh, for the love of …" I will try to wipe the stuff up with my fingers but the sticky concoction will smear all over everything like tacky glue. Tears of anger and despair will form in my eyes.

"Dammit."

Fifth, attach the wafer around the stoma and apply light pressure to perfect adhesion.

I will follow the instructions but the wafer will barely stick to my skin. It will slowly curl up and out at the corners. I will press harder on the wafer but it will continue to curl up. I will grab some bandage tape and anchor the wafer to my skin. I will smile at my handy work and ingenuity.

I will look at the commode and the basket of Cosmopolitans and Vogues beside it. I will realize I will never again sit on the toilet and read.

I will press harder on the wafer for added precaution. The paste will ooze out around the stoma. I will instinctively reach for a Kleenex and dab at it but the tissue will stick to the paste. In disgust, I will pick out the fragments of the tissue from around the stoma.

I will sigh in despair.

Sixth, the Exclusive Dart Comfort-Fit 9000 Resealable Pouch, with its patented Zip-Tech closure, fits securely around the plastic flange on the wafer. Simply snap the two together and you're ready to go!

Before I will be able to place the bag onto the wafer, the stoma will spew out a foul brown substance the consistency of thick gravy and spit out undigested English peas. The discharge will splat on my bare feet, then splatter onto the carpet.

"Oh, shit."

CHAPTER 1

▼

PAPA'S LITTLE GIRL'S GOT A BRAND NEW BAG

"Paper or plastic?"

"Excuse me?"

"The bag, lady. Paper or plastic?" the checkout clerk asks.

"What difference does it make?" I snap.

"Lady, please, just make a decision here."

"Paper. No wait. Plastic. Give me the plastic," I tell him like it really matters.

He places the contents of my pity party into the bags and hands them to me. I drag myself and my groceries across the parking lot and into my piece of crap compact car.

The drive is quicker to my apartment without the stop and go of rush-hour traffic and I barely have time to ponder my predicament before I turn onto the street where I currently live.

When I pull into my parking slot at the apartment, Jack, my neighbor, is ready to greet me, like he has the last three times I've come home at eleven-thirty in the morning, on a weekday, not including holidays.

"Lost your job again, huh Carmichael?" he says, matter of fact.

"You sit out on the front stoop everyday waiting for me to quit something, don't you?"

"It gives me a reason to live," He tells me as I pull my bags out of the car and slowly negotiate the steep front steps with the heavy groceries.

"Geez, Kelly, you look like a freakin' bag lady," he says.

"Funny, Jack. What are you? My mother?"

"You wish." He takes a last drag on his cigarette, then flicks it into the yard. "Cable man was here again."

The bags burst under the strain of the weight. Cans of Underwood Deviled Ham roll down the steps, a jar of picante sauce smashes, and a bag of Oreos goes crunch as I scramble to retrieve my provisions.

"Should have gone with the paper. Haven't you learned by now?"

"Was he really here?" I ask.

"You owe me eighty-two fifty."

"Oh, Jack, thank you. What would I do without you?" I ask him as I climb the steps with my arms full of junk food.

"Miss watching the 'Beastmaster' again, I suppose." Jack places a box of Cracker Jacks into my overloaded arms.

"Can I write you a check or something?"

"You're kidding, right?"

"No, but I'll pay you tomorrow or the next day. Is that all right?" I smile real big. "And I'll pay you in cash."

"Sure, what do I care? To all of my friends I'm First National Bank of Jack."

Jack helps me with my groceries and brings them into my apartment next door to his.

"Thanks again. I really appreciate this," I say.

"Ah, don't mention it." He puts the Oreos and a half-gallon container of skim milk on my counter.

"Stay with me today and participate in my shameless wallow of self-pity," I say as I dump the junk food out onto the dining table. "I have Ho-Hos and Yoo-hoo."

"Both? You really are on a shame spiral, aren't you?"

"I quit school today, too. My GPA's barely above a two. I can't get into law school on that, so what's the use in applying or, for that matter, continuing?" I shrug, then sigh.

"Well, I wish I could stay but Bennigan's calls, although the Yoo-hoo alone might be worth getting fired over. I'll bring you a Death by Chocolate when I get off work. Sounds like you're going to need it."

I give Jack a hug. "You're so good to me. Don't you want to be my boyfriend?" I plead.

"Sure I do, honey. But you ain't got no dick."

"Life sucks, doesn't it?" I whine.

"You could say that." Jack throws me a kiss and closes the door behind him.

I go to the cabinet and pull out my large jar of Tums and bottle of Mylanta and set them down on the counter by the phone and dial Daddy's cell phone number. I must be out of my mind.

I mean, here I am, twenty eight years old, a college and career drop-out who has been in and out of more offices and universities than Elizabeth Taylor's had husbands. I'm single and still relying on Daddy to make my car payment and send a little extra cash, all right a lot of extra cash, my way each month when things get slim and I can't even afford bologna to eat.

Today has been no exception to my life. I got mad at my boss, a hotheaded lawyer, and quit a decent job as a paralegal, a profession that I am starting to get pretty good at but lack the passion to be great at. Besides, it was a shitty firm anyway. I can do better than that. It wasn't even a firm, to tell the truth. It was a one-lawyer office with lousy wages and long, unappreciated hours of thankless drudgery. He got all the glory. I got all the crap.

I had skipped three days of classes at the college and worked until three in the morning to write what I considered to be the best written and best researched "Motion to Deny Summary Judgment and Brief In Support Thereof" of all time, and it had resulted in a quick and very profitable settlement of Three Hundred and Fifty four thousand dollars to our client, thirty-three percent of which was ours, straight off the top. I felt I deserved a bonus. Tightwad thought otherwise. I could see the job was going nowhere. Much like the last couple of years of my life as a struggling paralegal, I had held this job a whopping three months, sixteen days and two hours. A new world record for me.

I've been pursuing pre-law at Mississippi College, my seventh such institution of higher learning. I haven't been attending college ten years straight, mind you. Just every time I believe that a job or a major is not giving me the satisfaction and fulfillment I think it should, I quit and run back home to Arkansas and to my father, who I know will give me the guidance and wisdom to pursue my next phase of failure.

I don't want to do that anymore. For once I would like to make a career choice on my own. Right now I know the most about being a paralegal. I will resign myself to being one. Besides, I don't want to go home and hear the old pharmacist speech again:

"Kelly, honey, I tried to tell you. Pharmacy school would have been the best thing you could have done if you had listened to your old Dad. But no, you didn't want to take my advice. Well, look where it's gotten you. Nowhere." Dad always lectures me when I come home. Then he proposes my next pursuit of career, such as, "Maybe you should think about neurology. I hear women are doing well as brain surgeons these days."

My father means well. He's a pharmaceutical salesman with a devoted wife and a lovely home in an affluent neighborhood. He's done better than his parents. He only wants the same for me, his only child. For some reason, though, a husband never even enters into the conversation when it comes to my life and future. It's simply Kelly and her career. My high school friends have already fallen into matrimony and left me behind. I have more bridesmaid's dresses decorating my closet than a bridal shop. Everyone back home refers to me as the eternal career girl. If only I could find a career.

Growing up, I can't remember ever wanting to be a doctor, nurse, or lawyer. Mom was a housewife. I just assumed I'd be one as well. When I was little I played house, fed my dolls tea and cookies from my Fisher Price kitchen, and vacuumed the house with my pretend Hoover upright. Then I would bathe myself in Mr. Bubble and complain to Barbie and Ken what a tough day I had, that the sink was leaking again, the kid had a fever and the car needed a new transmission. Just like Mom would do with Dad.

"My daughter's not going to be some old boy's concubine. No sir. You're better than that," he always reminded me. I don't know how many boyfriends my father has run off just because he thought he saw a glimmer of a gold band and a Volvo in their eye. "A career woman is what you will be Kelly girl. I want to see you happy."

So after years of trying to please my father and failing miserably at the task, I have managed to flunk out of pre-pharmacy, pre-nursing, accounting, secondary education, occupational therapy, physical education, and now pre-law. I can't get a handle on anything, despite my IQ being over a hundred and thirty. Nothing my father chooses for me satisfies, stimulates, or interests me.

Between school and work, I've approached burnout and I'm becoming physically ill in the process. But that's what stress does to me. It makes me sick. Tums and Mylanta are my best friends. It's the price I've paid for trying to live up to Betty Friedan's ideals and Benjamin Carmichael's expectations.

I know I should go to the doctor and get this thing checked out. I mean, it's not normal for food to pass completely through you without digesting, is it? But it'll clear up eventually when I get some of this pressure off me. Besides, I can't go see a doctor right now. What if there's something big wrong? I don't exactly have medical insurance. I let that slip almost a year ago. Dad doesn't know and I don't want to worry him any more than I have to. As soon as I settle down, I'll get some coverage and take care of this problem.

Before I left work, I re-did my resume. It looks great. Hell, I'd hire me. I only wish I didn't have so many employers. It was hard to condense my work history down to one page. I heard from a legal secretary I know that Westward, Inc., a huge hotel franchiser, is always needing temporaries, which they sometimes hire permanently. She knew a girl who got on there. Said it was the best place she ever worked. It's worth a try. Memphis sounds better than running home to Daddy and there's definitely nothing left for me here in Jackson.

"Dad? Hey, how are you?" I say over the phone as I shove a Ho-Ho into my mouth and chase it with a swig of Mylanta.

"Hi, sweetheart, I'm great. And you?"

"I'm good. I'm good," I stutter.

"What's wrong?" he asks.

"Nothing really."

"Kel, it's the middle of the week. You never call during the middle of the week unless you need more money or worse. How much you need?"

"I don't need any money, Dad. I just …" I unconsciously take another drink of Mylanta as if it were a Martini.

"Well …?"

"I'm moving to Memphis to take a job with Westward. You know, the hotel chain," I begin. He doesn't need to know that I haven't even applied for the job yet or that I've flunked out of school.

"I know who they are. I just stayed at one of their hotels."

"It's a great company with benefits, high salaries, expansion, and even educational reimbursement. Dad, it's a chance at a real career. I think this would be good for me."

"Honey, that sounds nice and all. Really." His voice is flat. "But maybe you should come home and discuss this first. What about becoming a lawyer?"

"Dad …"

"I thought law school was what you wanted?"

"Dad, I'm sick of this crap. I just want to settle down for once."

"Do you remember Kimberly Simmons?" Dad asks out of the blue.

"Uh, vaguely. I think she graduated high school with me. Why?"

"Oh, nothing really. She's just bought a house down the street from us and Bob Elliott's hired her as a pharmacist. Drives a Lexus, too."

"That's nice for her." My mouth is suddenly chalky. Kimberly Simmons was the acne-riddled nerd of my class who we all thought would most likely end up as a librarian or fast food worker. Who knew?

"It's champagne colored. You know, the two-door model. Really top of the line luxury. Bob got her a deal on it from someone he knows up in Little Rock," Dad keeps on. "Speaking of cars, how's yours running?"

"The usual. What can I say? It's top of the line cheap." I hear Dad sigh into the receiver. "How's Mom?"

"Pretty good. She's taking a class in real estate at the college. She's thinking about getting a job, can you believe that? Like I don't provide."

"Perhaps Mom is bored. Maybe she's ready to get out and experience the real world like us," I say.

"I don't know why she'd want to do a fool thing like that. She doesn't know what it's like out there. It'll eat her up."

I lick the Mylanta taste from my lips. "Just tell her I love her and I'll see you both soon. Gotta run, Dad. I'll call you in a couple of days and let you know my new number. I love you."

"I love you, too, sweetheart. I just really wish you'd think about this, though. Law school would be good for you. Women are making good marks as attorneys these days. Look at that woman on CNN."

"I'm sure they are Dad. But I'm still going to Memphis."

"You're going to do this whether I want you to or not, aren't you?"

"Yes, Daddy. Like I said, I'm ready to settle down. This has gotten old. I'm tired."

"Well, I know people in Memphis. If I can help, you know I will."

"Thanks Dad." You've done enough helping, I say to myself as I hang up the phone and barely make it to the bathroom before I throw up.

*   *   *   *

The next morning I get up with a new determination for my life and drive to Memphis. I've been there before but I never really paid that much attention to it until now. I always thought of it as the place where Elvis lived and ate donuts, not a place where I'd ultimately end up living. Then again, I never dreamed I'd be pushing thirty and still trying to make it on my own.

It suddenly occurs to me that my life is just like Mary Richards on the Mary Tyler Moore Show. I even recall from the reruns that she faked her resume, so to speak, too. I begin to hum the theme music. Oh, God, how the hell did I get here? If I only had a hat to throw up into the air.

I drive past the Peabody and around the corner to where the Memphis Bar Association is located. I was told by my friend that this is where the Memphis legal profession does all its hiring through. I ride the elevator to the fifth floor and enter the small, unpretentious office.

A young woman about my age peers around the corner and smiles. "Hi, can I help you?" she asks in a deep southern drawl.

"I'm Kelly Carmichael and I'm a paralegal seeking employment," I answer with as much Mary Richards confidence and enthusiasm as I can possibly muster.

"Well, Kelly, you've come to the right place." She extends her hand. "I'm Debbie Sinclair. Nice to meet you, Kelly." She says my name again. I never know about people who always speak my name in every sentence. I'm not sure if they're being sincere or downright phony. "Are you looking for something temporary or permanent?"

"I'd like to be permanent, but I'll gladly temp until something good comes up," I say as I take a seat where she is pointing to.

"I was hoping you'd say that, Kelly, because most firms and corporations like to try out temps before they hire. We've found the system works to their advantage as well as to the employee. If you don't like it at one place, then you can work somewhere else tomorrow."

"Sounds reasonable."

"Okay, Kelly, first of all, let's get you to fill out all the necessary paper work and then we'll see about placing you." She opens a desk drawer and sifts through the papers.

"Great, Debbie." She looks up and shoots me a smile, then hands me several forms to complete.

Of course, the place where you put your work history is only three spaces long which will only cover this year. "Would it be all right if I attach my resume'?" I inquire.

"Oh, sure, Kelly. That'll be just fine."

I sit quietly at the edge of the desk and fill out each question: which business machines I can operate, previous addresses, mother's maiden name. Honestly, you'd think I was applying for sainthood as thorough as this questionnaire is. When I finish, I feel like I've completed my entire memoir. I hand her the paperwork.

"Kelly, you have some exceptional experience and background. You shouldn't have any trouble staying busy or finding something steady for that matter," she says as she flips open a notebook and peruses the pages. "Let's see now. Abercrombie, Tucker, and Williamson needs someone with tax experience."

"Forget that. I'm one of those people who waits to the last minute just to file an extension on a ten forty E-Z even when I'm getting money back."

She laughs and scribbles on my application, "'No tax.' Okay, how about personal injury and disability with Harold Lemmings?"

"Lemmings? Didn't I see his billboard on the way in?" I ask.

"Yeah, he's all over the highways. TV, too. Claims he makes house calls." She whispers, "I understand he can be a real son-of-a-bitch. I'm not supposed to tell you this, Kelly, but he's even got a couple of sexual harassment suits pending against him. You didn't hear that from me. Okay, Kel? You're not from here and I'd hate to see you get a bad taste in your mouth on your first job, if you know what I mean?"

"Oh, sure. No problem. Thanks for the tip."

"Okay, let me see. No, no, no," she flips through the book quickly. "That may be it today," She continues to turn the pages. "We get calls all the time. You never know."

No Westward. Well, if I have to wait for it, I have to wait for it. I can handle Lemmings for a couple of days. I have no breasts or ass. He'll have nothing to say to me. But I want Westward.

"Oh, wait. Here it is," She stops at the last page. "I thought this was still open. I haven't placed anyone over at Westward. They're the hotel chain, you know. They've got a spot in franchise and contracts. You have any experience in franchise?"

My heartbeat increases, and I can feel the hairs on the back of my neck stand straight up. This is better than luck. This is destiny. "I just finished taking a class on contracts at Mississippi College if that helps."

"Why sure it does, Kelly. Great, then, that's where you'll go first, starting Monday. Everyone who goes there loves it. They're asking for six weeks, only this order is almost two weeks old. But I've seen them ask for someone for three days and keep them over six months, so you never know. Oh, and they're trying to hire for that position as well. They tried internally but no one bit so they're opening it up to outside applications starting in a couple of weeks." She winks at me. "Hey, you'll already have your foot in the door. I've seen them hire lots of temps that way."

"Maybe so." I nod my head affirmatively as I try to contain my excitement. I don't want to jinx this. I haven't even been in Memphis an hour, and I've possibly landed the job of a lifetime. I take this as a serious sign from above that I have finally made it. When I get downstairs and out into the mall area, I throw my purse up into the air. It lands with a thud and I hear my compact mirror break into pieces. I should have waited for a hat.

*   *   *   *

I scarf down a Happy Meal at McDonald's and drive out to East Memphis, where Debbie told me is the best place to live for someone new.

The drive around the loop is pleasant and I easily find my way to Poplar Boulevard and begin my search for apartment complexes with the Newcomers Guide Debbie gave me.

The first four apartments I tour have no vacancies until next month and are way out of my ballpark price-wise. I'm beginning to get desperate. It's late in the afternoon and I need an apartment this weekend. I turn down a quiet little avenue and spot a high brick fence surrounding a beautiful Williamsburg-style complex of town homes. Expensive looking town homes. What the hell. I've got nothing but time.

The leasing agent shows me the cutest little apartment I have ever seen. Two bedrooms, one and a half baths with a washer and dryer and a covered patio and front porch.

"This is the perfect little place for an up and coming career gal such as yourself," the big-haired agent tells me. "Maybe I can get you into it this weekend." She flashes a grin toward me.

"It's perfect. I want it," I blurt out, not even asking how much the rent is. I look down on the brochure and notice that it's twice the rent I'm paying in Jackson. So what. This is my life. This is my career. I'm going for it.

"You're very lucky, sugar. This is our last unit. If you'd have waited until later to come by, I'd have had to turn you away. That's how fast these units go."

"And I can have it this weekend, huh?"

"For you, sugar, sure," She says as she pats me on the shoulder.

"I'll take it."

*   *   *   *

I pack up all of my belongings in my apartment in Jackson and push them against the walls. I put only what I think I'll need for a week's stay in Memphis into the car. Next weekend, I will rent a trailer and move the rest. I'm not even going to tell my friends goodbye. I've been to so many places over the years that goodbye scenes are just too emotional for me. There's the promises to write and visit but no one ever does. If you just leave town the way you came, you avoid the spectacle of those scenes and the adventure of a new place isn't clouded by any remorse. The only person I've told is my landlord, who hates to see me leave but understands my predicament. He promises to round up his sons to help me move next weekend when Jack is at work.

I put eighty-two dollars and fifty cents in an envelope and place it in Jack's mailbox. I can hear Madame Butterfly on his stereo. He always plays it when his significant other breaks up with him. Then he has to get me to come over and listen to him lip-synch "Une Belle Di" and feel his pain.

I rush to my car without his noticing me. "Bye, Jack," I whisper toward his apartment. I can see him through the window sheers dancing and prancing about his living room by himself. I'm sorry but thankful that my getaway is clean.

*   *   *   *

Armed with the basic necessities in my new overpriced Memphis deluxe palace: a microwave and Lean Cuisines, a television, toiletries, a sleeping bag and clothing, I feel I am set to spend the remainder of my working years here in my new dream apartment and at my new job, whatever the hell that is.

Unfortunately, it's hard to make a good first impression in a knock out Ann Taylor suit with grungy tennis shoes. Dammit. For some reason in the fury of packing, I did not pack my shoes, and at ten o'clock on a Sunday night there are few places to find choice footwear.

I find a discount store a couple of miles from the apartment and choose the only pair of shoes I can find in my size: an obnoxious pair of navy blue low heel pumps made of durable vinyl with ugly plastic anchors hot glued on top. These will have to do. A minor setback on my way to becoming Kelly Carmichael, paralegal extraordinaire for Westward, Inc.

At two o'clock in the morning my beautiful dream apartment turns into a nightmare. I wake up to find that the air conditioner has gone out and it's hotter than hell in here. I open the window and the unusually hot June heat just makes it worse. I call the emergency maintenance number but they can't fix the unit until tomorrow, in spite of my pleading and desperate sobbing. Sometimes it works and sometimes you just have to suffer.

I prop open the refrigerator and move my sleeping bag closer to the kitchen. There's only one bottle of ketchup and a can of Coca-Cola in there, so nothing of significance will spoil. I unscrew the light bulb so that the light doesn't keep me up, but I still can't fall asleep. I'm wide awake now.

I lie here, listening to my intestines churn from getting so worked up and I wonder if I've done the right thing. It's always been so routine to run home. This is the most impulsive thing I've ever done. Usually I let the failure sink in for a couple of months before trying the next venture.

Mom thinks that I'm a spoiled little brat and that Dad has overindulged what she perceives to be a reluctance on my part to settle down. Hell, both my Mom and grandmother wonder about me. They were long married by my age. I've brought less than a handful of boyfriends home to meet my parents. Mom hates it when I go sifting through Dad's closet looking for oversized shirts to wear with my jeans. She just knows deep down in her heart that her only daughter and chance for grandchildren is butch.

I'm not a lesbian. Romance doesn't come along that often for me, that's all. Mainly it's because I hop around from job to job, town to town, school to school. I don't stay put long enough for a second or third date, let alone a commitment. That and no one who's really struck my fancy has come along yet.

But I'd really love to plant roots somewhere. I look around my apartment which is bathed in the glow from the streetlights outside. I feel all warm and cozy in here and not because the air conditioner is broken. It's that same feeling I used to get at Christmas time. It's that sense of home and contentment. It would be nice if Memphis has the right soil.

*   *   *   *

I report to my new career at exactly eight fifteen as I was instructed. I'm feeling a little tired, but I'm determined to make it through the day. I don a smile and pretend I'm wonderful. I can't call in sick or look like there's something wrong. I have enough under-eye concealer on to hide Texas. Despite everything and the ugly shoes, I look pretty good.

A personnel representative escorts me to the law department. He doesn't make any small talk or chitchat. He just points my way toward franchise.

"Go to the end of the hall, take a right, then another right and ask for Glenda," he says. He acts like I've put him out.

"Thanks."

"Yeah, right."

I slowly make my way down the corridor of cubicles. People with their ears to the phones and their hands on their computer keyboards stay busy and don't even notice me. I round the corner and find a rather robust woman eating a donut and drinking a cup of coffee.

"Caught me red-handed," she says as she licks the sugar from her fingers.

"Excuse me?" I ask.

"Oh, I'm sorry, I thought you were my conscience, Amanda, from Risk Management. She's trying to get me into Jenny Craig, but sometimes a girl's gotta live, if you know what I mean?"

"I suppose. I'm Kelly. Kelly Carmichael. I'm the temp from the Bar Association."

"Oh, Kelly. Yes, yes. And I'm Glenda." She takes a quick nibble from the donut. "Oh, we're so happy they sent someone. Morris was getting worried. He'll be thrilled."

"Morris?"

"Morris Jacobson. You'll be working for him." She rises from her desk. "Come on. I'll introduce you to him." She stops at on office door across the hall from her desk. She pauses and looks down at my shoes. "Your shoes. They're so cute."

"You think?"

"Oh, yeah. I love 'em."

I look down at Glenda's shoes. She's got the same pair on only in red.

"You're gonna fit right in here," she says and winks at me as she opens the door.

I follow her into a large ornate office. Morris' ego wall is covered with diplomas and accomplishments: Bachelor's Degree from Yale, JD and L.L.M from Harvard, a Master's Degree from Princeton. The man must be incredibly smart. He sits behind a massive oak desk and speaks Spanish to someone on the phone.

"Si, Si, Hector. But the fact remains, you've got yourself a problem here. I don't know what else to tell you." Morris smiles and waves us in and points for me to sit down. "All right, Hector. I'll talk to you soon. Si. Si. Adios." He hangs up the phone and looks toward Glenda. "This is the temp?"

"Yes. Her name's Kelly Carmichael."

"So tell me about yourself, Kelly."

"I'm from Arkansas. I'm a paralegal. I've taken several pre-law and paralegal classes at Mississippi College. I'm anxious to settle down and work."

"Well, so you are, huh? All right. I've just gotten off the phone with Hector. He owns several Westward Star hotels in Cancun and Cabo San Lucas. I need you to examine the management agreement to his hotels. There's a group in there he wants out. Contract's virtually unbreakable. He's been getting complaints about them, and now he's turned to us to bail him out. Some of his hotels under this agreement have had some serious franchise violations of late. Review the contract. Tell me if you see a way out for him."

"Sure, Mr. Jacobson."

"Morris. Call me Morris, for cryin' out loud. Take some good notes. I like notes." Morris picks up a thick contract and hands it to me. "Glenda will show you where you'll be working. When you're done reviewing it, buzz me and we'll go over it."

I follow Glenda out of the office. "Trial by fire," she says. "He's testing you. He tests everyone. His bark is far worse than his bite. He's really quite the teddy bear. He just wants to see what you can do."

"I'll try not to let him down."

Glenda gives me the tour of the offices and introduces me to almost everyone in the department. Their names swarm inside of my head then fade away fast.

"And this is the supply closet where we also keep the coffee and what not. On Mondays and Fridays Morris provides the donuts," Glenda indicates as she takes a Danish. "What the hell. I'll diet tomorrow."

At this point in the tour, I'm completely lost. I'll never find my way around. This whole department is laid out like a maze.

There are several facets to the Westward Law Department: franchise, contracts, risk management, labor, corporate, trademark, and litigation. Glenda introduces me to Mitzi Tucker, a paralegal in trademarks who occupies the cubical next to mine. Susan Ellis is a young attorney in the office next to Morris', with drop dead gorgeous looks, a model's physique, and apparently a brain to go with it all. Why can't I be that lucky?

"We meet everyday at two thirty next to the file cabinet between my office and Morris' for a Tums break," Susan tells me.

"And we don't schedule any meetings or conferences at that time either," Mitzi adds. "Two thirty is sacred to us. So far, it's been just us two, but you're welcome to join us if you like."

I think I'm going to like this place.

The ultimate highlight of the tour, however, is my office. It just happens to be the largest cubicle. It has a desk which takes up two walls, a round conference table for four, a wall of file cabinets and a computer station. Glenda supplies me with my own e-mail address, voice mail, password, and temporary ID badge. She also supplies me with a file on Del Sole', the management company Hector needs to terminate.

"Well, I'll leave you to it. You have any questions, just buzz me. That's what I'm here for."

"Thanks, Glenda."

I sit at my new desk and look around the cubicle. I open drawers and thumb through the files. I glance over at the computer and spy my reflection in the screen. "You're on your own, kid, and this is it. This is as good as it's ever going to get," I whisper. "Don't screw this one up."

CHAPTER 2

▼

DOUBLE BAGGED REALITY

Daddy always says, "There's a fine line between bullshit and truth. It simply takes an artist to distinguish the left from the right, then erase the line." He's a terrific salesman because no one can tell which side of the line Dad's on.

When it comes to school and work, I tend to stand most notably on the left side, thanks to Dad and his constant pushing. When things are over my head, as they most often have been in my father's choices of career and curriculum for me, it's been a lot easier to bullshit my way through than to admit defeat. I suppose there's actually a fine line between bullshit and knowledge. Because of my vast and diverse schooling and experience, I know a little bit about a lot of things; therefore, it's easy for me to slide through life on a slick layer of ingenuity. The problem with that, however, is the more bullshit you create, the larger the pile becomes, and the smaller the shovel gets.

Everyone at Westward thinks I've got this natural ability for law and contracts. I can't help it if I interpreted a simple little paragraph into a major loophole. I was just doing what I was told and when you're called in by the boss and you want to keep your job, you do whatever it takes. Now these people are singing my praises. I hope they don't figure out I'm some sort of phony. Nothing would please me more than to show my father up by landing this job and getting him the hell off my back, once and for all.

Morris shakes his head at me. "I've had my best people on this and you, a temp for crying out loud, waltz in here and put them all to shame. This is nuts."

"Sir, I just did what you asked me to do. Paragraph 16-B," I say with a shrug as I approach his desk. "If it had been a snake …"

"Remind me not to send my people into the jungle. All right. I doubt very much that if an anaconda were dangling from a tree not a foot in front of them, they'd see it." Morris shakes his head again. "Judas Priest, a damn temp." Morris buzzes the intercom. "Glenda, get me Hector on the phone."

At 2:30 sharp I meet Susan and Mitzi at the file cabinet. They've already selected the flavor of the day: Grape, my favorite, in celebration of my coup.

"Way to go for you, girl. Not so great for us," Mitzi praises then moans.

"Outside looking in, you know," I say with modesty.

"I'll never hear the end of it. I'm head of contracts and I didn't catch it. I should hate you." Susan pops a Tums into her mouth.

"The last thing I'd ever want to do …"

"Oh, no, Kelly, you don't worry about what other people think. You worry about the company. The company comes first. Hell, I'd have done it, too," Susan says. "I wanted in here so bad, I probably did do it. Now that I'm here, I guess I've slacked off."

"So how did you get here?" I ask. "I mean, you don't have an Ivy League diploma on your wall like some of these folks."

"I have no idea," she confesses with a laugh. "I'm just a hick from Delta State, did law school at night, no honors to speak of, worked in an average, run-of-the-mill law firm for five years, applied here and got it. I hope to God it wasn't because I'm blonde, thin, and tall," she says as she pats her hair and shakes her hips.

"Don't let Susan fool you," Mitzi says. "She had an outstanding resume from that law firm, won ninety-two percent of the cases she handled, got lucky and landed contract work with Yellow Dog Productions. You know, the concert people who bring the big names into town." Mitzi smiles at her. "Girl's had lunch with everyone from Jagger to Pavarotti."

"Oh, do go on, girl. But it wasn't ninety-two percent, really," Susan blushes. "It was ninety-three, but who's counting. And Mick chews with his mouth open."

"Mick Jagger? The Mick Jagger? Oh, I'm way out of my league here." I clutch my stomach. It suddenly does a back flip. "Weren't you scared to negotiate those big contracts like that?" I ask.

"Yeah, but it was there, you know. I had to go for it. I just said, Susan, you can do this. I knew enough about contracts to get by and what I didn't know, I made up. Just like everyone else does." Susan removes another Tums from the container. "So here I am."

"So what's your story?" I ask Mitzi.

"I got in the good old fashioned way. Daddy!"

Mitzi, Susan and I raise our Tums in toast. "So here we are."

I shift my Tums from the left to the right side of my mouth.

＊　　　＊　　　＊　　　＊

"Mom? Hi. It's me. Kelly," I say over the phone, as if my mother has more than one child. I really don't think she could handle another me.

"Hi, Kelly, it's good to hear from you," she answers back. "How are you keeping yourself?"

"Fine," I say as I sniff the skim milk for freshness, then pour in the correct amount for my macaroni and cheese dinner.

"How's the new job? Is it what you want?"

"It's going all right, I guess. It's a job, you know. What can I say?" I can't let them know I'm just a temp. With my past history if I don't get on permanent then it'll be a lot easier to explain to them that it was a dead end job going nowhere fast, that I quit and I'm looking for something better, than to have to explain the truth.

"Dad said you're taking a real estate class or something. I didn't know you wanted to go work." I mix the fat free margarine into the macaroni, then take the pot, spoon, and Diet Coke into the living room and plop down on the sofa. "I think it's good that you'll have something to do during the day, plus have all that money to spend on clothes and stuff for the house. You wear the same old thing all the time. You should go buy yourself a wardrobe now that you're going to be a working gal like me."

"Kel, I'm not wanting to work to have something to do," she snaps at me suddenly. "I'm going to work because I have to."

"Daddy's making you go to work?" I ask.

"No. He's not."

"Because I never thought he really wanted you to work …"

"You're making me. It's you."

"I never told you you had to go to work," I defend myself.

"You really haven't any idea, do you?"

"Mom, please. Don't put the blame on me. I left home a long time ago to …"

"You may not live under our roof anymore but you certainly … Do you know how much money your father's spent on you this month? Do you even have a clue?" she asks.

"A couple of hundred, maybe."

"A couple of thousand, Kelly. Thousand."

"Mom, things have been tight with my moving and deposits and all that I couldn't make my car payment but I haven't asked for that much …"

"Six hundred dollars for your Visa bill. Four hundred and fifty dollars for your Dillard's bill, and we're still paying on your student loan from LSU."

I don't say a word. I just mimic my mom's tirade, eat my macaroni and flip the channels on the television set while she goes off on me. I can't help it if Daddy insisted on paying my bills. He didn't have to. Mom's just jealous over the relationship I have with Dad. She and I have always acted more like siblings than mother and daughter. All of my life it seems we've fought over Daddy's affections. I can see why she's hated me all these years. She thinks I've been the victorious one.

"Things have been tight lately since they cut your father's sales territory. He's not bringing home as much, but he's working away from home more than ever. I don't get it. That's the way these corporations work, I suppose."

I stop my mimicking. "When did this happen? I didn't know …"

"Five or six months ago. You just never listen or your father didn't want to get you upset so he just didn't tell you. I don't know."

"Mom, I had no idea." I drop the spoon into the uneaten pot of macaroni and put it on the coffee table.

"Your father's got three mortgages on this house, two of which are to cover your butt. Things have got to change, Kelly. I don't know what else to tell you."

"I'm sorry, Mom. I didn't know."

We say our good-byes and I hang up the phone. Did I really spend that much money? Damn, I hate reality.

*   *   *   *

"Kelly, I need to see you right now," Morris booms over my intercom. Every time he calls, I just know it's to give me the old heave ho. I've been here three weeks living on the edge. I hate being a temp. I push aside the keyboard, lick my lips, smooth out my skirt and make my way toward Morris' office. I sneak a couple of Tums from the file cabinet like I always do before I go into his office, then knock on the door.

"Come in, for crying out loud."

"You wanted to see me?" I ask.

"Sit down," he demands.

I immediately take a seat in front of his desk and clasp my hands in my lap. My left leg begins to bounce up and down and my stomach gurgles.

"You've been here what, a month?"

"Just over three weeks, sir."

"Yeah, whatever. I'm told you've been putting in a lot of overtime lately, true?"

"Well, yes, sir. You approved it."

"I know I approved it. What are you working on?"

"Well, I've been working on the Del Sole' matter, the Alberta Franchising, and adding in the new stipulations to the operations manual, I've ..."

"So what you're saying to me is that you've sort of gotten used to this position, huh?"

"I guess. I mean, it's the job I've been assigned. I'm going to do the work until you let me go," I explain.

"Do you want to go?"

"I don't know that it's up to me, sir. I'm just a temp."

"You do or you don't?"

"Excuse me, sir?"

"I'm asking you if you want to stay here or go somewhere else. What it's going to be?"

"I'd like to stay."

"Then you're hired. I don't have time to try to find someone and train them. Go over to the personnel department and sign the necessary paper work. I'll start you out at mid range salary for this position, seeing as how you don't seem to need much training and all. Does that sound fair?"

"Sir, I don't know what to say." I can't even breath.

"How about 'thank you'."

"Yes, sir. Thank you. Thank you very much." I rise from my chair and take his hand to shake.

"Yeah, yeah, whatever." He waves me off.

"This means so much to me."

"Uh, huh, sure, sure." Morris looks down at his desk and waves me out of his office. "And close the door, for crying out loud."

I shut the door, turn around and lean on the door handle.

There should be balloons, ticker tape or something when you land the job of a lifetime. After ten long years of trying, Daddy's little girl's finally got a real career.

*   *   *   *

I am almost shaking because I'm so giddy from this unexpected turn of events and thankful that most of my day is being spent filling out the necessary paperwork for my employment. I'm so excited I don't think I could do any real work.

There are payroll deductions, life insurance beneficiary forms, dental insurance, optical insurance, and the almighty health insurance form. This afternoon I will have to take a physical from the company's doctor. All routine, I'm told.

"Have you ever suffered from the following: …" the insurance forms asks.

I repeatedly check the "No" column. "Intestinal or Digestive disorders." I think about this one. I lean back in my chair and stare at the health insurance application form before me. My intestines gurgle and my stomach churns. Symptoms from my excitement and the stress of thinking I was being let go. "No."

*   *   *   *

"Way to go girl," Susan says as she pats me on the back during our 2:30 get-together.

"Thanks," I say with a smile. "It's great to be a part of such a wonderful corporation." I'm so excited I don't even feel the need for a Tums today.

"Yeah, well, don't count your chickens just yet," Mitzi cautions. "Westward is in the process of being bought out by some conglomerate out in Phoenix. When they buy, you can say bye-bye to the new people."

"What do you mean?" I ask. Suddenly I need a Tums.

"Downsizing, girl. That's the buzz. Cut the fat," Mitzi explains.

"Where'd you hear all this?" Susan asks as she fondles a Tums.

"CNN. Geez, don't you guys ever watch the news?"

"When do we have time?" I ask.

"We're always here," Susan adds. "You're the only one who's ever home by six."

"Oh. Well, I guess I do have one of the easiest jobs around here," Mitzi gloats. "Sorry, Kelly. All I'm saying is 'don't get too attached.'"

"A Phoenix conglomerate, huh?" Susan asks Mitzi.

"Hamburgers and ceramic tile. Now hotels," Mitzi says. "Maybe we'll all end up in the desert. I love Southwestern design, don't ya'll?"

"Temporary again. Story of my life," I say as I pop a Tums into my mouth. Mitzi and Susan give me a hug.

"Hang in there, Kelly. Morris wouldn't hire you for nothing."

*　　*　　*　　*

"Open wide," the doctor tells me. I open my mouth and say, "Ah."

"All right." He puts one of those Hershey Kiss things on the end of a lighted instrument and looks up my nose as if he's really going to find something of interest in there, then peeks in both of my ears.

"You've got a little wax build up in your left ear, did you know that?" he asks me, like I look up in there everyday.

"No, I didn't know that."

"I'll give you some drops. I have samples."

"So does my father," I laugh.

"You're father's a doctor?"

"Pharmaceutical rep. I bet I have more scratch pads, pens and refrigerator magnets promoting antibiotics and birth control pills than you do," I tell him.

"I'm sure you do," he says, not amused. "You look a little pale. Do you eat right?"

"You mean, am I eating fast food instead of real food?"

"Are you even eating?"

"I'm not anorexic or bulimic if that's what you're getting at. I don't always have time to eat, but when I do, I promise I eat plenty and I take a multi-vitamin everyday."

"Well, you look a little pale to me. You've got dark circles under your eyes. I'd like to get a hemocult test, if you don't mind. Company's paying for it, might as well."

"Sure," I tell him, shrugging.

He hands me two cups. "Urine and stool sample. End of the hall. Give them to the lab tech when you're done," he says. "Oh, and let them take blood, too." He scratches something down on my chart and leaves. Not so much as a poke or a prod anywhere else. Simply routine.

Apparently the doctors or lab technicians who do these tests have never had to provide a sample in a Dixie cup before. Urine is fairly easy. The other, well … When it comes, it is runny and slimy. It's obvious there is probably something wrong. I should eat better, I know.

I sit and wait patiently for the verdict. I have been caught, discovered, like a student waiting in the principal's office to take his licks for cheating. It was only a matter of time.

Dr. Mitchell tells me I must go to the gastroenterologist down the hall. And just my luck, there's an opening in a half hour if I'd like to stick around and wait. What the hell.

*   *   *   *

The waiting room of Dr. Baylor's office is packed to capacity. I find it odd that half of Memphis has some sort of intestinal ailment which warrants a visit to a gastroenterologist. I ask the receptionist is this just a busy day or is it like this all the time. She informs me this is a light day. I won't tell my father about this clinic's patient load. He'll have me pursuing gastroenterology, I'm sure.

After an hour and twenty minutes, I've filled out every form and read every Time, Golf Digest and Highlights magazine there is in the office when the nurse finally calls out "Carmichael."

I'm escorted, not to a cold examining room, but to the doctor's office where he sits behind the desk anticipating my arrival. I feel I'm here for a job interview instead of an examination.

He makes a little small talk with me then finally begins asking the serious questions of why I'm here and what seems to be the problem.

I tell him I've had a bad case of diarrhea for the past few months, probably from my lack of eating properly, what with school and work going on. I feel so uncomfortable talking about bowel movements and diarrhea to someone across a desk. I feel like I should whisper as if I were discussing sex. The pictures of his two sons, his beautiful daughter or is that his wife, seem to lean in closer in anticipation of hearing all of my deep dark secret ailments.

Doctor Baylor has got a degree from Vanderbilt, University of Tennessee Medical School and numerous other certificates and achievements lining his wall, much more than what Morris has on his ego wall. He seems qualified enough. He tells me the intestines are tricky organs and then directs me to follow him to the examining room.

I have no idea what he's going to do. I flash on a visual of the doctor taking one of those lighted instruments with the Hershey Kiss on the end and trying to look up my butt. I almost laugh out loud. If this is the case, I'm running like hell.

Instead, he sits me down on the examining table with his nurse present and listens to my heart then down around my stomach. My intestines gurgle. It doesn't take a stethoscope to hear them.

"I'd like to perform a sigmoidoscopy on you," he tells me. "If you will change into a gown, we can do this now."

"Sure," I shrug. "What's a sigmo ..."

"Sigmoidoscopy. I'm going to look inside of your large intestine and see if I can spot any problems. It's not painful or anything. A little uncomfortable perhaps, but not painful. Don't worry. Relax."

I take the gown the nurse hands to me and I wait for them to leave the room. Then I slip out of all my clothes, including my underwear, as instructed, and into this piece of thin cloth. I realize the room is cold. There is nothing for me to use to cover up. I feel extremely vulnerable.

The nurse knocks on the door and hands me a nightmare, an enema, which she instructs me to use as directed on the box in the bathroom through the door behind me. "Hold it for as long as possible," she says with a smile. I've never had an enema before. They have these colonic spas in California where the stars go to get cleansed. I try to imagine I'll feel all clean and fresh as a summer's rain just like the commercials for douches say on TV.

I do as I'm told and emerge from the bathroom feeling more like I was flushed out with a garden hose instead of purged with the essence of springtime. As I watch the nurse lay out the sigmoid scope thing, I realize I just had the easy part.

"A little bit more," the doctor says. I grab hold of the table with both hands and grit my teeth. I pray that Alan Funt is not somewhere in this building, as I am in a most compromising position. There is a long black scope being forced inside my ass by a doctor I've only just met today. There seems to be some sort of disparity in that as if we should have at least had dinner or lunch, cocktails even, before suddenly jumping into this sort of procedure. He's seeing parts of me I've never even seen before. Somehow, I don't think my mom would approve of this sort of thing. I let out an "Oew" as he tries to force the scope further into a space God didn't necessarily want us to see. If he had, well ... The doctor apologizes and tells me just a little bit more.

Finally....

"Well, you definitely have some inflammation, that's for sure. I'm going to give you a prescription for it. Should clear up in a couple of weeks, especially if you change your diet, take some fiber supplements and eat more fruits, cereals and vegetables. Stay away from milk and cheese for a while. That's about it."

"Huh, the staples of my diet. That's it?" I ask.

"That's it," he replies.

No handshake, no kiss goodnight, nothing. Just a prescription and a couple of words of wisdom. "Thanks," I say as he leaves the room and closes the door behind him. I rub my tender bottom and shake my head.

I have to pay for the doctor's services upfront since I don't have any insurance coverage yet. It's over two hundred dollars. You'd think they'd be upfront and tell you how much it's going to be before they dish out the services. No new clothes this month.

I walk outside, past a brand new Mercedes convertible with "Baylor" on the license plate. I feel more than humiliated as I get into my cheap compact car. I feel used, violated even. How did I even get into this shit?

*   *   *   *

"Oh, Daddy, I think this is it. Westward is definitely where it's at for me. I'm finally here," I say. "I really do like it." We sit in the living room, my first visit home since I moved to Memphis.

"I just don't understand you, that's all," he says to me, the same old speech I have heard more than a hundred times before. Now it's simply ritual.

I pretend to listen to him but my vision becomes more focused on the family photos which line the mantel. I look like such an obedient daughter in all those pictures. Maybe if I had been in real life, we'd be going over paint chips for a Lexus right now instead of rehashing my shortcomings.

"In order to get anywhere these days, you've got to have that degree. When are you going to realize that?"

"Dad, I try really hard. I don't know what's wrong with me. I like it at first, then I just sort of lose interest. I don't mean to flunk out. I just do."

"I really thought you were onto something this time. You're grades were really good last semester."

"Cs."

"For you, that's good. Besides, haven't you heard the old joke?" Dad scratches his head. "Let's see, the A grade lawyers are the teachers, the B grade lawyers are the judges, and the C grade lawyers make all the damn money." Dad laughs. "So see there, you were off to a great start."

"Daddy, don't you understand? I don't want to go to school any more. I'm ready to start my life. I'm restless and bored with it all."

"Nonsense. You don't know what restless and bored is yet and I'm trying hard to keep you from having to experience it." Dad looks toward Mom, who stands in the kitchen, washing the dinner dishes by hand, despite the brand new dish-washer.

"I don't want to be a lawyer, I don't want to be anything right now. I just want to work as a paralegal. I'm pretty good at it, you know."

"Paralegal, huh?"

"Yeah, Dad. They're in demand, especially with skyrocketing attorney's fees. My salary's better than some of the first year lawyers I know. I honestly think this is where it's at."

"School is where it's at for you, young lady. I paid out all that money. The least you could have done was waited until the end of the semester. You only had a month to go. I'm giving you the opportunity for a life. Why do you keep throwing it all away?"

"Dad, I'm sorry I blew all that money, but I told you when I started this semester that eighteen hours and a part-time job was too much for me. I'm burned out. I told you."

"But you could have graduated this December on that schedule. Then you could have rested. You'd have had some time before Ole Miss Law School."

"Dad, I didn't get in. How many times do I have to tell you that? There's no point in me continuing this nonsense. I'm not very smart. I'm lucky to have landed this job."

"Well, you take this little break but come time for summer school, I want to see you in some classes at Memphis State. Title or not, you're nothing without that piece of paper."

I look toward the kitchen again. Mom meticulously places the old grocery store dishes in the cabinet as if they were fine china. She's so lucky. Apart from worrying about me, she doesn't have a care in the world.

*   *   *   *

"Yes, my little sweetheart has gone and made it to the big time in Memphis," Dad announces to all his friends at the bar of the Spivey Country Club the next night. "She's a corporate legal assistant at Westward, Inc., the hotel chain. Got an office, top salary and lots and lots of perks, ain't that right, sweetie?" Dad beams and all his friends smile and clasp their hands together in congratulations. Mom just stands there in the corner, as always, the social bump on a log.

"Well, you could say so, Dad."

"You watch this one. In a few short years, she's going to be running the company, just you wait and see." Dad pats me on the shoulders.

Dad's best friends, Bob and Julie Elliot and Hal and Pauline Tourtellott congratulate me, Daddy's little darling. I watch Mom grab her bag and make her way toward the bathroom. She hates it when Dad makes me the center of attention instead of her. I can't help it. When I'm home for the weekend, the universe simply revolves around me. When I leave, then she can have her star back.

Julie turns around and looks for her. "Where's Olivia?"

"Bathroom," I point out.

"Well, come on, girls, let's go join her. Doesn't she know a lady isn't supposed to go to the bathroom without her posse? It just isn't proper." Julie and Pauline take me by the arm and drag me into the bathroom where Mom stands in front of the vanity mirror, putting on lipstick.

"Olivia, there you are," Julie says. "You know, I'm about to have my living room redone. You've just got to come with me when I start shopping for furniture. You're so good at that kind of thing. I mean, you helped Pauline pick out that wonderful bedroom suit."

"Sure, I'd love to help you," Mom says.

"We'll make a day of it, just us girls," Julie squeals. "And if you're here, Kelly, you come, too."

"Sure," I reply as I check my hair and makeup in the mirror.

"So, how is Memphis?" Julie asks.

"Oh, I love it. It's a wonderful place."

"Job's going good, I hear," Julie continues.

"It is. I couldn't ask for anything better."

"So have you met anyone in Memphis yet?" Pauline begins the interrogation, the reason why they brought me in here. Pauline and Julie are the worst gossipholics I know. They love information and Mom is their codependent. She seems to be one who provides all the fodder to keep their little mill running.

"I've met a lot of people at work and a couple of tenants at my apartment."

"No, I mean, men. Are you dating anyone yet?"

"No, not yet. I've only been there a month."

"Long enough to meet someone and have a couple, two or three dates, though," Julie emphasizes.

"Face it, she's almost thirty. All the good ones have already been taken," Mom comments as she blots her lipstick.

"Oh, come now, Olivia. She's just being picky. A girl's got to be in this day and age, what with all those diseases out there and all." Pauline counters.

"You do want to marry, don't you?" Julie asks.

"Oh, sure. I just haven't met the right person yet." I emphasize "person." Every time Mom's friends corner me, the conversation is always about my love life, or lack of it. I know I'm one of Mom's hottest topics with them. It's a lot of fun to egg them on and watch them try to decide on what side of the fence I like to graze.

"Well just what kind of 'person' are you looking for?" Pauline questions as we all walk out of the bathroom and back into the Club.

"You know, dependable, good-looking, nice sense of humor. A good, decent 'person.'"

"Oh, Kelly, I happen to know just the right fellow for you. He's thirty-one, owns a company, good-looking and a widower. He would be so wonderful for you."

"Julie, now you know better than to fix my girl up with some old boy who's got nothing more on his mind than to make her a mother and a housekeeper. She's better than that," Dad reproves.

I watch as Mom rolls her eyes.

"Oh, come on, Ben," Julie says. "He's a good catch."

"For someone else, maybe, but not Kelly. She's destined for better things, not domestication.

"You're knocking the whole institution of motherhood. What about your wife? And what do you think about us?" Julie demands.

"I love you girls, all of you. You know that. I just think that the days of the housewife are over. I'm a women's libber, just like that Alan Alda fellow. I want to see women living up to their potential. I love women." Dad rubs my shoulders. "And this is my daughter we're talking about here. She's going to make something of her life."

Oh, yeah, I am going to make something of my life all right. I believe they call it Jell-O.

*　　　*　　　*　　　*

I can never come home and not go over to Hampton to see my grandmother, Mimi. I call her Mimi because I couldn't say Memaw. My cousins still call her that but she won't answer to it with me. Only to Mimi. She's my only grandparent I have living, my mother's mother or Miss Alene Jennings as most folks around Hampton refer to her. Of course, everyone there refers to her as the Bird Woman of Hogskin County.

Dad has dubbed her yard as the Jennings Memorial National Bird Sanctuary and Critter Habitat. She has ten hummingbird feeders, twelve regular bird feeders, three birdbaths, and in the summer, her flower garden attracts every known species of butterfly known to man, and she has appeared on the cover of Southern Bird and Bee Magazine no less than three times.

"Hello, Mother, it's us," Mom calls out as she opens the screen door and pokes her head inside Mimi's quaint little white frame cottage.

"Oh, for Pete's sake, get inside this house before you let some more of those damn flies in here." Mimi yells from her vinyl recliner, the usual cigarette dangling from her mouth and armed with a fly swatter with the faded words of 'Faubus for Governor' still partially visible on the handle. "Kelly, honey, what a wonderful surprise. When was the last time you came by and visited your old Mimi, huh? Nineteen eighty-two?"

"Mimi, really. I saw you at Christmas," I tease.

"Oh, yeah, that's right. How stupid of me to forget. I must have that old-timers disease or something."

"Mother, we brought you some tuna salad. Thought you might enjoy some lunch and company," Mom says as she holds the Tupperware container up for Mimi to see, then crosses to the kitchen.

I give Mimi a big hug. She almost squeezes the air out of me, then blows her cigarette smoke into my face. I cough.

"Tuna salad, huh?" Mimi sounds disappointed.

"You like tuna," Mom insists.

"What kind of tuna did you use?"

"Bumble Bee, I think. I used whatever was on sale."

"Bumble Bee's that tuna with the dolphins in it."

"Mimi, they don't put dolphins in tuna anymore. None of them do. Not Bumble Bee or any one of them. It's all Dolphin free. Says so right on the can. I can vouch that Mom's tuna salad is Flipper free," I say as I take a seat on the well-worn couch.

"I saw Sam Donaldson on my own TV say so. And if he says so, then it's so."

"Mother, it doesn't have any dolphins in it. If I had made it with Starkist, you'd complain that it has Charlie the cute little tuna …"

"Kelly, how's your schooling thing going? Are you about to become something yet?" Mimi cuts Mom off. Mom places the container of tuna salad into the fridge, then sits down on the couch and lights herself a cigarette.

"I quit school."

"Oh, forever more, child. Why did you go do some fool thing like that after all that money Ben's done spent on you?"

"I got a job at Westward, Inc. They're the hotel chain."

"You quit school and got a job at some old sleazy motel?"

"No, I got a job in the law department of the corporation which runs the hotel chain. I've got a real full time job now."

"Well, I don't understand all this nonsense anyway about going to school all these many years just to get some damn job at a motel chain. What can they possibly teach you? 'Good evening, can I help you?' 'Can I show you to your room?' 'Please sign the damn register.' What's so hard about working at a hotel?"

"Mother, she's working as a paralegal. She's not working at the hotel. She's not a clerk."

"Oh. Paralegal? What the hell is that? A crippled lawyer?"

"I'm a lawyers assistant," I say. "I do a lot of research, prepare documents, draft agreements, a lot of stuff the lawyer doesn't have time for."

"I get it. You do all the dirty work so he can have time to play golf with the damn doctors, right?" Mimi laughs as she lights up another cigarette. "I tell you, I don't understand you. Must be something in that Carmichael blood. None of Phil's daughters work…. They've all got families to take care of and husbands who provide them with new cars every year and big houses which I've only seen on videotape and Polaroids, but I know they have them. Why can't you do that? Find a husband and settle down?"

"Maybe I want to be more than just a housewife," I say. "Maybe I want to do something else besides watching soap operas all day and squeezing out babies." Uncle Phil's daughters are all housewives. Fat, unhappy, miserable housewives who's idea of work is turning the channel to tune into their favorite soap opera.

"That husband of yours has really done a number on this one, hasn't he?" Mimi leans over and tells Mom.

"Daddy hasn't done a number on me. I want to have a career. It just took me a long time to find one, that's all," I defend myself.

"If she makes it longer than six months, then she can safely say she's had a career. Until then, it's just another item in the grocery bag of Kelly's life," Mom insists.

"I just hope she's been double-bagged."

I hate this. They just don't understand me, that's all. They're housewives. What do they know?

*   *   *   *

"Mom, I've got to go now. Where's Daddy?" I ask as I set my bag in the middle of the kitchen floor and look around for him.

"He's taking a nap in the bedroom," Mom says as she wraps up some roast beef for me to take back to Memphis.

"A nap? Really? That's not like him on a Sunday afternoon."

"Lately, it's been his ritual. The last couple of weeks he's been coming in tired and not eating. He's lost a couple of pounds."

"Maybe he should go to the doctor."

"I think it's just stress. Things are tight around here. The money isn't flowing like it used to. He worries."

I peek into the bedroom. "Daddy, I've got to go now. It's late and I've got a four hour drive ahead of me."

"Oh, all right, sugar." Dad raises up and gives me a hug. "You need any money?"

"Dad, I always need money. That's a stupid question.

"Here, take this and don't tell your mom." Dad slips me a hundred dollar bill. Things must not be so bad after all. "I want you to go over to Memphis State and pick up a catalog for this fall. We need to select some classes befitting a hotel business woman. You won't have to be somebody's assistant long if you play your cards right."

"Dad, I'm not ready to go back to school yet. Maybe next year."

"The sooner you jump on the bandwagon, the sooner you get to play."

"I know but I like it where I am right now," I say. "I'm happy."

"You wait 'til you're a V. P. then you'll see what happy is."

"All right. I'll pick up a catalog." I give in to him and hug him. "I love you, Daddy."

"I love you, too, sweetheart," he says as I leave the room.

"Make him go to the doctor for a checkup. He doesn't look so great." I tell Mom as I pick up my bags.

"I'll try but, you know how he is," she says.

"I know," I say as I walk out of the house and shut the door behind me.

I put my overnight bag in the car, start the engine, light up a well deserved cigarette, pop a Tums in my mouth, and place as many miles as I can between me and misery.

CHAPTER 3

▼

LOOKING FOR MR. GOODBAG

For many years now, I've tried to imagine what life would be like when I finally made it to the big career.

I've often pictured myself sitting back in my leather chair with my feet propped up, a cigar in my mouth, barking orders to my semi-nude Chippendale stripper secretary, my ear to the phone and my personal assistant, who looks amazingly like Brad Pitt, organizing my paperwork and giving me a toe massage at the same time.

Somehow, somewhere, the fantasy fairy got my wish wrong.

I sit here in the utility closet by my office, feeding eighty-two pages of a new management agreement into a fax machine for Hector to go over. It's almost ten p.m. on a Thursday night and Mitzi's waiting for me on the roof of the Peabody Hotel for one of their sunset parties. I've got fifteen pages to go on this lousy fax machine and I know damn good and well that Hector's not sitting there waiting to read this thing as I have been led to believe. No, he's probably sitting under a freakin' cactus tree drinking a lousy Margarita, eating deluxe nachos somewhere, and caring less that I'm missing the Rum Runners, according to Mitzi, the hottest reggae band this side of Montego Bay.

Hector must have heard me cursing his good name. Suddenly the pages start to slide sideways into the fax and jam up. I try several attempts to fax the remaining pages but to no avail. They just won't go. I have no choice but to call Mexico, tell them that the fax won't send any more and that they'll have to wait until tomorrow.

"Buenos Noches, Senorita," I say over the phone really loud, as if I'm speaking to a deaf Mexican. "No habla Espaniol. Is Hector there?"

She rattles off something to me in Spanish.

"No understando Espaniola."

Again, she tells me something in Spanish.

"Okay, porfavor. J'emapelle Kelly. Je suis American de Westward Hotel, Les Estas Unis." You never know if they might understand a little high school French. It's not everyday you get to use it and besides, all those romance languages are supposed to be the same. "Ou est Hector?"

Again, she rattles off something, obviously put out by me. I hate to admit that my father was right, but I should have listened to him when he tried to get me to take Spanish instead of French.

"No understando. Westward Hotelo, United Stato. El Faxo is brokeno. Comprenday vous? El faxo is brokeno. I sendo tomorrow."

I hang up the phone, yank the remaining pages out of the fax machine and give it up for the day.

*   *   *   *

The elevator opens to the roof of the Peabody. I look around only to find that the band is packing up and a few people are still denying that the party's over. I search around for Mitzi but she has long since abandoned me, I'm sure. I make my way around the roof and find myself in front of the duck cage.

"Hello, duckies, it's Kelly. What'd I miss? A bunch of quacks?"

The ducks look up at me and quack.

"You seem like a nice mallard. Come here often?"

"Oh, yeah, all the time. This place really quacks me up," a voice answers.

I look at the ducks, then to my left. A blonde-headed male of average looks and height stares at me.

"Oh, hi," I grab my chest out of surprise and embarrassment. "I don't normally talk to ducks."

"What, are you too good for them?"

"No," I answer in defense, then realize he's being cute and flirtatious. I throw my head back and laugh. "I don't have a problem with ducks, per se. I'm just not attracted to webbed feet, that's all."

He pulls his foot up and pretends to check it out. "Then it's a good thing I don't have duck feet, huh?" he pauses, laughs, then extends his hand for me to shake. "I'm Walt Mackenzie."

"Kelly Carmichael."

"Well, very nice to meet you, Kelly."

"Same here."

"I think the Peabody ducks are quite stunning, waddling around the fountain and all. However, they'd look even better mounted over a fireplace," he says.

"Ooo, no, I think I'd prefer you have web feet than to be a hunter."

"You don't like hunters?"

"I don't know. I just think the animals are so cute. And besides, what did they ever do to you."

"You've got a point there, Kelly. From this day hence, I'll give all the animals I'm hunting a gun, too. I mean, to make it a fair fight, you know."

This guy is way too much. What he lacks in the looks department, he certainly makes up for it with charm. It makes him incredibly attractive.

"Say, this place is trying to close up. How 'bout carrying this party elsewhere?" he points to the elevators.

"I was supposed to meet someone here but it looks like they've gone off without me."

"Damn bastard," he cusses.

"It was a girl, actually. A friend from work."

"Damn bitch, then," he says through a grin, then raises his eyebrows up and down. "But great for me."

"One question?"

"Shoot."

"I'm not the scrapings from the bottom of the barrel for you, am I?"

"Excuse me?" He's genuinely taken aback.

"Never mind," I say. "I don't know you at all. You could be some sort of ax murderer or something. Why should I go off with you?"

"Because, Kelly dear," he says as he snaps to attention and holds two fingers above his brow in salute, "A Boy Scout is trustworthy, loyal and courteous."

"You were a Boy Scout, huh?"

"Not really, but it does sound impressive, doesn't it?"

"If you're trying to gain some credibility, then the truth might help you," I tell him. "If you weren't a scout, then what were or are you?"

"Well, let's see. I went to Yale, actually. Got my MBA from Wharton, and now I'm an accountant with MidSouth Paper and Timber. An accountant. You can't get more credible than that, I tell you."

"Unless you're embezzling from the company."

"Well, they won't let me touch the real money yet, so there's probably no danger of that for me. I have to get paid the honest way."

"And you're parents weren't by chance Bonnie and Clyde, or something like that. You never know. Accountants could turn out to be ax murderers. You never can be too safe."

"My parents own three car dealerships in Tennessee. Cadillacs, Toyotas, Chevy's, the works. I doubt we even own an ax among us. If we need one, we just hire out for all our axing needs."

"Okay, Walt Mackenzie, I guess you pass. Where to?"

*   *   *   *

Walt swipes a bottle of Moet & Chandon from someone he knows at the bar, puts it under his coat with a couple of glasses and smuggles them out. I want to believe this is the first time he's ever done this but something tells me that I'd be living in denial. He excorts me into a white horse-drawn carriage which seems to be waiting just for us in front of the hotel.

"I want to know all about you, Kelly," he says as he pops open the champagne and pours us both a glass. The glass feels ice cold in the hot summer heat and the Memphis skyline looks a lot taller as I lean my head back on the seat.

"You really haven't wasted any time, have you? I've known you a whole twenty minutes already. I know who I am. You went to Yale and you have lots of cars. Ax murderers are not beneath driving and education.

"All right, I've come on a little strong, I understand. I'm Walt Mackenzie ..."

"You've said that already."

"Oh. Okay, I went to Yale, you know, blah, blah, blah ... My parents are June and Walt, I'm a third. My mother calls me Trey but I hate that. 'Trey,' sounds like a TV tray, or breakfast tray, or cafeteria tray. Everyone else just calls me Walt. My father goes by Walter. They own an Oldsmobile, Cadillac, Chevy, Honda Dealership out towards Cordova. I'm thirty years old and I like golf, duck hunting, and football, and I live alone in an apartment in Germantown. Well, not actually alone. I have Bosco. He's a chocolate lab and we both want World Peace and the Cubs to win a series. Now you."

"Me, okay. I'm closing in on twenty-nine. I'm a paralegal at Westward. I grew up in Spivey, Arkansas, home of the Spartans. I did not attend Yale or Wharton, but I have graced the halls of many of our more finer Southern institutions of higher learning," I say as I take a piece of my hair and curl it around my finger. "And I like underwater basket weaving, throwing poetry, and if I can't be a model, then I'd like to be a brain surgeon."

"Very cute, Kelly, very cute," he says. "So where did you get your degree?"

"Um, well, I haven't yet, actually." I gulp my champagne dry. "I'm close but I … I just haven't yet." For the first time I feel completely inadequate.

"But you want to finish?"

"Oh, sure. I was going to go to law school, took the LSAT and everything. I just didn't want to go."

"So, how did you do on it. Where were you going to go?"

"Let's put it this way, a guy at school who took it with me made two points less than I did and he's going to Harvard this fall." I shoot him a flat smile.

"Wow. Why not you?" He pours me another glass. I feel hot. I drink it fast as if it were lemonade.

"You have to apply to get in."

"Good point. Geez. And you didn't want to finish? I don't understand."

"I just didn't want to be an attorney, that's all."

"So what do you want to do?"

"Be a paralegal, I guess. There's a lot of room for advancement at Westward. I'll finish eventually. Right now, there's really no need."

"You say that but don't let yourself get caught in that trap. You need a degree these days. You're too good to waste it all like that."

"Maybe."

The carriage pulls up at the Peabody and stops. "You seem like a very nice girl, Kelly Carmichael." He leans over and kisses me gently on the cheek. "Can I call you sometime?"

"I'd like that."

He helps me out of the carriage and I realize that I'm a little tipsy.

"I should take you home," he offers.

"I can take a cab. But what about my car?"

"We have a towing service. I'll see to it that your car's home before the morning," he assures me. "Come on."

"Okay," I give in, trusting him. He walks me around behind the Peabody, takes my hand in his, and escorts me to a black Cadillac Allente.

"This is your car?"

"No. I don't know who's car it is, I just thought we'd take this one. I want to impress you … of course it's my car." He unlocks the doors with the keyless entry, opens the car door for me and eases me into the leather seat. When he gets in, he lets the top down. "I promise I don't do ax murders. Not on the first date, anyway."

"This isn't a date. This is just a taking me home thing," I tell him.

"Good point. But it is okay if I call you for one, huh?"

"Sure." I try not to sound so overly excited. "I suppose so." I let the hot breeze fly through my hair as we turn on to Union Avenue and head East. The radio plays Magic Bus, the least romantic song for such an occasion, and the champagne gives me a warm buzz which almost seems dreamlike. I look to my left and see Walt, happy and content in his convertible. His profile's a lot cuter than his front. Or maybe the car just makes him look really good. I've dated better looking before but right now I can't remember any of those guys features. They all look like Walt.

I catch a glimpse of a face in the sideview mirror. She's young, skinny and her hair shines and flutters all around her glowing complexion. In the soft golden glow of the street lights she looks beautiful, like a model for a makeup add. I close my eyes quickly then open them again. She doesn't go away. I pull my hand up to my mouth and the image does the same thing. Wow. I sink down in the supple leather seats. Damn, he looks good on me.

*   *   *   *

Always, when things are going pretty good, there comes a time when I hit the proverbial brick wall and slide down it in a big heap on the floor. I cannot get out of bed, eat or do anything. I will even hold my pee until I can no longer take it anymore before I drag my ass out of the bed to go and relieve myself. This is the turning point of my latest life. That, and Walt hasn't called and asked me out on a date like he said he would.

I call into work and try to sound convincing, that I have a bug, I'm throwing up and don't want to spread my germs around the office for anyone else to catch. I tell Glenda I have brought my briefcase home full of stuff so maybe later I'll do some work. "Right now, I just want to be left alone," I say. I'm very good at this calling in and sounding sick. So good, I'm surprised Dad hasn't picked up on it and suggested I try acting school.

I'm forever amazed at the talkshows on TV. There are people with problems I never in a million years could ever dream up, like my husband's got his ex-wives' name still tattooed across his ass and I want it removed, or I'm in love with my grandson's best friend. Please. I lay on top of the pillows on my bed and flick the remote control through the channels at least a dozen times before finally settling on the Weather Channel. There are thunderstorms in Florida, a tornado in South Carolina, and lots of wind in the Midwest. The wind is so bad in Chicago, they actually have some poor soul on location, barely standing, jacket and hair whipping in the wind, microphone hissing, and trying so hard to convince the nation that there really is a lot of wind in Chicago. "It's the Windy City, Bob," I yell at the television set. "Think about it."

*　　*　　*　　*

Lunch comes and goes. I'd eat but that would take too much time and energy. Besides, Bob is supposed to update me on the wind situation by the lake. I surely don't want to miss that.

*　　*　　*　　*

At six thirty, the wind has settled down to a tolerable roar, with Bob narrating over the clips of the Chicago area I've already seen all day. I finally get out of bed and carry my stiff body down the stairs. The mail is scattered all over the floor and I reach down and gather it up. I have a final notice on my telephone. They'll cut it off in a week if I don't pay. "Go ahead, who needs ya? You're never gonna call, anyway," I say to the bill, then the phone rings as if it actually heard me.

I let the answering machine get it, like I've done all day long, to avoid the bill collectors and siding salesmen, the usual callers, and make my way to the kitchen to pour myself a Diet Coke.

"Uh, Kelly, hey, it's me, Walt, the ax murder guy. Sorry I haven't called but, well, I won't make excuses. Sorry. Um, anyway, I'm calling about that date. I guess I'll catch you later. Bye." He hangs up before I can rush to the phone and pick it up.

"Dammit." I throw the bills on the desk, slink down in the chair, and laugh.

*　　*　　*　　*

"Mom, hey," I say over the phone at work. I love toll free calling.
"Hi, honey. How ya doing?"

"Just wonderful. I've met someone."

There is an unusual silence on the other end.

"How long have you been dating ... this person?"

"About a month now."

"You know, honey, I've prided myself in the fact that I've been able to advance with the times. And I've tried really hard to read up on these alternative lifestyles and to understand them. Really, I have. But ..."

I realize that I haven't been playing fair with Mom's emotions. I've carried out my little joke just a bit too far. "Mom, his name is Walt, Walt Mackenzie and I really like him a lot."

"Walt. It's a him? It's a him." I can practically hear Mom dancing around the house.

"He's an accountant, Mom, with a big timber company and his parents own a few car dealerships."

"Oh, my."

"I was wondering if I could bring him home to meet you and Daddy? Perhaps this weekend?"

"Oh. Well, sure. I think that would be wonderful. We're having a barbecue for a few people. Daddy's idea."

"Great. We'll see you on Friday."

I can feel Mom's elation through the phone line as she hangs up the receiver. She's thinking she's almost free of me.

CHAPTER 4

▼

A BAG IN THE HAND IS
WORTH TWO IN THE BUSH

Quite frankly, I don't really know why I do this to myself, bring men home to meet the parents. They always manage to scare them off, one way or another.

One time I brought home a multi-millionaire's son to meet them. Mom doted on the poor guy so much he finally had to tell her to get out of his face while Daddy kept asking him to verify his father's position on the Fortune 500 list. "Now, you did say your father was four hundred and fifteenth, right?" I can still recall Daddy mentally going over the calculations in his head, then saying to him, "Well, that's just not good enough for my daughter." I was crushed.

After that weekend, the guy never called to go out with me again. With every guy I bring home, it's always the same.

Walt's parents are well-to-do, though not Fortune 500 rich. I just know Daddy's going to ask him how big a diamond he plans on getting me.

"Sir, I plan on giving your daughter the Hope Diamond," Walt will say, whereupon my father will most likely reply, "Son, that's just not good enough."

"You look tense. Is something wrong?" Walt asks as he leans over and touches me on my leg. Despite the top being down on an unusually hot September day, I'm almost cold. "My parents aren't like yours."

"Oh, sure they are."

"My mom won't leave you alone. She'll cram cookies, roast beef and cake down your throat in order to make a good impression and Daddy won't like you at all. He'll think you're not good enough for me to date."

He laughs. "My folks were the same way. Didn't you notice? My father couldn't take his eyes off of you, he thinks you're just the best thing in the world. Now my mother, on the other hand, well …"

"Well …?"

"She thinks you're a golddigger."

"A golddigger?!"

"Yeah. She thinks you're just after our money."

"That's not true. Do you think that?" I ask.

"If I brought home a Kennedy or Rockafeller, she'd think she was a golddigger. So see, our parents are a lot alike. They only want the best for us. I just know how to charm 'em." He says with a cheesy grin.

"Yeah, well, don't hold your breath."

*   *   *   *

"God, Mom, I just know he's ruining it for me out there. I should never have left them alone," I say as Mom, Pauline, Julie and I watch from the kitchen window as Daddy and Walt fire up the grill. Hal and Bob watch. Daddy does all the talking. Walt sips his beer and nods.

"And ya'll wonder why I'm not married yet." I turn around to see Mom pulling out ingredients for cookies.

"You think Walt likes oatmeal raisin cookies or would he prefer chocolate chip?"

"Mom!" I roll my eyes at her and throw my arms up into the air. "I give up. He's going to think you're planning the wedding already while Daddy's trying to decide which gun to use on him. I give up."

"Don't be silly, Kelly. If he wants you, he's gonna get you, despite what Liv and Ben do to him," Julie says with a laugh.

"And he's a good catch, too. Rich and good looking," Pauline adds.

"And a bird in the hand …" Mom says and points her finger at me.

"Mom, I don't even know what that means."

"It means hang on to this one, honey!" Julie squeals. "He's got his mind made up."

"I think he does, too, but don't tell Daddy," I reply.

Daddy and Walt walk into the kitchen, arm and arm.

"I like this boy, Kel," Daddy says.

"You do?" I'm completely caught off guard. "I mean, you do. Great."

"We've got a lot in common, the two of us," he says as he pats Walt on the back and fetches him another beer. "Why we were in the same fraternity and everything. Yep, I like this fellow."

Walt stands in the middle of the kitchen and gloats as Mom offers to bake him cookies.

*   *   *   *

"So Daddy, you really did like him, huh?" I ask him over the phone the minute Walt leaves my apartment and I unzip my overnight bag.

"As a person in general or for a husband?" Daddy says, not really asking.

"Well, you know," I say and bite my lower lip.

"He's an ass kisser, Kel. He uses people. When he's done, then he's done. What else can I say?"

"But I thought you liked him." I knock the suitcase off my bed. My underwear and socks sit in a heap on the floor. I kick them across the room. "You said so all weekend."

"What did you expect me to say? We practically spent the entire weekend in front of our friends. 'Sorry, bud, but you're not good enough for my daughter.' How would that have looked?"

"That hasn't stopped you before." I make my way down the stairs.

"Kelly, you've got a fantastic future ahead of you. Why are you trying to spoil it?"

"Because I like him and if he asks me, I want to marry him. For once I would like your approval on something I want. Not just what you want."

"Kelly, look, you're going to do whatever you want to do anyway, whether you get my approval or not. I'm simply trying to spare you the frustration of going down the wrong path. You've never been one to make decisions for yourself. You've always chosen the wrong thing or nothing satisfies you once you make it half way through the process. Look at your track record, for god's sake. I believe you deserve better than Walt Mackenzie. I don't want to see him break my little girl's heart."

I open the kitchen cabinet, grab the Mylanta and drink from the bottle. "Daddy …"

"I mean it, Kel. You just wait and see. Just like your job. It's not going to last."

"You haven't even noticed that I made my car payment this month without asking you for any money," I whine.

"But did you pay your light bill?"

"Yes, Daddy, I paid my light bill, my cable bill, and my credit card. So I won't eat this month."

"Really, Kelly. I'm serious."

"I'm serious, too. I'm making it just fine without you." I drink another sip of the antacid.

"Well," he responds followed by a long silence.

"How are you feeling? You seemed tired all weekend. More than my last visit. You didn't even take Walt to play golf."

"I don't know. Maybe I'm getting older. What can I say?"

"You're not old, Daddy."

"You sure you don't need anything?"

"I'm sure," I say. "I'm doing terrific. I've got it together and I'm happy for once."

"Watch out for this guy. I don't want my daughter's heart broken."

"Daddy, he's not like that."

"Don't say I didn't warn you."

We say goodbye as I chug the remaining liquid from the bottle, hang up the phone, then wipe my mouth with my sleeve.

*   *   *   *

So how do you like pastel colors?" Morris asks me as he sits down at the table in my office.

"What does that have to do with franchising in Alberta?"

"It doesn't. I just didn't know an easier way to break it to you that we've been transferred to Phoenix."

"But I just got here to Memphis." I glance down at my watch. Almost an hour before the Tums break.

"So you'll get situated again in Phoenix. This time the move's on the company and a raise for your trouble. So what."

"Is everyone in this department going?"

"No."

"Why me?"

"Because I asked for you to be. For cryin' out loud, Kelly, it's an honor to be asked. Some people aren't this lucky and they've been here more years than you. You've been here, what? Months? Just be a good puppy and take the bone."

"Phoenix?"

"Memphis in the desert, only instead of white frame houses with front porches, you have adobe houses with no front porches. Big deal. It's still the same job. Still the same Big Mac."

"So I'm moving to Phoenix." A million miles away from my parents. I smile. A million miles away from Walt. I frown.

*   *   *   *

"I don't believe this. I don't freakin' believe this." Mitzi shakes her head. "You're going, and you're going, but I'm staying here. I don't get it. I'm the one who loves Southwestern design. This is not fair."

"My husband's not going to like this but I want to go," Susan states. "He's a teacher. I make more than him. Me moving up means I can provide a better life for our daughter. For once it's about me. Besides, what can he possibly give her?"

"It's hot out there," I comment.

"But it's dry heat. No humidity. Talk about paradise," Mitzi explains.

"Which means my skin will turn into lizard hide all by itself," Susan laments.

"I can't believe they wouldn't ask me to go. I mean, I have a degree from Vasser. I've been here six years." Mitzi shakes her head again.

"You have a small workload as it is. Everyone's envious of you," I say. "You get home by six. We're still here at eight. Two people could do what you do and still get their work done. That's why you're not going."

"What will you do?" Susan asks.

"Go to work for my father and brothers in their law firm, I suppose. Less money, twice the hours, and under their control. It's just not fair."

"Sorry, Mitz," I say and hand her a Tums. She pops it into her mouth followed by three more.

"Phoenix, huh?" Susan raises her Tums.

"Yeah, Phoenix," I toast, "and I don't even like cactus."

*   *   *   *

"Daddy, what a surprise," I say into the phone. "I was going to call you."

"Well, I know you're busy and all at work, but …"

"What's wrong?" I sit down in my desk chair.

"Well, I went to the doctor this morning."

"And?"

"And, well … they think I have hepatitis."

"Oh, Daddy."

"Well, it's curable, treatable, you know. They should get the results back tomorrow but the doctor's pretty sure that's what it is. I have jaundice, I'm tired, run down. That's me lately."

"I'm glad you finally went to the doctor. Mom and I have been worried sick about you."

"I know."

"You want me to come home?" I ask.

"No. Let's see what the tests say. I'm sure it's nothing. If it's something worse, well, then you come."

"Sure, Daddy."

I hang up the phone and sit back in my chair and sigh. How the hell am I going to tell him about Phoenix?

A lawyer from labor law saunters by my door singing. "It never rains in Phoenix, Arizona."

"Hey, Douglas, that's Southern California, you doofus, not Phoenix," Mitzi scolds. "Cut it out."

"Make me," he answers. "Well, I've never been to Phoenix. But I kind of like the weather," he continues.

"Rub it in, Doug. Rub it in, why don't you?" Someone else yells from an anonymous cubicle.

"Do you know the way to Phoenix, A-Z? Do, do, do, do, do."

"I'm warning you, Doug …" Mitzi yells.

"By the time I get to Phoenix, you'll be gone …"

I look out of my door in time to see a paper weight fly up and over Mitzi's front cubicle wall. It hits Doug square on the forehead and knocks him out cold.

   ✳   ✳   ✳   ✳

"I don't have to take it, you know. It's just the job of a lifetime, for me anyway," I say to Walt as we lay in bed together at his apartment.

"If you don't want to take it …"

"So you want me to stay?"

"I want you to do what you want."

"I don't know what I want."

"And that's your problem. You've never known what you want because Daddy has always made the decisions for you. And you haven't liked what he's chosen for you so far," Walt says. "I don't want this decision on my head."

"But what if I make the wrong choice?"

"So what. I mean, at least you're in the driver's seat now. Put your foot on the pedal and drive. If you don't like that direction, turn the damn car around."

"If this was your job, what would you do?"

"Take it in a heartbeat. Sometimes a transfer's the only way to move up in a large company."

"So, I guess I'm going to Phoenix."

"Then what about us? Are you just going to forget about us?"

"Okay, so I'm not going to Phoenix," I say.

"I mean, we can't keep up a relationship long distance. I don't want that. And I'm definitely not going to give up my job to go to some shithole in the desert," he says.

"You think Phoenix is a shithole? Have you ever been there?" I pull the covers up around me.

"Have you?"

"I asked you first," I insist.

"No, I've never been there, but …"

"Then you don't know. You might actually like it out there."

"The guy does not follow the girl for her job. The girl follows the guy. That's the way it is."

"Why? Why is it the way it is?"

"It just is. It's the unwritten rule."

I grab my clothes and begin turning them right side out to put them on.

"Where are you going?"

"Phoenix."

"Wait, wait …"

I stop and turn around.

"Don't go."

"I'm tired. It's late. I don't want to argue."

"No, I mean, don't go to Phoenix."

"Why?"

"Because things are really good between us, that's why. And I don't want you to go."

"And you won't go with me …?"

"I make a lot more money than you, Kelly. I'm up for promotion. If I was to go with you, I'd have to start all over again. I'm not playing for the same stakes as you. I have a Master's Degree from Wharton. I've sealed my fate with this company. You've got what? … Some college and a couple of years of experience? Think about it, Kelly."

I drop my shoes in defeat.

"Don't throw it all away. You've got a good thing, here."

"So what are you saying?" My stomach does a flip flop.

He pauses. "That's it. Don't walk away from a good thing here. That's all I'm saying." He gets up from the bed, goes into the bathroom and shuts the door.

I sit naked on the bed with nowhere to go.

*   *   *   *

"Kelly, baby," Daddy says softly on the phone, almost in a whisper. I sit in my office and push my work aside. "You better come home."

"I'll be there tonight, Daddy." I hang up and knock all my papers off the desk. It does not relieve my anxiety. It's not even ten o'clock in the morning yet, and I do believe I can eat whatever Tums are left in the file cabinet. I make my way to the stash and peer into Mitzi's cubicle. She has all her personal effects boxed up.

"Hey, Mitz. You going to be all right?"

"Sure, Kelly. What's the difference between now and six months from now. I was going to have to leave anyway."

"He shouldn't have done that. I heard you warn him."

"Well, Doug doesn't see it that way. He's threatening to sue me."

"Doug's a lot of hot air. I doubt he'll sue you. Too many witnesses on your side."

"Maybe you're right," Mitzi says as she tapes up a box and wipes her eyes. "It's just not fair, that's all. Look at you. You're moving up and I'm moving out. God, Kelly, how I envy you right now."

CHAPTER 5

▼

FOR WHOM THE BAG TOLLS

Daddy didn't look ill when he came here to the hospital. Not hospital sick anyway. He looks like the picture of vitality ... well almost. His yellow skin and a cigarette hanging from his mouth doesn't exactly paint the Surgeon General's portrait of perfect health but apart from that, Dad still looks like Dad. My Dad.

He places his jacket around my shoulders as we stand in the hall outside the doctor's office waiting for the results of his tests. The hospital corridor is cold. The longer we wait, the colder it gets. Finally, the doctor emerges from his office.

"So what did you see?" My father asks as he smashes out his cigarette and mindlessly reaches for another. No one seems to notice the 'No Smoking' sign displayed prominently in front of him.

The doctor doesn't even scold him about the hospital policy. He looks like he could use a smoke himself. "Ben, I'm not going to sugar-coat this. It's not good. There's something on your liver and pancreas."

"How bad?" Dad takes a long drag.

"We won't know until we get in there."

"When do you want to do this?" Dad questions.

"Tomorrow."

"No week-long vacation with my family before all this?" Dad sucks hard, pulling in every ounce of nicotine he can from his cigarette. "I mean, if I'm going to …"

"If we don't do this now, you'll be dead before mid-week." The doctor shifts his stance.

My mom sits down on the window sill. Suddenly the temperature in the hallway soars. I can't catch my breath. My father's face is void of expression.

"I see."

"Ben, we've got one of the best staffs in the country here. I'd let them cut on me."

"Okay. Do what you have to do."

"All right." The doctor gestures for us to get moving, as if my father's going to croak right here in the hallway if we don't get him to a room quickly. "We'll put you up on seventh, the VIP wing, my request. Just go to the nurses station up there and they'll get you checked in."

"Sure."

Dad just stands there, dazed. Mom reaches for her cigarettes and lights one as the doctor marches down the hall and out of sight. "I think you need a second opinion. M. D. Anderson is where you need to be. They've got …"

"No," Dad cuts her off.

"They're the best, Ben. You need the best."

"These people know me here. They don't know me from Adam down there. I'm staying here." Dad slowly makes his way down the hall, toward the elevator, leaving me and Mom behind.

"Ben … Ben …" My mom calls out. "Ben … I think we should discuss this."

I look at Mom, then toward my father, who has already punched the button to summon the elevator. Mom gathers her things and rushes after him. This whole moment is so surreal to me. These sorts of things happen to other people. TV people. I can't possibly go on without my Dad. My mom and I barely get along. God wouldn't do this to me.

*   *   *   *

Dad's room is private with an extra bed for Mom. I suppose the recliner is for me. Our nurse tells us that Senator Wheatley occupied this room last month when he had gallbladder surgery. Why can't my Dad just have gallbladder surgery? That's pretty routine.

Mom finds the telephone with its extra long extension cord. She sits out in the hallway, makes phone calls, asks questions of people, and basically gets educated on becoming a wife of a cancer patient. Dad and I can hear her talking to some airport reservations clerk about getting a flight for tonight to Houston. Dad just shakes his head.

"What are they going to do for me there that they can't do for me here? Huh?" Dad asks me.

"I don't know. Mom just seems to think they're the best."

"They didn't do anything for Eddie Graham. He died anyway. Barbara said the place is so big you get lost. So many people," Dad says and leans back on the bed.

"Eddie Graham died?"

"Last year. I didn't tell you?"

"No. I didn't even know he was sick." Eddie Graham was a neighbor who lived up the street from my parents. I guess Barbara, his wife, still lives there. Eddie was famous in our neighborhood for erecting at Christmas a Santa Claus dressed in hunting clothes who sat in a duck blind and pointed a shot gun at the cute homemade wooden mallard ducks which decorated the Tourtellots lawn. It made the papers and everything. Dad even helped him build the duck blind. Since I moved away from home, I've sort of lost track of Mom and Dad's friends and neighbors. I hate to hear that Eddie's gone. But everybody reacts to cancer differently.

"Are you scared, Dad?"

"I don't know."

"They don't give you much time to prepare, do they?"

"No, they sure don't."

"What would you do if they did give you time?"

"Probably nothing special anyway … except worry. I don't really feel like worrying right now. I just sort of feel like resting." Dad closes his eyes.

"You want me to leave you alone?"

"No." Daddy takes my hand and holds it. "You just stay right here. I don't get to see you much anymore now that you've gone off and become a career girl."

"I thought that's what you wanted me to do."

"I just want you to be my little girl right now."

I move over to the edge of the bed and sit next to Dad, like I used to do, nuzzling close in the safety of his embrace. All of my problems would simply vanish when he would hold me close and whisper, "It's all right, Kelly, dear, it's all right. You're just fine. I won't let anything happen to you." This time, though, it's me who holds my father close. We just sit there together and contemplate tomorrow in our own minds as Mom sits outside the door and tries desperately to make this moment go away through a phone call or two. "It's going to be all right, Dad," I whisper. "You're going to be just fine."

✳   ✳   ✳   ✳

Mom's phone calls bring her the support group she needs. Even the pastor of my parents' church is here despite their lack of attendance. He pats my mom on the back, consoles her as if she were a front row Methodist, then asks for all of us to bow our heads in prayer. I guess it's worth a try. I'm not hugely religious and I'm especially not one for praying in public. I think it's fake. I've already said my own little prayer, so this is like extra credit supplication as far as I'm concerned. But hell, anything for Mom.

As Brother Carroll goes on and on, I know I'm supposed to be praying but I can't help thinking of Dad and what kind of lives are we going to have after he comes out of surgery. Cancer. My grandfather died of the shit, an awful horrible death. I was just a little girl at the time. Mom sat at his side through most of it and all I can remember is the suffering and the imposition on everyone. And I remember my mom saying, after months and months of agony on everyone's part, "It would be a blessing on us all if he were to go." And finally he did. I could never imagine wishing someone to die. I guess her little 'prayer' has always stuck in my mind. I hope she's not praying for that now.

The Elliotts and Tourtellots are here—the inner circle. They're always there for each other. Julie and Pauline for Mom. Bob and Hal for Dad. I'm here by myself. I guess I don't need consoling. It's just surgery. Dad's going to be fine. I know it. I told Walt not to come, that I'd be just fine. I lied to him and told him it wasn't serious. He knew better but honored my wishes and stayed in Memphis.

I'd call a couple of friends who live here in the area but I don't want to put them out. I know I'd hate to sit in a waiting room with them if the tables were turned. Their Dads are in perfect health. I wouldn't want to ruin their Saturday.

Mimi's here. That's probably all I need or can handle as far as a support group anyway.

"Damn hospital," she swears. "You know, I've had my breasts removed, half a lung gone, a good size portion of my intestines extracted, got one good kidney left," Mimi lists, counting on her slim, long fingers, "survived a bad case of shingles, scarlet fever, too, and to top it off, got rheumatoid arthritis and I'm only eighty some-odd years old, for Christ's sake. Ben's had what, his damn tonsils removed? Give me a break."

"This is cancer, Mimi," I say. "They're almost sure of it. That tops ..."

"What the hell do you call a radical mastectomy, elective surgery? Think I had those babies sliced off because they were sticking out and in the way?"

"I was only saying that ..."

"You know, you'd think these damn doctors would come out here and keep the family informed from time to time so they don't have to sit here for hours on end in the dark." Mimi rattles on.

"Mimi, we've only been waiting about fifteen minutes. He's probably not even under yet," I explain.

"Well, still. I need a smoke," she says as she fumbles in her oversized and over-stuffed purse for her cigarettes. "Damn hospital policy making us smoke outside in the weather. Gonna catch my death yet." Mimi rises from her chair and shakes her cigarette case at me. "These damn things are the key to a long life, I'm telling you, girl. You want one?"

"No thanks, Mimi. I don't care for one right now. Maybe later."

"Well, would anyone care to escort this unescorted lady out to the designated smoking area or is the South truly dead?" Mimi demands.

"Mom, I'll go with you. I need one, too." My mother makes her way with her support group in tow, leaving me with Brother Carroll.

It doesn't take the preacher long to feel the duty of breaking the silence. I was beginning to enjoy the quiet. "You don't smoke. That's good. Real good."

"I smoke sometimes. Just not in front of my mother. I'm almost thirty years old. Go figure."

"Well ..." He has no answer. "Care for a Cert?"

"Not really, but thanks." I've eaten three rolls of Tums already. Close enough.

"So you're still in college?" he asks.

"No. I'm out now."

"Oh, yeah. You're a legal secretary, right?"

"Paralegal. I have a secretary."

"Oh. You're father mentioned you work for a law firm or something like that in Memphis."

"I work for Westward, the hotel chain, in their law department."

"You enjoy the big city?"

"Well, if you call Memphis the big city I suppose. They're thinking about sending me to Phoenix, though."

"And you like it there?"

"I don't know. They haven't flown me out there yet. They're just talking about it right now. We'll see."

"I went to Phoenix once as a missionary on my way to California …"

I pretend to listen to him but my thoughts are elsewhere. I watch as a woman about my age comes into the waiting area, alone. She sets her Dooney & Bourke bag down, then rummages through a pile of magazines and chooses a year old Cosmopolitan. She sits and nervously flips through it, looking up from time to time and smiling at me. She is so beautiful sporting clothes I'll never in a million years be able to afford. She wears a diamond necklace and matching bracelet with diamonds so large I can see them from here. She fondles the bracelet and fidgets with the necklace as she glances toward the double doors of the operating room.

No wedding band. She's all alone. I feel sorry for her, keeping watch over a relative or boyfriend all by herself. I feel an instant kinship toward her that I can't explain.

I realize that I am staring at her and direct my attention back to Brother Carroll as Mom and her crew return. The smell of Benson & Hedges and Virginia Slims replace the sanitized air of the waiting room. A young couple have followed Mom into the room. They sit next to each other on the opposite wall from where we sit, near the single woman. They hold hands and stroke a well worn Raggedy Ann doll. They look up from their vigil, stare at us occasionally, and give a sympathetic nod or flat smile toward us as we return the same. So does the single woman. Welcome to the Waiting Club.

$$*\qquad*\qquad*\qquad*$$

Three hours later a surgeon pops out of the double doors. All eyes turn toward him. The waiting couple rise and wring their hands for the news. He's here for them. The doctor smiles and escorts them aside to a private little room to talk. I can see their heads through the small window in the door. The woman cries, then hugs her husband and the doctor. Faint laughter filters through to the waiting room. Our group looks around at each other. We hope we'll hear the same news.

The smokers don't say a word to each other. They just grab their packs of cigarettes and solemnly withdraw from the scene, leaving me alone once again with Brother Carroll. I pretend I'm really into this article on Lyme Disease and avoid any contact with the preacher. Our doctor suddenly bursts through the double doors and my heart begins to race.

"Where's …"

"Gone out to smoke," I answer.

The doctor does not display any expression on his face.

"Shall I get her?" Brother Carroll responds.

"That would be nice," the doctor answers.

"How is he?" I ask.

"Well ..." the doctor scratches his chin. "Why don't we wait for your mother."

"Oh, okay." I try to be matter of fact. Instead I feel like a minor, like I'm not old enough to hear. It's nothing probably. He's a busy doctor. He just doesn't want to tell it to us twice.

The group dashes into the room and the doctor escorts my mother and me into the private little cubicle. Through the window I can see everyone watching for the reactions on our faces. Even the single woman stares at us intently.

"Olivia, I promised I'd be straight forward with you." He pauses, then wipes his chin. "It's not good."

Mom sits down in the chair. I can feel the blood flowing away from my cheeks.

Outside the room, I can see Brother Carroll turn toward the group and shake his head.

"Basically we had to re-route his liver. We've fashioned a sort of bag for his bile to drain into, on the outside, kind of like an ostomy. The cancer is widespread throughout the liver and the pancreas. We'll be starting him on chemo and radiation in the next few days."

"Is he going to recover?"

"I'm not going to make any predictions until I see how he responds to the treatment," the doctor replies. "He's a strong man in fairly decent shape. We'll just have to wait and see." The doctor pats Mom on the shoulder, gives me a sympathetic smile, then exits the room.

Our support group peeps in. Then Julie and Pauline rush to Mom and cry. Hal and Bob walk back into the waiting room. This has got to be hard on them. This is their best friend. I suddenly feel very mortal.

I look for someone to cry with but all I see is Brother Carroll looking my way to be the shoulder. For some unknown reason I search for the single woman but she is gone.

Luckily Mimi grabs my hand and whisks me down the hallway to a quiet corner.

"You know your mother is a very fragile person. This whole thing could send her over the edge."

"Mimi, I don't ..."

"I'm telling you, child, you're going to have to be the cement that holds everyone together. I know you and Livy have your differences, but you're going to have to drop it and help each other. She's absolutely dependent on Ben and now he won't ever be the same."

"But he'll get better with the …"

"I know what I'm talking about. I've been there, where your Mother is now. This ain't no piddly lump. I saw the doctor's face.

"No, it's not."

"Well, then, you're going to have to give up the little selfish act and think of someone else for a change," Mimi orders, dumping the grouser trademark and turning stoic on a dime. "Damn lump." Mimi pulls out a handkerchief from her purse and begins to sob as she pushes me back toward the group and my mother. "Go on. Go be some cement or something. I need a goddamn cigarette."

I can't believe what my grandmother just said to me. I know this is going to be a tough time. Lots of families have tough times. But Dad's going to be just fine. And I'm not selfish, I lament to myself. I sit down on a chair in the waiting room to sulk. How can I possibly be cement when I have nothing to bond to?

"Oh, you dear child," Brother Carroll kneels down to me and grabs my hands. "We must pray now."

Dear Lord, please rescue me from this hell!

∗   ∗   ∗   ∗

Phoenix is supposed to be this wonderfully therapeutic place where one can achieve a complete catharsis and be purged from an impure existence. At least that's what some Westward VP kept telling me on the plane out here.

Ordinarily I'd feel all giddy and beside myself flying halfway across the country on a corporate Leer jet, but all I feel right now is guilty.

Mom is taking Dad home from the hospital today, and she really wanted me to be with her for assistance. But work's important, you know. So she told me to go to work. But I know that deep down inside her, she's cursing me for leaving her with the burden of Dad. How can I possibly enjoy myself at a time like this. They don't even know where I am right now. They think I'm slaving away in my cubicle in Memphis, negotiating contracts and dictating letters to big people in foreign countries.

The plane touches down at the airport at a little after nine in the morning with a limo to escort us to the new corporate offices. Phoenix is such a long way from home. Other than a job, there's nothing for me out here.

I can't even see the scenery out of the limousine window. I'm stuck in the middle between my boss and a junior VP from accounting. Occasionally I catch a glimpse of a recognizable fast food chain or a strip mall here and there. With the exception of cactus instead of magnolia, it looks like any other major city I've seen.

The new corporate offices are posh and totally state of the art. It's enough to impress the hell out of any corporate executive let alone a degreeless chick from south Arkansas. Our tour finishes in a board room where nameless Armani pin-stripes and first rate Chanel knockoffs are seated. I feel underdressed in my J. C. Penney career coordinates as I take my seat next to the so called chosen ones in the new downsized corporation.

"We're prepared to offer, on Morris' recommendation, a five percent salary raise and a moving allowance of up to five thousand dollars. That should take care of cost of any living increases and your move across country and deposits, should you have any. Just remember to save receipts and we'll take care of the expenses," some corporate big-head says. "And should you be...."

I don't hear the rest. I nod when I feel I need to and smile back at my boss occasionally. My father's got cancer half way across the continent and I'm stuck here watching a video tape about how three of the countries top interior designers were called in to decorate my new office. Suddenly I hate Southwestern art.

*   *   *   *

"Dad, hey, how you doing?" I ask him on the phone in my Southwestern designed hotel room.

"Better, sweetheart, better," he whispers

"I didn't think you would be answering the phone yet."

"Mom's got it placed next to me on the bed here. Damn thing's been ringing off the hook, people asking me how I'm doin'? I'm thinking about just taking an ad out in the paper that reads, 'Don't bother calling. Ben Carmichael's doing just fine.'"

"Oh, Daddy, they're just concerned about you. Like me. Are you pissed I went back to work?"

"Oh, honey, no. I told you to go. Your mother and I made it just fine although we're going to have to fumigate the car."

"What?"

"I got a little car sick. Nothing to worry about."

"I'm sorry, Daddy. I should have stayed to help. Morris told me I could take as much time as I needed. I should have stayed."

"You're doing the most important thing you possibly can do right now. Your career is important."

"Sure it is," I say and flick a Westward pamphlet on the floor. "How's Mom?"

"She's fine."

"She's pissed, I know it. I can hear her huffing and puffing in the background."

"She and I told you to go back. Don't worry about me."

"But I do," I say. "Oh, by the way, I got a hundred dollars cash from your credit card. Is that all right?"

"Well, sure, hon. If you need it."

"I didn't want to but …" I hate to tell him I'm out in Phoenix. "… I got caught short. Oh, and I charged a couple of things at Gantos and Penney's with it, too. I needed a couple of business suits."

"It's okay. I told you it's for emergencies. I suppose that's an emergency."

"You know how corporate expects you to look. I've seen your Armani suit."

"Touché. You can't ride the express unless you look the part."

"So you do approve of me working for Westward?"

"All I'm saying right now is that I think maybe you might be on to something, that's all. I want to see you succeed in something."

"Oh, Daddy. For you, I'll try. You just get better, you hear?"

"Have I ever let you down before?" Daddy asks.

We say our good-byes as I look outside my hotel window at the desert beyond the parking lot. There is nothing out there but forsaken landscape as far as the eye can see. I put down the phone, pop a Tums into my mouth, and cry.

CHAPTER 6

▼

THERE'S A LITTLE BIT OF SELFISHNESS AND SORROW IN EACH AND EVERY BAG

No one wants to see their loved one sick. Especially me. That's why God invented the excuse.

Excuses come easy to me. Hell, I've been a walking excuse all my life. Busy? Sure. The career, you know how it is? Cruising fast on the executive express. If I make any sudden departures, the whole thing might derail. Yeah, right.

"God, if my father was sick right now, I'd want to see him," Walt says, shaking his head as he drives us down Poplar boulevard toward Corky's Barbecue.

"He's in Little Rock again at the hospital. No big deal," I say. "It's nothing serious. Just a couple of nights, to regulate his chemo, that's all."

"Jesus, Kelly, the last time you went home was when?"

"I've been to Little Rock twice to see him," I explain. "He's responding well to the treatments. It's kind of a waste just to go see him in the hospital because his chemo makes him a little bit nauseous, don't you think?"

Walt turns the car around, almost in the middle of Poplar.

"Where are we going?" I ask as I hang on for dear life.

"Little Rock."

"Damn it, Walt ..."

"I don't get you," he screams. "Why won't you go see him?"

I start to cry. "I hate seeing him like this. Please turn the car around and take me home," I plead. "I'll see him when he gets better."

"You're going to see him now and that's that."

*   *   *   *

"Daddy, hey, it's me," I say as I peek into his room.

"Pumpkin," he says weakly. He doesn't look at all like my father, more like a holocaust victim than a pharmaceutical rep. I glare at Walt as we enter the room.

"Mom."

She gives me a feeble wave.

"How are we doing? What do they say?" I ask as I try to sit next to Dad on his bed. I more or less lean on the mattress for fear of touching a tube or making a sudden motion that might set him back.

"You know …" Dad says with a sigh then looks up at Walt. "You brought the fellow, huh? How ya doin', Walt?"

"Actually he brought me," I tell him.

"'How are you doing, Mr. Carmichael?' is the more pertinent question of the day." Walt pats Daddy on the leg. Dad winces but Walt does not see it as he moves toward Mom to pour on the honey he knows she loves so well. "Hello, Mrs. Carmichael. You look lovely, as always."

Mom smiles, takes Walt's hand, pats it sweetly.

"I don't know what's worse, the disease or the chemo," Dad says, then coughs.

"The doctor says he's doing just fine," Mom explains. "That this is normal and to be expected. I still think …"

"Drop it, Liv, please …" Daddy says, then begins to cough uncontrollably until the phlegm is released in his throat. He leans back onto the bed, defeated by the effort as Mom crosses her arms and frowns at him as if to say I told you so.

I've never seen my father like this. He looked better after the surgery. I hate this shit.

"So what's new?" Dad finally asks.

"Not much. Same old thing," I say.

"The job still going good?"

"Still going," I say, trying hard not to elaborate any more than I have to.

"So what do you think about Kelly going to Phoenix?" Walt blurts out.

My heart stops cold. I shoot him a look. He looks puzzled. He didn't know I hadn't told them. I just didn't think it would come up so soon.

"Phoenix? What about Phoenix?" Mom perks up, shakes her head and rises with her hands on her hips as if I'd taken the car without permission.

"Oh, God, you didn't tell them, did you?" Walt asks.

"No," I whisper.

"I'm so sorry," Walt apologizes then backs up toward the door. "If you'll excuse me?" He walks out of the room.

"Walt," I call out.

"Phoenix?" Dad asks.

I pause, then look him in the eye. "Westward's transferred me to Phoenix. Pay raise, moving allowance …"

"Why haven't you told us this?" Mom demands.

"You're fighting cancer, for god's sake. I didn't want to worry you."

"And it's okay now?" Mom retorts.

"Livy," Dad scolds. "So what's going on in Phoenix?" he asks, genuinely interested.

"Westward was acquired by another company. They want the headquarters moved out and scaled down. They're only taking key people."

"And you're key?" Dad sits up. A small shimmer of color returns to his cheek.

"I work for one. I guess that makes me one, too." I shrug modestly.

"They're eyeing you for promotion then. Go to night school. Get the degree. Get the masters. They'll move you up fast." He's up from the standing eight count and begging for another round. If it gives him pleasure and makes him feel better, I guess I should oblige him.

"I'll look into it, Dad. You're probably right."

"See there, Livy. It's a good move," Dad says as he nods and smiles at Mom.

"But Phoenix is so far away," Mom says.

"Liv, that's why we have airports."

"What does Walt say?" Mom asks.

"He doesn't want me to go."

"Figures," Dad says. "Wants to hold you back."

"But do you want to go?" Mom asks.

"I don't know."

"Sure you want to go," Dad says. "Don't be a fool."

"And throw her chances away at a good and decent husband who can take care of her?" Mom interjects.

"If she makes vice president, she can take care of herself."

"Dad. Mom. Please."

"What?" both reply at once.

"It's my career. My life. This time let me make the decisions. Okay?"

"Don't throw your chances away," Mom pleads.

"Kelly, don't be stupid."

A nurse walks into the room and interrupts us. "Mr. Carmichael, I need to check your pouch."

"Sure," he says, then mouths the word "go" to me as the nurse pulls back the sheets.

"You want me to go?" I say to him and point to the door. I know what he means.

"No, no," he sighs. "Stay here this time. It's just a lousy bag. You should see this thing."

The nurse lifts his pajama top up and pulls back his bottoms to reveal a small bag attached to his right side and a road map of scars. My stomach churns and I feel faint and hot.

"You're fine, Mr. Carmichael," the nurse says as she pats the bag and pulls Dad's pajama's back into place. "Nothing much there. I'll check you again in an hour," she says, then leaves the room.

"Does it hurt, Dad?"

"What? The bag?"

"It looks disgusting," I tell him.

"I thinks it's just beautiful. After all, it's supposed to keep me alive, isn't it?"

I rush into the bathroom and vomit.

*   *   *   *

Upon Walt's insistence and because of my conscience, I leave work early on Friday and go home for an official visit.

There's a different smell to my parent's house. The kind of odor you smell when you visit relatives at the nursing home. Urine, disease, and worse.

"God, Mom, it stinks in here," I say as I put my purse and bag down on the kitchen floor.

"It's good to see you, too," she says. "I don't smell anything." She sniffs around the kitchen as I make my way toward the master bedroom.

I peek into my parents bedroom. Hal and Bob sit beside Dad and discuss the past. I turn back toward the kitchen. "You got some Lysol or something? It really reeks in here."

"It's cigarettes, isn't it?" she asks and nods as if it's the discovery of the century.

"No, worse," I tell her.

"I don't smell anything. Hal and Bob haven't said a word about it."

"And they won't." I look under the kitchen cabinet and pull out a can of Glade and begin saturating the atmosphere with the fresh scent of Lilacs.

"Where's Walt?" Mom asks as she removes a sheet of chocolate chip cookies from the oven. "I thought he would come with you."

"No, he's in Seattle for a company meeting. I think they're discussing his promotion. He's been looking forward to this meeting longer than we've been dating."

"He's just so wonderful to you."

"He is nice, isn't he?" I dip a spoon into the cookie dough and stuff a wad into my mouth. "How's Dad?"

"They changed his chemo."

"Again? Why?"

"They thought this one would work better. I don't know."

"Funny, but why hasn't he lost his hair yet?" I ask. "Isn't that what's supposed to happen when you take chemo?"

"The oncologist assured us that he won't. Newer chemos don't do that, he told us," Mom says as she places a fresh sheet of cookies into the oven. "Speaking of losing hair, the other night we were staying at the motel by the hospital. Ben went to the bathroom and I suddenly I heard him scream, 'Livvy, come quick. My hair's falling out.'" She laughs like it's just riotous. "See, there were all these little short hairs all over the bathroom. My hair. I forgot I cut my bangs and hair was on the floor." She laughs out loud.

"God, Mom, it's not funny. He looks awful. He's got to have lost at least fifty pounds or more."

"They said to expect it. That's why we have all those cans of Ensure in the pantry."

"He needs exercise. Just walk a little bit. Does he do that?"

"To go to the bathroom."

"Mom, if he doesn't get up and walk, he's going to ..."

"I know. I know." Mom slides the cookies off the sheet and onto a piece of wax paper. "But he's just so sick from the chemo. If they'd just give him a break from it ..."

"Tomorrow, he's going to walk, even if it kills him," I announce.

*   *   *   *

"Daddy, wake up," I say as I shake him gently on the shoulders. "I want you to get up and walk around the house. You need to exercise, get your strength back. It'll make you feel better."

"I do feel better. Don't worry," he says and closes his eyes.

"Then get up and walk if you feel better. Exercise. You need the energy to fight this thing," I tell him. "Come on, Dad. Fight with me. You know you love it."

"For you, okay. I'll get up."

"Good, Daddy. I love you. I just want you to get better, that's all. But do it for yourself, not me."

"Sure, sweetheart," he says and sits up. He looks like a feeble old man. His brown whiskers and hair take on a gray cast through the subtle light of the drawn drapes.

"I'm going to get some breakfast. You want some coffee to get you started?"

"No. Let me work up an appetite," he jokes.

"Okay, Daddy."

I leave Dad sitting up in the bed. Mom stands at the kitchen sink polishing her silver. It's barely eight o'clock.

"Don't you think that can wait?" I ask her as I reach around her to get a bowl from the cabinet.

"It keeps me busy, occupied. Later I'm going to clean out the closets."

"Not me." I take the bowl, milk, and Lucky Charms into the breakfast area and sit down at the table. Dad slowly creeps up behind me and grabs a chair. He tries to smile for me but just from the bedroom to here, he's already winded.

"Daddy, sit down. Take it easy. You're panting."

"No, no. You're right. This is good for me." He lets go of the chair and almost like a toddler, waddles toward the living room.

I crunch my cereal and shake my head at Mom.

"Ben, sit down, for god's sake. Take it slow. You can walk more later."

"I'm fine," Dad says as he waves her off. "Kelly's right. This is good for me."

"He really should take it easy," Mom says to me as she picks up a silver candle stick. "You haven't seen him that much lately. He's weaker than you think."

I feel bad for asking him to walk. "Dad, forget it and come on back to bed," I call out, still eating my cereal. I look up and see that he's made it to my room and sits on my bed.

"Kelly, go help your father back to bed. Enough's enough."

"Mom, he's fine. He's resting. I'll get him when I'm through eating."

She drops the candle stick into the sink with a thud. "I'll go get him then. Eat your damn cereal." She glares at me as she walks by.

I stare at my cereal bowl. No wonder she hates me so much. I'm such a selfish bitch. I pull the spoon toward my mouth but the delicious morsels have long since wilted and lost their magic.

"Kelly!" Mom screams. I drop my spoon. Milk splashes the faded chintz placemat. "Oh my god, Ben!"

I rush to my room. Dad is sprawled out on the end of my bed, legs hanging off. He has urinated all over himself, staining the Laura Ashley comforter. His eyes have rolled back into his head.

"Now look what you've done! Get the doctor. Get someone!" she commands as she tries to call his name and revive him.

I run to the phone in the kitchen, not realizing until after I get to it that there is a phone in my room. I grab the receiver and go blank. I don't remember how to make an emergency call. I almost dial information to get the number for 9–1–1. I complete the call.

"Yes, we're at seventeen ten Oakwood Lane … My father has passed out. He's unconscious. He has cancer. It's bad. Hurry." I hang up the phone and hesitate before I go back into my room.

My mother tries everything to get him to wake up.

I stand helpless and ashamed in the doorway.

CHAPTER 7

▼

E=MC^{BAGGED}

OR

THE THEORY OF RELATIVES

I've thought very little about my own mortality. I've thought even less of the mortality of my parents. I think of them as being like taxes. Always there. They are certain and reliable. A fixture of my existence.

I find it hard to believe that I will no longer catch the smell of Aramis on my clothing after a warm hug from Dad. I'll never be able to walk down the aisle with my hand in his arm at my wedding. Nor will I ever again argue about my future career path with him over the phone.

Right now the house is empty. My cereal bowl is still exactly where I left it. Dad is gone. Mom retreats to the bedroom for the difficult task of contacting family and friends and making arrangements.

Soon the house will be flooded with mourners, lemon poppy seed pound cakes, and platters of cheese and cold cuts. Someone will have the foresight and consideration to bring a bucket of chicken, pot of baked beans, and a mound of coleslaw. I remember my grandfather's funeral, and more recently my father's parents' funerals. They were all exactly the same: one great big party when you're not really in the mood for one.

The door bell rings and the party begins. Julie and Pauline rush in with hugs and sobs. I'm still too numb from all that has happened for an all-out cry. There are things I must do before I let myself go.

"What can we do?" Julie pops up.

"We're here for you, sweetie. Just anything. You name it," Pauline adds.

"Mom's in the bedroom. I need to take a shower and go pick up Mimi. We don't want to tell her over the phone."

"I just don't believe it. Our Ben," Pauline sobs. "Ben." She buries her face in a pressed and starched handkerchief that she has no doubt saved in a drawer lined with lilac sachets for just this sort of occasion. She shakes her head in disbelief. "Ben," she mutters again.

"He was so …" Pauline follows suit, hanging on a sob. "Young."

Right now I don't feel like participating in this scene. All I care about is getting to Mimi's.

"Julie. Pauline," Mom calls out from the bedroom. They rush to her side as I disappear into my bedroom for a quick shower and a fix up.

I realize as I am searching for something to put on that I have packed very lightly for this weekend. Shorts, T-shirts and a ratty pair of Birkenstock's are all I possess at the moment. No doubt I will need to do some shopping this afternoon.

As I pass by my bed, the scene of Dad sprawled out, gasping for his last breath fills my mind and my senses. I quickly remove the bed clothes and mattress pad. Luckily the stains haven't soaked all the way through. The stench of death clings heavy in the air. My room will never be the same again.

*   *   *   *

The birds at Mimi's are thick and numerous. I can hear them fighting over the morsels of sunflower seeds she so religiously feeds them as I make my way up the brick path to her door. Flowers and roses are in full bloom. Spring sunshine beats down. A mocking bird calls out. Weird how the world seems oblivious to sorrow.

"Mimi, it's me, Kelly," I call out. I open the back door to the kitchen.

Mimi sits and snaps beans in the living room while she watches the last college basketball game of the regular season.

"Come on you damn Razorbacks. You worthless pieces of shit. Gonna piss it all away like you always…. Oh, hey Punkin', you surprised me," she says as she puts her pan of string beans down, hugs my neck, then lights a cigarette. "Ain't this a change. Usually I have to come over there to get a visit out of you," she says, puffing on her Virginia Slim. "Sit down, for cryin' out loud." She picks up an extra pan, puts a few handfuls of beans in it and hands it to me. "Go on, make yourself useful."

"Sure," I say, humoring her. "Where'd you get the string beans? Isn't it a little early for 'em yet?" I ask as I start my snapping slow. Then I get to a good, quick rhythm that summers with Mimi developed.

"That's my girl," she praises my technique. "Got 'em at the A&P. Too early for 'em. I know," she says as she examines a bean, then goes back to her rhythm. "I imagine they come from Brazil or Ecuador or some third world country that doesn't know squat about gardening. Hell, they probably taste like shit but that's what pork fat's for, isn't it?"

"Mimi, I ..."

"Can you believe this weather? Why, I don't know when I've ever seen such a beautiful day before. Hell, I've been sleeping with my damn windows open at night and it ain't even bothered me."

I continue to snap the beans and pray that Mimi will eventually shut up long enough for me to remove this burden from my lips.

"Alice Shrewsbury got a new car yesterday, did I tell you? A Cadillac at that. So what if it's five years old and was her son's. A Cadillac's a Cadillac, you know. And it's loaded to the nines. She came by this morning and took me around town in it. Had to stop off at the grocery store and show off in it. That's how come I got the beans, see. Hell, I didn't even need anything but you can't just drive up to the A&P and not buy nothin'."

"Dad's dead."

"Dammit, I know that," she says as she lights another cigarette with her last, takes a long deep drag and sighs. "Why the hell else would you be here?" Mimi rises and smashes out the previous cigarette in a cheap metal ashtray that's older than I am. "I'll get my things."

*   *   *   *

Sandra Rogers has always been the person I turn to in Spivey for friendship. We met several years back at someone's wedding shower and have remained loyal friends since. She has been the one friend in my adult life that I have hung on to. I have long since severed ties with my high school friends and I don't keep up with the friends I've made in college or from the various towns I have lived in. I don't have to work at my friendship with Sandra. It's just there.

She's ten years older than I am but she's never been married, has no children, and like me, she's only recently found a permanent career path. She teaches kindergarten. Now we share an even larger bond. We both are fatherless. She lost her father about a year before I met her.

"How's your mother holding up?" she asks me as she settles into my car.

"Hasn't hit her yet. Too busy," I reply as I pull a Virginia Slim from the pack I stole from Mimi. "Want one?"

"Oh, do I." She takes a cigarette and we both light up as if we're still in high school and hiding the habit from our parents.

"Mother was the same," she says. "Took her about a week before she finally broke down and had the big cry. Liv will be just fine. She's a strong person."

"You think that?"

"Well, sure. At least she seems that way" Sandra insists.

"She's just so dependent on Dad."

"My mother was, too, but look at her now."

"Your mother has grandchildren to occupy her. Your brother's kids are her saving grace. My mother doesn't have anything but her mother, me, and her brother."

"He lives in Cleveland, right?" Sandra recalls. "What's his name?"

"Phillip. He hardly ever comes home to visit, nor do his kids or grandkids. They're not close. Pisses the hell out of Mimi, though."

"Your mother's stronger than you think. You'll see."

I roll my eyes as I park the car in front of Wiseman's, our local department store.

"Can't you borrow something from your mother?" Sandra asks.

"She's too short and our tastes aren't the same."

"Shame to have to buy clothes for just a couple of days."

"Well, what am I supposed to do? Run up to Memphis?"

"I guess not."

I sort through racks of skirts and dresses and find nothing appealing. "I can't do this, Sandra. I can't." I push the clothes away from me and bite my lip to keep back the tears.

"Here. This looks like you," she says as she thrusts a black and tan houndstooth suit toward me. "And you can do this and you will get through it. I promise. Just don't watch any of those long distance telephone ads or camera commercials for a while and you'll do a lot better. Trust me on that."

My sorrow turns into laughter.

"Come on, let's get out of here for a minute," she says.

"But I …"

"The clothes will still be here ten minutes from now."

We stroll around the town square and pause at the fountain which graces the intersection of Washington and Main Streets. The water dances out of the top spout and trickles down the three bowls to the main pool which is about a foot and a half deep and at least twelve feet wide.

"I remember when they put this here. I was almost in high school then," Sandra says. She removes a penny from her pocket and tosses it in.

"I was pretty young but I remember, too. Daddy brought me down here when they dedicated the stupid thing," I say. "For city beautification. Got my picture in the paper, though."

"That was you! I remember that," Sandra squeals. "Your Daddy was holding you up on his shoulders as you were throwing pennies in. Wow."

"Yep, that was me." I nod as I play with a penny inside my pocket.

"That's a good memory and you'll always have those, you know."

"Yeah, I know. No one can take them away from me either, can they?"

"Nope. No matter what, he'll always be your dad," Sandra says.

I throw my penny into the fountain without any wish at all.

*   *   *   *

Sandra and I return to my house with two pairs of shoes and three coordinating outfits to get me through the next couple of days. The house is full of people, with more pulling into the driveway all the time. A woman passes me in the foyer with a bucket of chicken and a casserole dish of baked beans.

"Some rituals never change," Sandra states as we inhale the comforting aroma.

"Five bucks says there's a platter of cold cuts and a pound cake in the kitchen," I counter.

"I'm not going to take that bet," Sandra says.

Mom sits on the couch sandwiched between a distant cousin of Dad's and Brother Carroll's wife. Brother Carroll and the men circle in the kitchen and sample the food while Mimi enlightens them on all the many ailments from which she suffers. Julie and Pauline greet the well-wishers, take their platters of food and direct them to the guest book like good hostesses at a bridal shower would do. It's one great big party.

Sandra is ushered to the book while I try to make my way to my bedroom.

An hour later I get there. I must admit that I am not good at this. I do not have the patience to recite the same plastic civilities over and over again to people I either don't know or haven't seen in years.

Unfortunately, I have to get used to it. I have two more days of this. I close my door and try hard not to look at my bed as I search for my jar of Tums.

*   *   *   *

"My father died today," I tell Walt over the phone. I am almost matter of fact.

"Oh, Kelly, I'm so sorry," he says. "I'm in shock."

"Me, too," I tell him. "I just called to tell you that the funeral will be on Monday, that's all."

"Monday. Oh, well, I guess you want me to come home and go to it with you, huh?"

"I don't know, it's …"

"I mean, I suppose I could leave the meeting and catch a flight out there … I guess …"

"I don't know. It's up to you."

"Well … God, Kelly, I'm … I mean, we're … Oh, shit, Baby, I mean I can't leave here right now. I just can't."

"Then it's okay. I understand. I really do." Right now I really don't care. Quite frankly I don't even want him here. I don't want anybody here. If he can't make this all go away, then I don't need him right now.

"I mean, if things were different …"

"Different? My father's dead. What other …"

"You know … Different," he says again.

"Oh, yeah. Right. Different." I get it now. For some reason a gold band changes protocol. I see how it works now.

"I am sorry, Kelly."

Yeah, I'm sorry, too.

*   *   *   *

Mom, Mimi, Hal, and I arrive at the Ellington Funeral Home by three o'clock with Dad's Armani suit. We are escorted to an office to begin the task of planning Dad's glorious funeral service. I had no idea there were so many things to arrange.

Thomas, the funeral director, takes us upstairs where the coffin showroom is. Arranged around the showroom is every model of casket they make from the tiny no frills model all the way up to the Cadillac of them all. Thomas takes us through the cheaper coffins, past satin lined caskets, caskets engraved with roses, bible verses and eight-point bucks, to the more elaborate models, ornately appointed with silk and nickel plating. I feel like I should test drive it, lay in one or something, to make sure this is the one we want to buy and place my Dad in. I touch a beautiful oak casket with brass fixtures and Hal loses it, excuses himself, and flees from the room as if I had just done something totally forbidden.

Then Mom loses it between the metal caskets and the cherry vaneer. "Oh, I can't make this sort of decision now. I just can't …" She sobs, then bolts from the room.

"Many people find this task to be the hardest."

"I see." I look at Mimi for some guidance.

"Oh, Lord child. Pick a good one, for god's sake. If you don't, it'll be the one thing people will talk about."

"I know."

I make my way down the line of coffins until I see just the one, a beautiful platinum hued casket with brass handles and a soft ivory bed. I run my hand across it as if I were checking out a Mercedes, classically understated yet exquisitely engineered.

"That's a fine model, ma'am," Thomas tells me and pats me on the shoulders. "Reasonably priced but still gives a mighty good show."

"Yes, it does, doesn't it? We'll take it," I say as I smile at Mimi. Daddy would be proud.

"That's my girl."

*   *   *   *

It's a bizarre ritual, this sitting with the body at the funeral parlor. We assemble all around the room and face the body. We marvel at how good he looks in his heavily padded suit and Max Factor makeup, considering what all he went through.

From time to time, Mom points at Dad and recollects how they went all the way over to Dallas and bought a real honest to goodness Armani suit but that she never dreamed he'd actually be buried in it.

Mom's brother, Phillip, slightly worn out from his flight, sits quietly beside me with his face down in his hands while Mimi wanders from flower to flower, removing cards from the plants and commenting on their expense or lack thereof.

"Like this one, for instance. My sister Erna has more money than God and this is what she sends."

"Mother, they don't know what they're sending. They're at the mercy of the florist, for cryin' out loud," Uncle Phillip breaks his silence.

"Not Erna," she replies, shaking the card at Uncle Phil. "She knows." Mimi picks up another card. "Look at this one. 'With all my love and sympathy, Eleanor T.' Is this one of your friends, Kelly, 'cause I don't know who the heck she is. No address. Nothin'."

"I don't know her." I look towards Mom who shrugs. So does Phillip.

"Well, whoever she is, she didn't leave an address to send a thank you. I think that's tacky."

"It's probably a client or a business associate or someone like that," I say. "Daddy knew lots of people through work that we didn't know."

"Don't worry about it, Mother. We'll figure it out later."

"Tacky, that's what it is," Mimi says. "Just plain tacky."

We all sit back in our chairs and ignore Mimi's rantings as we try desperately to come up with a new comment or reflection about Dad.

The opening of the front doors to the funeral home and raucous laughter interrupt our friendly little wake. Hal's duck hunting story trails off, Mimi looks up from her task, and Mom's skin turns white as Dad's brother and his wife crash into the room, cocktails and cigarettes in hand. The smell of liquor and filterless cigarettes is overwhelming; it's a wonder they haven't set each other on fire with every puff. Edward and Cookie have arrived.

"Oh, sweet Jesus, Ben, what the hell have you done to yourself?" Edward turns on the tears. "Oh, shit, Cookie, come here. Oh Lord, come look at him." Cookie and Edward grab hold of each other as they gaze at Dad. "He looks so good, doesn't he? Oh, shit, Cookie."

No one moves or speaks. We all just watch as they take over the wake. Edward turns to Mom and plants a big wet bourbon soaked kiss and hug on her. She barely returns the embrace. "Oh, goddammit, Livy. Why? Why?" Edward breaks down and kneels on the floor beside her.

Cookie set her sights on me. I get up out of the sheer politeness and respect my parents conveyed to me growing up, but oh, how I long to send them back to trailer park they came from. Cookie hugs me tight and transfers the smell of ashtrays and no name liquor to my new skirt and blouse. I suddenly feel the trickle of gin running down my back from her sloshing cocktail. My skin crawls, I'm repulsed and there's nowhere to run. Dad just lies there, peaceful at last, not bothered or embarrassed by his brother's arrival.

"Cookie. Cookie, where's my goddamn lighter?" Ed mutters, taking a seat next to Mom as Hal and Bob rise and take their cue to exit and usher their wives away from the scene. The others follow suit.

"Do you have to go so soon?" Mom extends her hand toward Hal with a look of desperation in her eyes.

"It's getting late and tomorrow …" Hal looks toward Dad.

We say our good-byes to Dad's dearest friends and hug them, wishing the exchange would last a little longer. But when everyone departs, it's just us and *them*. Mimi doesn't say a word. Even she is too stunned for speech. She's only seen Dad's brother and sister-in-law once or twice, the last time was when I was in junior high and we had them over for Thanksgiving. It was the year Dad's father passed away.

Uncle Edward searches through his pockets and finds his Zippo, lights his cigarette, then shows the lighter to Mom. "Got this in Germany while I was in the service. Got it at the PX over there back in the fifties. Can you believe this goddamn shit?" He lights the Zippo, extinguishes the flame, then lights it again repeatedly. "Can you believe this shit after all these years. Amazing. They don't fuckin' make 'em like that anymore. I got Ben one back then, too. He still got his?"

"I don't know," Mom answers him. "I don't think so."

"Fuckin' shame." Ed says and lights the Zippo again for emphasis.

"You know this is a funeral home," Mimi breaks her silence.

Cookie half laughs, half spits as she tries to kick back her cocktail. "I certainly hope so or else he's in the wrong place." She points at Dad and Edward laughs with her.

Mimi starts to say something but Uncle Phillip places his hands on Mimi's side, keeping her from saying something derogatory.

"Uncle Phil, I didn't see your name on the guest register. Why don't you do that now," I say, trying to lure him from the room.

"I did … n't. Why don't I do that now," Phil catches on in an all too obvious manner but Cookie and Ed seem too drunk to notice. Uncle Phillip follows me out of the room.

"Why can't you do something? Say something? This is horrible," I plead to him.

"What do you want me to say. He's your father's brother. He has a right to come see him here."

"But Uncle Phil, he's drunk and foul-mouthed. There's a certain type of decorum ..."

"I know what you're saying but I can't do anything about it. They have a right."

"But what about our rights?"

"Kelly, I don't know what to say." Uncle Phil goes back into the room. I utter an expletive and follow him back.

"There's a no smoking sign up there, you know," Mimi says, pointing to the sign.

"No one pays attention to those things," Cookie says as she dumps her ashes in a potted Sansavera plant.

Uncle Phil grabs Mimi by the arm as she begins to comment. Mom just sits there silently, waiting for Dad to rise up and take control of his drunken brother as he used to do so many times in the past.

"Don't you think we ought to be getting on home?" Mimi states as she shoots Phil a look.

"I think so. I'm tired. It's been a long day," Mom says as she slowly walks over to Dad and strokes his arm.

"Oh, shit, Livy, we know you're tired so don't you worry none now about us back at your house. You just go on about your business like we're not even there."

Mom grabs Dad's arm tightly as if she's going to faint. Uncle Phil rushes to her to catch her.

"That's right, Livy, honey, you just pretend we ain't even here," Cookie adds.

*   *   *   *

Edward and Cookie have taken over my room and bathroom, so I have moved my things into Mom's room. Mom's room. Dad used to be in there somewhere. I shake my head at the thought. Nothing has sunken in yet. We're all just going through the motions.

I hang my dress next to one of Dad's suits and place the box of new shoes next to a new pair of Florsheims Mom said Dad never got a chance to wear.

Mimi sits in the rocking chair in the bedroom, puffing away at her cigarette and rocking back and forth vigorously. "I can't believe they come from the same cloth," Mimi starts. "I mean, I know Ben cussed a little. Hell, I cuss, dammit, but I've never before in my life heard such words. And in a funeral parlor no less."

Mimi points at Mom with her cigarette. "And you … you're putting up with it." Mimi shakes her head. "You and Phillip both. I thought I raised you two to stand up for yourselves."

"Mother, please. If it bothers you that much, then you say something."

"It's not my place. And you let them into your own home. Your sanctuary, for cryin' out loud. Why, I don't even believe you let this happen."

"Mother, what do you want me to do? He's Ben's brother."

"Ever heard of a motel?" Mimi counters.

"This is hard enough without …" Mom pauses.

"Without? …"

"Just leave it, Mother. They'll be gone in a day or so."

"Dad never could establish a relationship with them no matter how hard he tried," I say. "Funny, he's a lot closer to Phil."

"Phillip's a good, decent man. Lives too damn far away, but otherwise, he's a good man. And he's staying in a motel."

"I tried to get Phillip to do something."

"Yes, I noticed," Mimi says. "A lot of good it did."

"They've always been this way," I tell her. "It's gotten worse in the last few years, hasn't it, Mom?"

"Oh, yes. But it's always been bad. Always," she insists.

"Did you know I had my first drink at Uncle Edward's house?"

"When did this happen?" Mom questions as if she's going to punish me now.

"When they still lived here in Spivey and I was about eleven. When you and Dad went to Hal's fortieth birthday party. Cookie fixed me a glass of Cold Duck."

"Oh, forever more," Mom gasps. "Why didn't you say something?"

"I was eleven going on twenty-one. Would you have said something?"

"That's it." Mimi rises from her rocker. "I'm going in there and kick some pickled butt."

"Mother, stop it." She grabs Mimi and pushes her back down in the rocker.

"Dad would tell us just to let them be."

"I don't know what it is about you two.

Livy, you've always been one big welcome mat and you, Kelly, you push the task off on someone else as usual."

"I'm not afraid … I can … They're …" I begin to cry uncontrollably. Mom joins in, followed by Mimi.

*   *   *   *

The door bell rings and I quickly rush to the front door to answer it. It's the limo driver. We've been hiding out in Mom's room waiting for the time to leave. Mimi even slept with us, all three generations tucked snug in the king sized bed. I rush back to the bedroom.

"I'll tell Uncle Edward we'll meet them there, that the limo is here for us." I march back across the living room as if reclaiming my territory again and Edward and Cookie meet me half way across the living room.

"I thought I heard commotion out here," Edward states. "We were wondering if you were even up yet."

"Oh, we've been up."

"Shit, we just helped ourselves to the coffee and whatnot," Edward keeps on.

"Well, just make yourselves at home. The limo is here and ..."

"Great!" pipes Cookie. "I just love limos. Makes me feel like I was one of them country singers or Hollywood stars."

"... so we'll meet you there," I trail off.

"What are you talking about, little lady?" Edward asks. "We're riding with you."

Cookie and Edward squeeze me between them in the limo. Mom and Mimi ride backwards, clinging to the doors while Edward and Cookie light up cigarettes and exchange swigs from a flask.

Cookie does that insipid half-spit, half laugh of hers, flinging saliva all over my new houndstooth coat dress. I cringe.

Mom turns her head and looks out of the window.

"It's just a cryin' shame the girls couldn't come," Cookie says. "Too busy playing house and all that other bullshit, if you know what I mean?" Cookie nudges and winks at me.

"So how is Peggy doing?" I ask. Peggy is the daughter closest to my age. She's a couple of years younger.

"She's doin' a lot better now that she moved out from that son-of-a-bitch asshole she was living with," Edward says.

"He beat her up a couple of times," Cookie adds.

"He's a goddamn alcoholic, is what he is." Edward takes a sip from his flask.

"Now she's pregnant," Cookie reveals.

"You mean they weren't married?" Mimi is shocked.

"Hell, no. After three failed marriages, she's sort of given up on the damn institution."

"So what's she doing now?" I ask.

"Living in a trailer park and working at a convenience store. She's already got three kids," Edward says and takes another swig.

"One from each marriage," Cookie says as she pulls out her wallet to show off the pictures of her grandchildren. "That there's Dakota Blue, we call him Cody, he's almost fifteen. And that there's Austin Dillon, who's eight. And that's Madison Montgomery, she's seven. Ain't they just as cute as they can be?"

"Handfuls is what they are," Edward points out.

"Where'd she come up with all those names?" Mimi asks. "Rand McNally?"

"No. Just made 'em up," Cookie explains. "Got Cody's and Austin's names from soap operas. We loves to watch 'em . They got the best names there. They really do"

"So when you gonna give poor old Livy some grandchildren?" Edward pokes me in the ribs. "She's gonna need 'em now."

"I haven't thought about it much," I tell him.

"Well, sugar, you better think about it and start getting your life and shit together. You ain't gettin' any younger." Cookie laughs, saliva spraying on Mom and Mimi.

My life? I could care less about it right now.

✳   ✳   ✳   ✳

For some reason, at the funeral home they set the family off in a little room to the side of the chapel so all we can see is the coffin, the preacher, and all the flowers we know we've got to send thank-you's for. I have no idea what the turn out is like but if the flowers are any indication, it's a full house.

Thank God my mom took the advice Phillip and I gave her and requested a closed casket service. I don't think I could make it through with that lid up and my Daddy there helpless while some preacher he never really cared for tells everyone how wonderful he was.

With the exception of Dad's name being called out every once and while, it's pretty much anybody's funeral. At least that's what I keep telling myself. This isn't Ben Carmichael's funeral. This is somebody else who happens to have the same name. It doesn't always work, my believing that, but I've only gone through three tissues and Mom's gone through a whole travel pack.

*   *   *   *

Before we can load back into the limo to go to the cemetery, Mom has to examine the sign-in book one more time. I know she's mentally compiling a list of all the people who weren't here.

"Eleanor T," Mom almost squeals. "She's been here." Mom looks around the chapel and tries to see who doesn't belong.

"Any of these people could be Eleanor T. and I wouldn't know it. Don't worry about it. She's probably a wife of someone Dad knew."

"That's true. Don Simmons died last year and I think his wife's already remarried. Maybe that's her. I think her name was Eleanor. Or maybe it was Elaine. I don't know."

"What difference does it make, Mom?"

"I just wanted to thank her for coming."

"Perhaps she's shy."

"Perhaps." Mom takes one last glance around the chapel and out into the parking lot. "Oh, well." She grabs my arm and directs me toward the limo.

CHAPTER 8

▼

THERE ONCE WAS A BAG LADY FROM NANTUCKET ...

I open my apartment door and find a pile of mail on the floor. There is a dark, cold emptiness in the air. I put my bags down and flip on the light but it doesn't come on. The street light is my only illumination.

I march to the kitchen. Everything's dead. My refrigerator is warm. The ice cubes are liquid. I hear the faint bass of my neighbor's stereo and realize the power outage is isolated to my apartment. A red card nestles among the mass of junk mail and bills and indicates my power has been out for three days. I haven't been here for over a week.

I phone the electric company. A not-so-nice woman tells me that a service man will be here when he can. "Dammit."

I light a couple of candles and watch shadows dance across the room. I don't feel like being here by myself. I try to phone Mitzi and invite her out for a beer but she doesn't answer. I have to be here when the electric company comes anyway so I pick up the phone and call home.

"Da-..." I catch myself. "Mom. It's me. I made it hom ... to my apartment."

"That's good. I was worried about you," she says. "You looked tired when you left."

"I was. I hate writing all those thank-yous. As if we don't have anything else to do or burdens to worry about. Don't they know we're appreciative?"

"That's just how things are done," Mom says, "I can't change formality."

"I know. Just seems like such a hardship on an already burdened situation. Well, I'm here. That's all I really wanted to say."

"Take care," she says. "Maybe you can come home early on Friday. Then we can get an early start filling out all of this paper work. I want to get it behind me, you know."

"I'll see what I can do. Give my love to Mimi. Bye."

Sandra said I needed to have one big cry, by myself, to let it all out. She promised it would make me feel better. Now seems to be a good time for it. I sit down on the couch to prepare for the gush. The candlelight makes me feel lonely. But my tears do not flow. I can't even find a sob. Nothing. I feel empty. I lay on the couch, stare at the shadows, and think about nothing.

✳   ✳   ✳   ✳

Morris has been looking for me all morning. I can't help it if I have the absolute worse case of diarrhea the universe has ever seen. It's so bad there's blood in it. Blood and mucous. That's not normal, is it?

"Kelly, are you in there?" Glenda calls out. I look under the stall door and see her red sailor shoes scuffing along the tile.

"I'm in here," I call out.

"Morris wants you to review this contract right away." She slides it under the door.

"Right now?"

"Well, you've been in here half the morning, Morris thought you might like something to do," she explains.

"Gee, that's so thoughtful of him." My intestines gurgle as my poor raw behind throws up.

✳   ✳   ✳   ✳

"Don't you think you'd better go out to Phoenix this weekend and find yourself an apartment or someplace to live, for cryin' out loud?" Morris rants as he leans into my cubicle.

"I've still got plenty of time for that," I say to him. "I've got three more months."

"Weeks, Kelly. You've got only three weeks until the move, dammit."

"When did this happen?"

"Don't you pay any attention to your voice mail?" he asks. "I mean, everyone knows I don't, but you're young. You know how to operate the damn thing."

"I guess I didn't get it," I say and stare at him blankly.

"Best get packin' girl. You're heading up and movin' out."

My intestines suddenly surge. I make a mad dash to the bathroom.

*   *   *   *

"If you want to take a short little trip this weekend the company will fly us out to Phoenix at their expense. It might make a nice little get-a-way," I say to Walt as he flips a steak on the grill at his apartment.

"Why would I possibly want to go to Phoenix?" he asks. "Besides, you're supposed to be going home this weekend to help your mother."

"I was but they want me to go out to Phoenix and look at apartments."

"You're still serious about this transfer, aren't you?" He flips the other steak and the grill flames up.

"I'm just checking it out."

"Then what are you going to do about your mom?"

"What about her?" I ask as I peel the label from the long neck bottle of beer I've been nursing for the last hour.

"She's just lost her husband. I mean, Kelly, you're her only daughter. She's reaching out to you. She apparently needs you right now."

"Walt, this is hard enough for me as it is without you making me feel guilty about taking control of my life for the absolute very first time."

"I'm not trying to make you feel guilty. I'm just trying to get you to think about someone else besides yourself for once in your life." He slides the spatula under the steak and slaps it onto the platter.

"You think I really am selfish, don't you?"

"No. I think your priorities are just ill placed at the moment, that's all," he says and hands me the platter of overdone beef. "Besides, you've got almost three months to decide. Three months to milk this thing and then find another job here if you want."

I look down at the charcoaled flesh. "Three weeks. It's three weeks. Not three months," I mumble to him.

"Jesus, Kelly!" Walt slams the hood down on the grill. "I don't get you some-times." He hurls the spatula off the balcony. It lands on an unoccupied chaise lounge by the pool.

"I didn't know until today. Honest," I plead and slide the platter onto the patio table. "I'm sorry. This is so hard for me. So very, very hard."

"I know it is and I'm sorry, too," he says. "Come here." He takes me into his arms and kisses my forehead. "I'm just now getting to know you, Kelly Car-michael. I'm not sure I'm ready to lose you just yet."

"Then convince me to stay," I tell him.

He takes me in his arms and holds me close, then kisses me so hard I can barely breathe. He picks me up and carries me into the bedroom. As he slides my T-shirt off, I see Walt's dog on the patio. Bosco eats the charcoaled New York strips in three quick bites as Walt kisses my naked breasts. I don't care about the steaks. I'm not hungry and I'm not sorry anymore. I'm being convinced.

∗   ∗   ∗   ∗

"Don't be crazy, Kelly. You don't even have a ring on your finger," Mitzi tells me over the phone. I sit at my desk and stare at the paper work which hasn't moved since eight o'clock this morning.

"I know," I tell her. I look up to see Glenda at my door. She's on her way out for the day.

"Have a nice weekend, Kelly honey," Glenda says to me.

"I'm talking to Mitzi," I whisper to Glenda and point to the phone at my ear.

"Tell her I said hi," Glenda says and disappears.

"You have to think about yourself," Mitzi continues telling me. "Screw Walt. You are Morris' wonderkind. Don't be stupid, Kelly."

"I know. I've finally made it. I'm in," I tell her. "Why should I even be having doubts? This is what I've wanted my whole entire life, independence. And you're right. I'm going to take it. I can't pressure him into popping the big 'M' word on me and I'm not going to try. I don't even know that's what I want right now. I just know that I've finally made it. I don't need him, do I?"

"Nope, not at all."

"So how are you doing?" I ask her.

"Great, if you like working for your father and brother," she says. "I'll find something else eventually. But you, you get your ass out there to the desert, girl, and start living your life for a change," Mitzi says. "You hear me?"

"Loud and clear," I say. "I'm going back home this weekend but next Friday I'm going to fly out there and make the necessary arrangements. You've given me motivation, Mitz. Thanks. I'm going for it."

"God how I envy you, Kelly."

*   *   *   *

After staring at the paper work too long, I realize that I need to leave for Spivey or I'll be on the road all night. I'm not sure if I'm merely procrastinating or if I'm simply trying to linger in a place I've sort of grown accustomed to. Although it's still the same job, I feel as though I'm reverting to my old ways by moving again.

I'm going to make you proud of me, Daddy, even if you are dead and buried. You wanted me to be an executive. Guess what? Here I am.

I grab my purse and decide I need a handful of Tums for the road. I have four hours of isolation ahead of me and I need to come up with a way to tell Walt I'm leaving. It will break his heart. But like Mitzi said, I don't need him. I don't need anybody. I have to think of myself for a change.

I look into Susan's office on my way to the file cabinet. She's always the last one to leave. She packs her belongings into empty liquor boxes.

"Getting ready to go out there early, huh?" I peep into her office. She looks up. She's been crying.

"Nope," she says. "I quit."

"What?"

"I quit. I'm no longer with the company. I'm out," Susan replies. With each item she puts into the box, the harder she shoves the next one.

"God, Susan. I'm so sorry."

"Oh, don't be sorry. I'm not sorry." She chunks the box on the floor and grabs another one to load. "I've given my life to this company. That's the problem. Now I have no life."

"I don't understand. You love it here. Why you're the most dedicated ..."

"Dedicated? Yeah, right. Motivated?" She leans over the box. "Look, you have to work your ass off to the bone here to get promoted. You put in sixty-five, seventy hours a week to prove that you can hang with the big boys despite having tits and no dick. Well I hung in there, baby. I put in my time. I got the career and dammit ..." She begins to tear up. "... my husband threatens to leave me and take the kid if I decide to accept this transfer. Geez, Kelly, look how far I've gone. Look where I am." She throws her arms up in the air. "I thought it was the most important thing in my life. Turns out my husband and my kids are. You see, you can't be a woman, have a career, and have a family at the same time. It just doesn't work that way. The Feminine Mystique and Cosmopolitan are a bunch of crap."

"Maybe if we told your husband how great a job you do and how hard you've worked for …"

"The thing is, Kelly, I don't want it anymore. I'm here because I went to college like I was told to do. I pursued a career because I was told I could do it. The truth is I don't need a career. What I need is a life." She slams a book into the box. "You know I missed my little girl's school play last week because I had to finish drafting that Orleans Star contract. I'll never get that back. She'll never ever again be a little mouse in a first grade play again. Never."

"Your husband's a teacher, right?"

"Yeah. Teaches math and science. He works hard, too. Don't get me wrong. But he gets time off for family things because of not having a demanding career. If I had taken the same time off, somebody else would be sitting in this office instead of me. It's just not fair, you know?"

"I'm sort of having trouble deciding if I really want to go to Phoenix, too" I tell her. "I just don't think I should pass up such an opportunity."

"Well, I can't tell you what to do. I only know what I have to do." Susan picks up her boxes and purse. "It's been nice knowing you, Kelly. I wish you all the best in whatever you do."

I watch her as she strides down the hall. She turns around and uses her back to push the door open. I hear her shout as the door closes. "I'm free!"

*   *   *   *

Like my apartment, my parent's house is also cold and empty. What's missing is my father's laughter. What's added is my grandmother's complaining.

"You need to eat something. Anything. You look like hell," Mimi screeches.

"Mother, I'll eat when I'm hungry and not until," Mom replies. She sits at the dining room table, smoking her Benson & Hedges and wearing a coffee stained housecoat.

"Just an egg sandwich. A lousy egg sandwich. I'll make it for you." Mimi looks up at me as I enter the kitchen. "Kelly honey, you're just in time. Talk some sense into your mother. Tell her she needs to eat."

I look at Mom. She looks like she's lost a little weight. She actually looks quite good. She had been looking a little dumpy the last couple of years. "You're looking good, Mom. You look thinner."

"Dammit, of course she's thinner. She hasn't eaten in three months."

"Mother, don't you think it's time you went back home. I'll get Kelly to take you tomorrow."

"Not until you eat," she insists.

Mom pulls a roll of Certs from her housecoat pocket, takes one piece from the open end, and pops it into her mouth. "There. I've eaten. Happy now?"

"Cute, Livy. Real cute." Mimi looks at me. "Nibble here. Nibble there. Like a damn rabbit." Mimi puffs on her cigarette. "Phil cooked steaks last night. Damn good ones. Expensive, too. Had to throw hers away."

"I told you not to cook me one," Mom says.

"Where is Uncle Phil?" I ask, looking around.

"On his way back to Cincinnati."

"It's Cleveland, Mother. Cleveland, Ohio."

"Cleveland. Cincinnati. What's the difference? It's up there." Mimi points toward North. "One of the grandkids has a piano recital or something. Says he's going to videotape the damn thing and send it to us. Never does, though. Can't even get a lousy picture out of his wife."

"It's not Madeline's fault, Mother. They just have a busy life. I've done the same on this side. Time gets away from you." Mom says as she puffs on her cigarette. Her eyes are glassy and her fingernails are all broken and ragged.

"You should go easy on the smokes, Mom," I tell her.

"Oh, right, like you should talk," she scolds.

"Mom, I just …"

"Don't antagonize her, Kelly dear. She doesn't need it right now."

"I'm sorry," I say.

Mom waves her hand and taps her ashes in reply. She does not look up at me.

"Go get your things out of the car. I'll make you an egg sandwich," Mimi tells me.

"Take her up on it, Kelly. She's dying to crack something."

*   *   *   *

"This one's ten thousand, this one is twenty thousand, this one is five thousand," I say as I sort through the insurance policies in the fireproof lock box. Mom sits down at the dining table beside me and examines the papers.

"What about the one from work? He has the big one from work."

"This one?" I hold up a folded policy and slowly open it up. It is big. "I think this is the one you want." I hand her the policy.

"Oh my," she says as she reads the amount. Her hands begin to shake.

"Mom, are you all right?"

"Your father used to dream of this kind of money. Always hoping that someday he would win the lottery and retire," Mom laughs. "He'd think up ways we would spend the lottery winnings as we'd drive down to Louisiana or Texas on a Saturday afternoon to go buy a ticket." Mom starts to cry. "It's just so ironic that he's worth all this money dead."

"Daddy was always the dreamer, I'll grant you that one," I say.

"What am I supposed to do with all this?" She hands the policy to me.

"Invest it. Spend it. Enjoy it. Do whatever you want to with it."

"You know we were barely getting by," Mom tells me. "It took everything your father had just to make it every month. And what was left, he sent to you."

"Mom ..."

"Ben always said he'd take good care of me. We ate beans when we were first married because we couldn't afford anything else. Then after you were born, I made all my own clothes so you could have the nicest things. We almost lost our car one month because for your birthday your father had to buy this stupid coat he saw in the store window. I wore the same old clothes so you could wear clothes from Wiseman's. I patched up my wool coat to make it through another year so your father could have a real, honest to God Armani suit to wear to a pharmaceutical convention. This is the life I've had."

"Mom, it never seemed like you struggled. You both had a good life. You've got this wonderful house, a Cadillac ..."

"The Cadillac was just one of his ways of showing off. I never wanted it and we couldn't afford it. Last year did you know the bank tried to foreclose on us?"

"What?"

"Yeah. Ben hadn't paid the house note in four months," she says.

"Why? I don't understand."

"Because he paid for your tuition."

"You never told me this ..."

"I offered to go to work but he said no. Don't worry. He'd take care of everything. Always, his famous last words. That's when I started taking the real estate course."

"So how did you get the house back?"

"I sold a few things," she says and waves her right hand at me.

The twenty-fifth anniversary ring is missing from her finger. "Oh, Mamma, no."

"I don't care. It wasn't worth that much but …"

"But Mom, that was yours. Yours. I didn't know." My eyes begin to tear up. "I'm so sorry."

"Well, it's done." Mom picks up her pack of cigarettes and shakes it. The pack is empty. "He said, 'Don't worry Livy. We'll buy another one. As soon as Kelly graduates and gets on her feet.'"

"Mom, you just always seemed like you were doing well."

"I don't know why I'm telling you all this. I shouldn't even be complaining. You thought your father was some sort of god. Well, I'm telling you he was only a man."

I look down at the policy in front of me. Mom wants me to feel guilty. Why should I? I can't help it if Dad wasn't good with money or that he wanted to spend more than he had. I can't help it if he spent it on me or a lifestyle he couldn't afford. My father always did want more than he had.

"Now look at me," Mom announces. "I can have anything. Anything at all, and what do I want? I must be out of my mind." Mom rises and searches the drawer for a pack of cigarettes in the kitchen. She removes a pack, then slams the drawer shut. "Dammit, Ben."

Mom stares right at me and the guilt sets in. I keep flashing on that Saturday morning. If only I hadn't been so demanding, so selfish and insistent that he do that for me. If only I had come home more often to see to it that he kept his strength up. If only I gone to pharmacy school like he wanted me to in the first place. If only …

*   *   *   *

"Has it hit her yet?" Sandra asks me over the phone.

"Like a ton of bricks. She's in the bedroom, locked away and feeling sorry for herself," I tell her. I flip through the channels of the muted television set and finally settle on the Weather Channel.

"It's normal. My mother got in her car and drove away a week after my father died. Called me two days later from West Texas and said to come get her. She didn't think she could make it back. At least your mother is safe and sound in her own house. Imagine what it must be like to get hit with grief just outside of Abilene," Sandra says.

"Were your parents a happy couple?" I ask.

"Yeah, I guess so."

"Mine weren't. I mean, they were great parents and all. They just weren't happy. Dad was always dreaming for more and Mom always felt unappreciated. I know that's why I'm so damn miserable." I look up at the television set. It's raining in Memphis.

"My mother felt unappreciated, too. I think it comes from that nurturing instinct mothers from that era must have. They didn't work so their family was their job. We never thanked her for the clean sheets, the hot suppers, the peanut butter and jelly sandwiches in our school lunch, nothing. Yet she went on doing those things anyway. Hell, I wouldn't. Maybe that's the problem," Sandra says.

"Maybe so."

"Your mother's just grieving. I wouldn't worry about her too much. She's a strong woman. She loved your dad. She'll get over it eventually."

"I know."

"Wanna go down to the White House Grill and grab a beer or two?" Sandra asks.

"Oh, Sandra, I'd love to but I can't. I've already taken Mimi back home and no one's here. I'm sure Mom'll be all right but I hate to leave her alone. Besides, I'm going back to Memphis tomorrow. I've got to get packing for the move to Phoenix."

"So you are going. What about Walt?"

"What about him? We're not joined at the hip or anything. I'm making this move because that's what Daddy would want. I don't need Walt. I don't need anybody."

I finally hang up the telephone. I look at the television set. A commercial for insurance is on. I turn my gaze to the pictures on top of the TV and find myself staring at an Olan Mills portrait which has always graced the top of the television set ever since I was five years old. In the picture I am wearing the velveteen coat which Mom claims almost cost them the car. Dad's beaming in a shining black pin stripe suit and Mom wears her same old Sunday dress I thought was simply her favorite and a scowl I thought was just a permanent feature on an otherwise beautiful face.

*   *   *   *

It's after five p.m. on Sunday and I really do need to go back to Memphis but Mom hasn't come out of her room yet. The door's locked.

"Mom," I call out as I knock gently on the door. I hear the television set go mute for a moment than back on again.

"I could fix you some supper if you like. Then I've got to go back to Memphis," I say. The television goes mute again.

"Bye." She says. The sound returns.

I go back to my bedroom and phone Mimi.

"Still in there, huh?" she asks.

"Mimi, I don't know what to do." I begin to cry. "I've got to drive to Memphis. I have to get ready to move out to Phoenix and ..."

"Now, now, Pumpkin'. I know you're suffering, too, but you think about your Momma. She's lost someone she's known a lot longer than you. She's grievin'. This is her way."

"I know that, Mimi, but I've got ..."

"Child, you listen to me, and you listen to me good. You only had one father and you've only got one mother. Together they have given you the world and you've taken it. Now it's your turn to give it back."

"But ..."

"I'm serious, Kelly. You're mother's a fragile woman. She's not as strong as you and me. You can't leave her now."

"I guess you're right," I give in.

"I'll get Alice Shrewsbury to bring me over there. Don't you worry. I'll be there soon."

∗   ∗   ∗   ∗

Mom's door opens at eleven thirty that night. Mimi dozed off hours ago, and since then I've been watching a storm free evening on the Weather Channel. "Would you like to sign my yearbook?" Mom asks me as she walks up to the couch.

"Do what, Mom?" I ask her. Maybe I didn't hear her right. Our conversation wakes Mimi up.

"My yearbook. I would be so happy if you would sign it next to your picture," she states as she hands me her high school yearbook. "I love your new flip," she giggles.

"Mom, what's wrong with you?"

"Go with me to the bathroom. I swiped the old lady's smokes." She grabs my hand and tries to pull me up off the couch.

"I'm going to call the doctor," Mimi says as she rises from her chair and marches across the room. "She's not right."

"Oh, geez. Um, I'll get her coat, and we'll take her to the emergency room."

"Aren't you going to the Anchor Club meeting with me today?" Mom asks me. I decide to play along with her.

"Why yes. I've got the keys to my dad's car. Why don't you go with us."

"Your old man's car? Really? Oh, I hope it's not an Edsel. I hate Edsels. My father has an Edsel. It's ugly."

"Why no, it's a Cadillac actually."

"Oh, goody," she squeals with glee. Mimi rolls her eyes at me. I want to laugh at her. She's kind of funny like this. Instead the tears roll down my face as I grab Mom's purse and car keys and try to usher her into the car.

"My stars, it's a big Cadillac. I hope I can have one of these when I grow up."

*   *   *   *

"Olivia's been going through the change for sometime now. I've had her on hormone therapy for a couple of years now," Dr. Wallace tells us in the waiting room. "It appears she hasn't been taking her medicine. She's been through a lot this past week. It's finally catching up with her. But she's going to be just fine once I get her hormones back in line. We'll get her admitted and then go from there."

"How long will this take?" I ask him.

"A few days. She's going to need someone to watch her for a while," he says, looking at me. "At least until we get her completely regulated."

"Sure," I say. I slouch down in the chair. "I'll stay with her."

Mimi pats me on the leg. "That's a good girl."

*   *   *   *

"Help me, sir, oh please, help me find it," I plead as I sift through a garbage dumpster. The man gives me a go-to-hell look and walks on.

"Ma'am. Ma'am, can you help me find it?" I say, turning my desperation toward a smartly dressed woman who happens by.

"What have you lost?" she inquires.

"It's in here. I just know it." I point to the dumpster.

The woman shakes her head and hurries down the street.

"Won't somebody help me?" I scream. I frantically claw my way through the trash.

"Over here, Kelly. Over here," a voice calls out. I turn around and see my father far off down the busy city street. He waves for me to come to him. He has found it.

I push my rickety grocery cart toward him. The basket overflows with the things I have treasured my entire life—my tattered Raggedy Ann doll, pink ballet slippers, Malibu Barbie, Mod Ken, Growing Skipper, and the velveteen coat.

"Kelly, it's in this one," my father says. "I promise this time."

I look at him with all the faith and certainty I've always shown him and peer into the bin. I look back toward him to smile at him in appreciation, but he has disappeared.

"Daddy?" I say. I fling bags of waste and refuse out of the way in my desperate attempt to find what he wants me to find. I discover a pastel painting of the desert at sunset. I take a long hard look at it, then toss it aside with the rest of the garbage. I keep digging and searching. "Where is it? I know it must be in here!" I say.

At last I find myself standing alone inside an empty dumpster. I am clothed in a tattered rag doll's dress and the velveteen coat. My hands and face are covered with filth. "Daddy, you promised it would be in here," I whimper. "You promised."

I crawl out of the dumpster and push my cart on further down the sidewalk. Business people scurry off to their jobs, glare at me and direct snide comments toward me as they pass by.

"Bag lady, get out of the street. You don't belong here."

"You stink, you worthless piece of garbage. Go back where you came from."

"Get a life, lady."

"Kelly, over here. It's in this one," my father calls out again. "Hurry, it's in here."

My spirits rise again when I see him across the busy intersection. "I'm coming, Daddy. I'm coming." I ease my cart onto the pavement and smile at him as I cross.

I try to dodge the traffic which whizzes by me. Cars swerve around me and drivers honk their horns and scream obscenities at me. It doesn't matter. My father is across the street waving for me to come. Nothing can possibly happen to me now. He has found what I need at last.

A pothole derails my buggy and my belongings scatter all over the street. I bend over to retrieve them but I cannot get to them. The air turns still and the street begins to rumble louder and louder as if a storm is about to strike. I look to the right. There is nothing. I turn to the left. A monstrous Mac truck barrels toward me. There is no time to run. I look to my father for help, but he has disappeared. I cover my eyes from the glare of the truck lights and I cringe.

"Ms. Carmichael," a nurse calls out. "Time for your pill, Ms. Carmichael, wake up."

I sit up in the recliner in my Mom's hospital room and shake the dream from my head. The overhead lights hurt my eyes and I squint until they adjust to the glare. Mimi slowly rises from the other bed and we both look at Mom. The nurse tries to give her a pill, but she pushes it away.

"Ms. Carmichael, you can't get better unless you take your medicine."

"So what. Who's going to care for me, anyway?"

"I am, Mom," I say. "I'm going to take care of you now."

Mom stares at me for a long moment then pops the pill into her mouth.

CHAPTER 9

▼

THAT'S NOT SOME OLD BAG, THAT'S MY MOTHER

They say everything comes full circle. If that's the case then my life is just one big twister.

"This seems so stupid, Kelly," Walt says as he removes a chair from my apartment, carries it out the door and into the rented U-Haul. "I mean, we could have put your things in the warehouse at the dealership for a couple of months until you return," he shouts to me from inside the truck. His voice sounds hollow and remote. He comes back into the apartment again. "It is for just a couple of months, isn't it?"

"Until my mom gets on her feet," I assure him. "I thought we went over this on the phone."

"We did," he says. "But this moving everything to Arkansas when you're going to come back in two months is silly."

"Maybe so but it's my stuff and I want it with me," I say as I wrap the sports section of the Commercial Appeal around a drinking glass.

"That's just like you, Kelly."

"What do you mean?" I demand. I put the glass into a box.

"Nothing. Just nothing." He picks up another chair. "I've been thinking that maybe I ought to start looking for a new place. You know, something bigger like a house perhaps."

"Why? Your place is plenty big enough for you and Bosco."

"For me and Bosco, sure, but …" He carries the chair outside where his voice trails off into a mumble. He returns to the doorway. "So what do you think?"

"About what?" I shut the box and seal it with tape.

"The living together thing. What do you think?"

I suddenly hear the words Daddy ingrained into my head, "No daughter of mine is going to shack up with some horny-ass boy. That will be the day I no longer have a daughter." It plays over and over in my head.

"So …"

My intestines rumble and the urgency for a bathroom becomes imminent. Before I can rise from the kitchen floor I feel my panties go wet with mucous and stool. "Ah, shit," I say.

"Come on, Kelly," he says, exasperated. "I'm really trying here. You know, sometimes I just don't get you."

"Yeah, I know." I rise up and pray that Walt cannot see what has just happened. I slowly try to make my way upstairs to the bathroom.

"You don't even want to break away from your family, do you?"

I stop halfway up and hold onto the banister. "Look. I've just lost my dad, quit the first job I've ever succeeded at, and now I'm moving in with my mother again. I'm almost thirty, Walt. I don't exactly want to live with someone right now."

"Then what the hell do you want?"

"Nothing right now. Nothing at all." I make my way upstairs to clean up the mess I've made.

*   *   *   *

I can't recall the last time my life was calm and effortless. There are no pressures or deadlines hanging over me; no worries about utilities being shut off, and nothing to study for. Living at home may not be the ideal circumstance for a twenty nine year old single woman, but I'm trying to look on the bright side of things for a change. I haven't had a Tums in weeks.

Remarkably, the days go by really fast. Mom and I have cleaned every square inch of the house twice. We go shopping almost every day. We've even tried to establish a better relationship. Sometimes it works. Sometimes it doesn't.

Today we have boxed up Dad's clothing to distribute to the needy. The good stuff has already been sifted through by Hal and Bob.

"Should we give them to the church or what?" Mom asks me.

"If you give them to St. Marks, the Thomas boys will be wearing them every Sunday. Do you really want to see Dad's Brook's Brother's suits on a couple of lowlifes?"

"I see your point. Maybe if we took them to El Dorado we could drop them off at the Salvation Army. Then we can go on to Monroe and go shopping," Mom suggests enthusiastically.

Since the doctor put her on a light antidepressant along with her hormone therapy, Mom has been nothing but a non-stop shop-a-holic. I've never ever seen her buy three pairs of pants in any given day, let alone month, and on that same day buy three separate pairs of shoes to match. She's gone absolutely bonkers.

"Maybe Pauline and Julie would like to come. Mom picks up the phone and calls Julie. "Oh, hey Bob, it's Livy ... Fine ... Doing much better, and you? ... Oh that's good ... Well, I was calling for Julie ... Oh, she is ... Oh, well, no, that's okay. It wasn't important ... Sure ... Bye, Bob.... Nice talking to you, too." Mom hangs up the phone and frowns.

"What is it?"

"Pauline and Julie went up to Little Rock to buy some furniture for Julie's living room."

"Oh, Mom."

"They didn't even ask me to go." She looks like she wants to cry but can't. I don't know if she's being stoic or if it's the drugs. Her eyes don't even glaze.

"But I thought Julie wanted you to help her pick out ..."

"It doesn't matter," she says, shaking her head. "We'll go to El Dorado anyway. Who needs them. It'll just be us."

"Sure, Mom. We'll have a good time. I just don't understand why they ..."

"And you won't. Not until you are a widow."

*   *   *   *

"Kelly," Mom calls out from behind a rack of cardigan sweaters. "Kelly, over here. How about this one?" Mom holds up a sweater with pink and green kitty cats all over it. "This is so sweet. It would look so cute on you."

"Mom, I can't possibly wear that thing, especially not in public."

"Why? What's wrong with it? I think it's absolutely precious."

"Mom, I don't like it. It's not me," I protest.

"Well, beggars can't be choosers, can they?" Mom hangs the sweater back onto the rack. I cringe from her words.

"I like this jacket." I hold up a brown tweed fitted riding jacket with patched sleeves. "Now this is me."

Mom looks at the price tag. "Of course, you would like that one. Two hundred and fifty dollars. Your father taught you well." Mom takes the jacket from my hands and places it back on the rack. This is like utter deja vu to me. I'm not pushing thirty. I'm going on sixteen and my Mother believes she is, well, my Mother. So what if I live under her roof, that she has paid off all my bills, pays me a small allowance every week, and spent thirteen grueling hours of intensive labor bringing me into the world. Just who the hell does she think she is?

We give up on the clothing and circle back toward the makeup counter. We take the shortcut through electronics. The Weather Channel is playing on all fifteen television sets. It's sunny and seventy-two in Phoenix.

*   *   *   *

I whine to Sandra over the phone the next evening. "I honestly believe she thinks I'm twelve years old." I reach into my purse and remove a roll of Tums.

"Kelly dear, the cure for your gloom is some serious drinking. A cold, wet, lathery mug of delicious beer. That and a reason to flirt. What do you say?" Sandra tells me.

"I say I'm buying the first round." I pitch the half-eaten roll back into my purse.

Sandra swings by fifteen minutes later to pick me up.

"Mrs. Carmichael, how are you doing these days?" she asks Mom.

"'Bout the same, I guess. I don't know," she replies. "How's your mother getting along?"

"Wonderfully," Sandra says. "Jeff and Stacy are expecting another child and Mother's so excited I swear she's going to bust."

"That's great, Sandra. Tell her I'm happy to hear she's doing well."

"I will. And don't wait up for us. I plan on keeping Kelly out for a good long time, if you catch my meaning."

"Still looking?" Mom half asks, half jokes.

"Well, I'm going to try my best to find one tonight." Sandra laughs. "Let the husband chasing begin!"

I lean over and give Mom a kiss on the cheek. "We won't be out too terribly late. This is Spivey. Where are we going to go?" I tell Mom.

"Just be careful." Mom stands at the door and watches us drive off into the night. It's just like when I was in high school.

"Your mother is so sweet and funny. Livy really is taking your Dad's death well."

"You could say that," I answer her. She doesn't see me roll my eyes.

We enter the White House Grill and find a booth in the back. The place is packed tonight. We both order two light beers.

"I don't know why I even try to get out and be seen. Here I am pushing forty. Shouldn't everyone know by now I'm single and ready to be snatched up? I'm never going to find somebody," Sandra laments. "I must not be good for marriage."

"Then what are you good for?" I ask her.

She stops and pauses for a moment. "Well I'd say sex but I haven't had any in a long time and I'm not sure if I'm still good at that either."

"Like riding a bicycle," I tell her.

"Only without a seat." Sandra laughs. Sometimes her humor gets a tad bit carried away, especially when she's going through a dry spell.

"Walt probably doesn't want me anymore. Nobody wants an almost thirty-year old chick still living with her mother. Sandra, she's going to drive me to drink." I take a big swig of my beer.

"She already has," she points out.

"She thinks of me as her little rebellious twelve-year old instead of her grown daughter. I don't know when she's ever treated me like I'm a grown up."

"That's because you're single. My mother still treats me the same way. Not as much now. She sort of stopped when I hit thirty-five and was still husbandless. Every now and then she reminds me of who brought me into the world."

"What gets me is that I gave up a really good job for her. Probably the best job I've ever had. I didn't want to come home. I did it out of sheer devotion to my family."

"Now that everything seems to be on track, couldn't you get your old job back?" Sandra asks.

"I doubt it. I'm sure they've hired somebody from Harvard to take my place. They prefer Ivy Leaguers. I can't compete with that."

"Do you want to work?"

"I don't know. It's expected of me. I know that. I just don't know what I want to do now."

"Be what you were."

"Paralegal? Not in Spivey. They use legal secretaries. They don't pay squat for my services in small towns. Not enough billable hours."

"Then be a legal secretary."

"Oh, right. You see, I had a secretary at Westward. I couldn't be one because I would need one to keep me straight. I'm horrible at it," I tell her. "I doubt they would let me stay the whole first day, let alone for a career."

"I didn't want to be a teacher but I had to. Teaching and nursing are about the only two professions in Spivey where a woman can actually make any money."

"My father wanted me to be a pharmacist. Don't forget the pharmacists," I say.

"I just about faint at the sight of blood, so I had to be a teacher."

"If you didn't want to be a teacher, then what did you want to be?"

"You're going to laugh."

"No I won't. Try me."

"A housewife."

I laugh. "A housewife! Like our mothers?"

"Sure. Oh, Kelly, I'm so jealous of all those moms driving around in their Suburbans. They drop off their kids at Karate. They go to the grocery store, head up the PTA, join the Junior League. I really want that."

"But that's not a career," I argue.

"Like hell. Oh, girl, those mothers work harder than I do. Families do more now. It takes some serious devotion and dedication to be a good housewife." Sandra sighs. "That's what I really want to be."

"I guess if that's what melts your butter …"

Sandra looks up from her beer. "Oh, look. At the door. Two guys. Real meat this time. Damn, they're good looking."

I turn around in my seat and spot two clean-cut average men in their thirties searching for a place to sit down. They choose the booth behind us. The slightly pudgy blonde sits facing our booth. The younger, clean-cut dark haired man, sits with his back toward me. Sandra smiles wide.

"Blue," she says.

"What?" I shake my head.

"Blue. I want my Suburban to be blue." She winks at me and laughs the little school girl laugh of hers which makes her seem younger than she is.

I feel a pat on my shoulder and Sandra's eyes grow wide with surprise. I turn around and find myself staring at the two guys.

"Excuse me but we're new in town and thought maybe you ladies could recommend something from the menu. Something we might like," the dark-headed one says to us.

Oh, geez, what a line, I think to myself. I bet they use this one in every town and every restaurant they've ever been in. I wonder if any woman has been dumb enough to fall for it.

"Well I like the steaks. They're big and juicy and the best you'll find any-where," Sandra tells them.

Oh, Sandra, no, no. Not these guys. They're hustling and you're playing right into their hands.

"What about you? What do you recommend?" the blonde one continues with me.

"Well, I like their super-duper burritos. They're hot, spicy, loaded with lots of onions, garlic, and beans. Sticks with you for days."

"You don't have a boyfriend, do you?" the dark one inquires.

"Why do you ask?"

"Two people. Beans and onions. Not quite a desirable combination, if you know what I mean," he says.

"You two look like traveling salesmen. Unless you both have something for each other, beans and onions shouldn't matter," I tell him.

"I'll have the super-duper burrito with everything," he replies. "I'm not afraid."

"I'll try the steak," the blonde states as he winks at Sandra.

Sandra giggles. "You won't be sorry."

"I'm Mike Endicott," the dark one says as he extends his hand for me to shake. "Steak man over there is Dan. Dan Simonson. Do we really look like a couple of salesmen?"

"It's the way you carried yourself in here. Not sure of yourselves. Then you took a seat next to a couple of cute, hopefully single girls who might occupy your evening in an unknown location. Spivey folks, on the other hand, walk in and make themselves at home. They don't scout."

"We work for Dart Pharmaceuticals," Mike states.

I turn toward Sandra and place my finger on my lips just as she is about to speak.

"Her ... um, I'm Sandra and that's Kelly. Why don't you join us?" Sandra blurts out instead. I shoot her a look and she shrugs. "You seem like nice guys. Dart. Wow."

"You know our company?" Dan asks as he settles in next to Sandra.

"I've taken your drugs before," Sandra says. "They seem to have worked. I'm cured."

"So what brings you to Spivey?" I ask. I'm not quite sure if I'm being polite or downright nosy.

"Our man down here died a couple of months ago. We're from headquarters and we're covering his territory while we find a replacement," Mike tells me.

"Interesting that the company has to send two men down to do one man's job." I wink at Sandra.

"The man was one hell of a salesman," Mike boasts. "What a guy."

"Wouldn't you ladies like to order something? We've talked about the company already. That means Dart can pay for this," Dan laughs.

"Oh, well, if the company's buyin' … I'll have steak." Sandra smiles.

"And I'll have a super-duper with everything," I say.

*　　*　　*　　*

"What are you doing?" I ask Sandra in the White House Grill's bathroom.

"I have my own place. I can invite whoever I want over."

"But you don't even know these guys," I plead. "It was fun here, but geez, Sandra, what if they …"

"But they knew your father. Doesn't that count for something? They all work for the same company. I don't see the problem. I'm having a great time. How often do we get to have some nice men over?"

"Obviously not often enough," I tell her as we exit the bathroom. We greet the guys. They stand and wait at the cash register to pay for our meal. Maybe I should have had steak.

"Why don't I ride with Sandra," Dan says. "Mike, you and Kelly take the company car. That way neither one of us gets lost." Dan throws Mike the car keys and winks at him.

"I think that's fair," Mike says.

I hate being separated from the safety of my friend. I'm sure nothing's going to happen. Then again some girl probably thought the exact same thoughts when she was getting into Ted Bundy's car.

Luckily we don't become statistics yet and make it to Sandra's house. She immediately sets the mood for the evening with some Memphis blues that I turned her onto. She breaks out the canned frozen pina coladas which she has most certainly been saving in the freezer for just this sort of occasion.

"Wow, Sandra, you're all set up for a party," Dan comments.

"I read in Bon Appétit, that's a magazine for gourmet's and hostesses, that you must always be ready for unexpected guests. I stay prepared." Sandra pours pretzels into a basket. "Hors d'oeuvre?"

Mike and I chit chat in the kitchen as Sandra and Dan retreat into the living room to dance. She has turned the lights down low. The mood is set for romance. I don't really think she's had a good date in quite some time. It's hard to find someone in a small town. I begin to feel sorry for her. I begin to feel lucky I still have Walt.

"So where do you live, Kelly?" Mike begins. He pulls up a chair next to me at the kitchen table.

I laugh. "I live with my mother."

"Oh, really," he says. "You don't seem like the live-at-home type."

"There's a type like that? I didn't realize."

"What I mean is you seem a little more independent than that," he says. "I would have taken you for a lawyer or a law student even. Something along those lines."

"I used to be a paralegal. Well, I guess I still am. I don't know. I moved back home for a while to decide what I'm going to do with the rest of my life. You might say I'm sort of on hiatus from my career for a while."

"I envy you," he says. "I wish I could do that. Sometimes this job is so absolutely cut throat. The pressure really gets to me. I never expected work to be this unbelievably stressful."

"Tums are your best friend, too, I see." I point at the label showing faintly through his shirt pocket.

"Yeah, I eat them like mints, one after the other," he says as he takes the roll and removes two tablets. He hands one to me. "If it weren't for the money, I'd find something easier to do. I'm probably going to kill myself before I'm fifty. So much for retiring early. But I'm trying, anyway."

"I don't know why it's so important to have such jobs," I say. "I know my father pounded it into my head that I must have a good paying career to be happy. I have pursued employers and college majors all of my adult life. I still haven't found what will make me happy."

"I think it's a myth," Mike says. "But as long as I'm driving Beemers and living in upscale apartments, who the hell cares." Mike takes a large gulp of pina colada. He winces and holds his forehead.

"Ooo, ice headache." I snicker.

"Wow." He shakes his head. "I'm not used to frozen drinks. Reminds me of popsicles when I was just a kid."

"Yeah. My best friend and I used to race each other when we were kids. We'd lick a popsicle as fast as we could until one of us got a headache first." I shake my head. and I gulp the frozen concoction. I don't feel anything.

Mike and I talk for a couple of hours without realizing it. He would love to be doing what I suspect Dan and Sandra are doing in the living room but I refuse to budge from this seat.

"Hey, Mikey buddy," Dan says as he enters the kitchen holding Sandra by the hand. "Why don't you take the car, man. Sandra says she'll drop me off later."

I give Sandra a hard look. She smiles and shrugs sheepishly.

"I, uh, guess I could get Mike to take me home." I look to Mike who nods his heads affirmatively.

"You don't mind, Kel?" Sandra half asks, half states "I really do appreciate this."

"Sure," I say. I try to stall for a little time to talk some sense into Sandra but Dan keeps a firm grip on her hand. I think he's played this scene before.

"It was nice meeting you, Kelly," Dan says. He ushers us out of Sandra's house.

"Call me tomorrow. Okay, Sandy?" I say as Mike and I walk out the door and down the sidewalk.

"Sure," she says, then shuts the door quickly. I turn around and I hear the two of them laughing. I feel helpless.

"So where to now?" Mike asks.

"Home," I say. "I need to go home."

He opens my door like a gentlemen. Then we drive off down the street. I point him toward my house.

"Do you have a big day tomorrow?" I ask, trying to break the silence and restart the conversation.

"Yeah, we've got to meet with a couple of pharmacists and the hospital people. You know, try to take up where old Ben left off."

"Your salesman's name was Ben, huh?"

"Yeah, Ben Carmichael. What a guy," Mike chuckles and shakes his head.

"Nice guy?" I ask.

"Nice? Oh, the man was a non-stop party animal."

"Really?" I try to act like my interest is casual, strictly conversation.

"Yeah. He used to come up to headquarters and treat us young guys to steak dinners and all the fixin's. He was one of Dart's top salesmen. And when his sales territory was increased … Geez, you should have seen the cash flowing."

"Yeah?" My heart pounds. I'm surprised Mike can't hear it.

"He was so good in fact," Mike continues, "that he barely had to work the territory at all. Hell, we didn't know he was dead until somebody called and told us that he'd died. That's how good he was. Turned me onto Armani suits. The guy had six of them."

"No shit?" I ask. I bite my upper lip.

"Really. Once he left his wife, he became a wild one, let me tell you," Mike says. "You know, I think maybe he was from Spivey, as a matter of fact. Did you know him?"

I remain silent.

"Anyway, he got a divorce and rented this kickass apartment. Got himself a girlfriend up in Little Rock, too. A young thing, younger than us. Man, he sure was a swinger. I only partied with him a couple of times," Mike says. "It was like the man went middle age crazy. His girlfriend was an aerobics instructor. A real looker, not like the pictures of his ex-wife I saw once. What a bag."

I've got to get out of this car before I suffocate. "This is my house," I tell him. "You can just pull in on the street." I try hard to choke back the tears and rage I feel right now. Maybe what I'm hearing is just a bunch of bullshit. Bullshit to impress me. Only there's no reason to impress me with someone else's antics.

"Kelly, I would love to call you sometime. Maybe when I'm in town again or you could come up to Little Rock," he says. "You seem like someone I'd like to go out with."

"Maybe," is all I say without my voice cracking.

"You know I never did get your last name?"

"Um ..." I stutter and pause. "It's, uh ... well, it's Carmichael. Kelly Carmichael. I'm Ben's daughter." I open the door and run as fast as I can to the front door. I fiddle with the keys. Finally I open the door. I hear Mike call out to me as I close the door. I hear the car start up and drive away. I sob as I lean against the door.

"It's three-thirty in the morning, Missy. Just where the hell have you been? And who the hell was that?" Mom demands. She stands in front of me, clad in her coffee stained bathrobe. With her cigarette in hand she uses the other hand to nervously run through her hair. It's greasy and slicked back from hours of worry. I stop my sobbing and hang my head down low for what I know will come next.

*   *   *   *

"I don't know what else to do with you," she says. "I have given in to you all of your life. Thirty years I've sacrificed, worried and suffered for you."

"Mom please." The tears roll down my cheek.

"No, not this time. I've given and given and given and what have you done?" she asks. "You've taken and taken and taken. Well, that's it. It's over. I'm not going to take this crap from you any more."

"I don't know what you possibly want from me?" I ask her.

"God, I don't believe you're saying this," Mom puffs on her cigarette and paces the kitchen floor. She's always wanted me to be a mind reader. Unfortunately, I never was. The attempt always got me into worse trouble than I already was in.

"I'll tell you what I'm going to do. You know I don't need you. I don't need all this hassle from you. I had enough of it from your father. Well, he's gone now. So, Missy, I don't feel like I should have to take it from you either."

"I don't understand you, Mom."

"Of course you don't. You never have. You never stopped long enough to find out. Well, who cares anymore. I certainly don't." Mom walks toward her room. She grabs her purse and pulls out her check book. "Will twenty-five thousand dollars make you happy?"

"What?"

"You heard me," she says. "Will twenty-five thousand make you happy? You don't ever have to come into this house, call me, write me, kiss my ass, or anything. I write you a check for twenty-five thousand dollars. You get the hell out of my life."

I don't understand what I'm hearing. My mom thinks she can just buy me off? Where the hell is she coming from?

"Thirty? Will that do it," she bargains. "I'm not going any higher. I've got to live, you know."

"Mom, I don't want your money." I try to stay calm but I fear I'm about to lose it. I begin to cry uncontrollably. I can't stop."

"Oh please, Kelly. Cut the act. You know this is what you want."

"Mom, why are you doing this?"

"Because I've had enough. You've had enough. I'm tired of playing this little game you and your father have been playing with me for as long as I can remember. I'm not going to take it any more."

"Mom, I don't know what it is your talking about. You're talking madness."

"Madness? Please. I've spent over thirty years being mad. A thousand dollars a year isn't too much to sacrifice for a little freedom."

"Mom, I'm sorry if Dad treated you like shit," I say. "I'm sorry that Dad spoiled me into thinking that I'm better than everyone else. I'm sorry that you were nothing to him but some old bag that he came home to on the weekends to do his wash and cook his dinner."

Mom slaps me. Hard. It stings. She never laid a hand on me growing up.

"So you see me as some old bag?" she demands.

"I know about Dad's girlfriend and their apartment up in Little Rock."

Mom starts to cry. I begin to bawl some more. We finally hug and she whispers she's sorry and I repeat the words. We walk to the bathroom and retrieve the box of Kleenex. We sit on the bed and sob.

"She's twenty-two years old, did you know that?" I ask Mom. "Did you know about her?"

"How did you find out?"

"That guy I was with tonight, Mike Endicott, works for Dart. He told me. He just didn't know who the hell I was, that's all. I pried it out of him. He said Ben Carmichael was divorced. Why would he say something like that?"

"I don't know. We weren't, I can assure you of that," she says.

"And no one at Dart knew he was dead. They just thought he was out selling until you called them."

Mom nods her head. "You thought your father was a saint. He was just one big asshole."

"Why didn't you divorce him, Mom?"

"After a while it's easier to stay than to leave. We've been together for thirty three years. He promised he would give me the world someday. I believed in him."

"Why didn't he leave?"

"He knew he had it good. Me on the weekends and her during the week. Why should he leave?"

"God, Mom. I feel like my world has suddenly caved in. I did everything to please him but I never could. He was never happy with the choices I made or the direction I wanted to go. He always wanted me to follow his path. Why didn't I rebel?"

"Why didn't you?" Mom asks.

"Because I believed in him."

I take the check which Mom has written to me and tear it up.

CHAPTER 10

▼

A Bag a Day Keeps the Doctor Away

When I was young, I was a very healthy person. I had an almost perfect attendance record from kindergarten straight through high school. Oh sure, a cold or a virus here and there on some rare occasions. But that's it. I don't know why my adult life has to be plagued with illness. Maybe it's because when we grow up and work, we automatically acquire health insurance. Gee, I wish I had some right now.

I know I should have gone to the doctor when this thing reared its ugly head, but I really thought it would go away on its own. It hasn't been that much of a hassle to tell you the truth. Okay, so I've had to replace almost all of my panties and I've started buying aspirin and Tums in bulk. But apart from that …

"God, Kelly, you look like hell," Walt says as he greets me at his door. "Are you sure you're up for the weekend?"

"Gee, thanks, Walt. I've only been on the road for four hours. How am I supposed to look?" I ask as I set my bags down in the entryway.

"No. I mean …" He gives me a hug and a kiss. "Oh, baby. I just mean you look ill. Do you have the flu or something."

"I've got this bug I can't seem to shake," I tell him. "Don't worry about me. I've almost got it licked."

"You should have waited until next weekend to come," he says.

"I wanted to see you."

We embrace and kiss for a long time. It feels good to be back in his arms.

"So how are things back home?" he asks. "Your mom's doing okay, huh?"

"Much better. She's getting there. It's just going to take some time, that's all."

"Did you get the Sunday paper I sent you?" he asks.

"I got it. Thanks."

"Well?" he asks.

"Well, what?" I pick up my bag and make my way toward the bedroom.

"Did you send any resumes out?"

"Oh sure. I sent a couple," I lie again. I don't want to admit to him that I've enjoyed the time off and the lack of pressure. Mom and I are getting along wonderfully and beginning to really know each other for the first time in our lives. Besides, I hate to think about leaving her and trying to find something new to do again.

"Somebody'll snap you up. You've got wonderful qualifications. You'll just have to pound the pavement for a while." He follows me into the bedroom. "You know, if you want, you could probably get a job out at one of the stores in the mall. Then you could finish your degree."

"I suppose I could do that." I roll my eyes. He doesn't see me.

"As a matter of fact, that would probably be the best bet," he says and pats my shoulder. "Yeah. Get yourself a degree in literature or art history."

"What?"

"Literature or art history," he says.

"Why those?" I ask him.

"Why not? Easy degree."

"And what am I supposed to do with a degree in art history? Visit museums for God's sake? What?"

"You're getting defensive, Kelly. I just thought maybe you might like the opportunity to finish a degree without any pressure. I make good money. I can take care of you while you study."

"Art and literature?"

"Or whatever you want. I just thought you would probably pursue something sort of interesting and fun instead of something stressful and demanding like law. I mean, you won't really have to work at all once we're ... you know?"

"Oh yeah. You know."

"My friend, James Glenn, you'll meet him on Sunday, his wife Chelsea got an art history degree from Vassar. Or maybe it was from Wellesley. Whatever. She's just so fascinating to talk to at parties."

"So that's what she does with her degree? Small talk? No career?"

"Why? She's a housewife. She has no need to work. James is an optometrist."

"If she's so fun at parties, perhaps she could create a new party game for me. How about pin the degree on Kelly. The degree that sticks wins."

"Kell, I'm only suggesting here," he pleads and throws his hand up in the air.

"I'm sorry. I know you're trying to help. But I've been here five minutes and you're already trying to change my life." I groan. "Can't you just be happy with me the way I am at this moment?"

"You're right," he says and takes me into his arms. "I just want you to be happy."

I force myself to smile and say, "I know you do."

*   *   *   *

Piazano's is my absolute favorite place to eat in Memphis. Usually. I look at the menu. Even the thought of salad makes my stomach churn. Despite taking four aspirins and drinking almost a full bottle of Mylanta, I still feel sick.

"I've gotta have the veal tonight," Walt says. "How 'bout you?"

"Spaghetti and meatballs," I say. What does it matter? It all makes my stomach churn.

"Oh, come on, now. No stops," he says. "You can do better than that."

"With this bug I've got, I don't think so. You'll probably have to box it up anyway," I say.

"I'm sorry, Baby. I thought you were almost over this thing. We can go home ..."

"No," I say. I can feel the aspirin kicking in. The hair on the back of my neck feels wet. I'll be okay in a few minutes. "Let's stay."

Walt orders for both of us.

"Anything else?" the waitress asks.

"I'd like a glass of ice water. Lots of ice in it, please," I tell her.

The waitress leaves and quickly returns with a bottle of Merlot and my water.

"Oh, wonderful," I say as she sets the glass of water in front of me. It has tiny bits of crushed ice in it. I like it like that.

"So I was thinking that maybe in a couple of weeks we could move you back here," he says. "Your mother's got to get on with her life sometime." Walt takes a sip of his wine. "We should go look at houses while you're here."

"Maybe," I say. I crunch the ice. It tastes so good in my mouth.

"God, Kelly, do you have to do that?" he scolds.

"Do what?" I ask.

"The ice ... I mean ... geez ..."

"Sorry," I say. "It just tastes so good."

"When did you start doing that?"

"I don't know. Since Dad died. It's weird. I'm just so hungry for ice. I can't help it."

"It's obnoxious," he points out.

I apologize but sneak one last bite of ice before I push the glass away.

Walt goes on and on about us living together but I don't really hear him. I just stare at the glass and daydream about eating snow.

*   *   *   *

I wake up wide-eyed and ready for the day only to find it's two thirty in the morning. I'm bathed in sweat and my hair sticks to my neck. I turn over and find Walt sound asleep. He snores lightly. It's kind of cute.

I ease out of bed and go to the bathroom. There's lots of blood in the toilet. It's not my period.

I sneak out of the bedroom, ease past Bosco, and carefully wind through the living room and into the kitchen.

Like most men, Walt has few appliances. But he does have a blender. I take two or three hand fulls of ice from the freezer and fill up the container. I press 'crush.' The ice crunches and whirs in the blender. The sound wakes up Bosco. He barks and charges into the kitchen as if he's doing his job and caught a prowler.

"It's just me, Bosco. It's just me," I say to the dog. He barks at the blender.

"Enough, Bosco, please," I plead. I turn the appliance off.

"What's going on?" Walt asks, still sleepy. He stands in the doorway.

"Oh, nothing, really. The dog just heard me and thought I was an intruder or something."

He looks at the ice in the blender. "What the hell are you making?" He glances at the clock on the stove.

"Ice."

"Ice? What's with you, Kelly?" He shakes his head.

"I don't know. I just want some." I pop the top off of the blender, scoop up the ice with my fingers, and shove it into my mouth.

"I don't get you sometimes, Kelly."

"I know." I crunch the ice between my teeth.

He turns around and shuffles back to bed. He calls the dog but Bosco doesn't obey him. The dog begs for the ice.

"You want some ice, Bosco?" I ask the dog. He whines and wags his tail.

"Here you go." I toss Bosco an ice cube. We both chomp the ice with pleasure. "You understand me, don't you, dog?"

Bosco barks and puts his paw out.

"I thought so."

*   *   *   *

"So these are your best friends?" I ask Walt as we drive through Germantown.

"We were real close in high school and sort of drifted away. Lately we've been getting back in touch. Since you've been away I've had to find something to do. James Glenn, my friend, he's married, so ..."

"To the art history phenom, right?" I ask.

"The what?"

"The one from Wellesly?"

"Oh, yeah, something like that," he says. "Anyway, I went to school with James. I didn't go to school with Chelsea."

"Oh."

We pull into the driveway of a home I don't think any of my parent's more affluent friends could even afford. I can't help but notice the Mercedes and BMW in the garage. There are also several affluent vehicles parked on the street.

"Wow," I say.

"Nice house, isn't it?" Walt says as he gets out of the car. I remain in the seat.

"You're nervous, aren't you?" He laughs.

I nod my head.

"Don't be. They're going to love you." He extends his hand for me to get out of the car.

"They're going to eat me for lunch," I tell him.

"Not on the first visit," he says.

We walk up to the massive leaded glass double door. I can see people milling around in the living room. My stomach churns and my intestines gurgle.

"You're hungry, huh?" Walt asks. He's heard. "Maybe you'll eat them for lunch." He squeezes my hand as the door opens. A tall slender woman with a cocktail in her hand greets us.

"Walt, sweetheart, you made it," she says. She gives him a sorority hug and a half kiss. "Jamie. Walt's here!"

She escorts us through the foyer and into the living room where three other couples mill around. "And you must be Kelly. I'm Chelsea Glenn. It's so nice to finally meet Walt's girlfriend. We've heard so much about you. We were worried he was making you up." She laughs.

"No, I'm real," I say. I try to be charming.

"Don't you know it, dear," she says. She introduces us to the other couples whose names escape me before the echo in the cathedral ceiling does.

Like all couples parties, the guys go off to the barbecue grill while the girls are left behind in the kitchen. I don't know these women. I feel like I'm on display.

"So Kelly, I heard you were an exec out at Westward. Wow. Practically a VP, huh?" one of the girls asks.

"Oh, I wouldn't call being a legal assistant anything close to being a VP. Besides, I'm not there anymore. I was transferred and didn't want to go."

"Paralegal. Paralegals are hot right now, huh?" one of the women asks.

"I suppose."

"Oh, yeah. I read about them in Cosmo. It's still one of the hottest trends," Chelsea says.

"So what are you going to do now?" the other woman asks.

"I'm not sure. Perhaps go back to school. I'll decide when I move back," I say.

"Walt tells us you're having to handle your father's affairs. I'm so sorry," Chelsea says. She touches my hand as if she cares. "Inheritance is tough. But hey, I love my new house." Chelsea winks at her friends.

"I know it must be tough on you," one of them sympathizes. "Grief always is."

"It's hard," I tell her. I smile at her. She seems so sympathetic. "I'm learning how to get through it."

"There's only one cure for grief that I know of," she counters.

"What's that?" I ask her.

"Xanex and Europe," she exclaims. The women all cackle.

"What can't that combination cure?" another woman asks as they continue to laugh.

"Tell me about it," Chelsea says. "If it hadn't been for those little pink pills and Christian Dior, I'd have never made it through the grief Uncle Sidney caused me." They all cackle again.

I feel ill and the room becomes unbearably cold. "Where's your bathroom?" I ask.

"Down the hall, honey," Chelsea says.

"Thanks." I walk quickly toward the bathroom with my purse in hand. I can feel the fever rising in my body. I close the door and fumble for the aspirins in my bag. I pop three in my mouth and wash them down with the water from the tap.

I stare at myself in the gilded mirror above the marble countertop. I sort of look like them. Then I look at my clothes. I realize that the plaid wrap-around skirt I'm wearing came from Wal-Mart.

I hear the girl's laughter through the door. I must make wonderful fodder for their conversation. What the hell am I doing here?

*   *   *   *

"My friends liked you today," Walt says as he starts the car.

"They're nice," I tell him back, not wanting to tell him how I really feel.

"They're a bunch of fakes," he says as he pulls out of the driveway and waves at Chelsea and James. "I know you hate them."

I laugh. "Then why do you hang out with them?"

"I don't know. I went to school with them. I don't have a reason," he says.

"Why me, Walt? Why do you hang around with me?" I ask him.

"Because you're the genuine article. You're sincere. What about me?" he asks as he backs out of the driveway.

"The same, I suppose. I enjoy being with you. I don't know," I say.

"Love's funny that way, I guess," he says and touches me on the leg.

"I guess so."

*   *   *   *

I barely make it to the outskirts of Little Rock on my way home when I have to pull over and throw up.

I took three aspirins just as I left Memphis. They don't seem to be working. I feel more feverish than I ever have.

I pull into a convenience store a couple of miles down the interstate. I hardly make it into the bathroom before I throw up again. "Please God, please let me make it home."

I purchase several bottles of water and a large cup of ice. I don't care that I have to pay full price for the ice. I need it. With a stolen roll of toilet paper in my purse, I try to make it home to Spivey.

The nausea comes about every half hour or so. I pull over, run to the other side of the car and throw up nothing. Then I feel great. I crunch my ice, rinse my mouth out with the bottled water, and start the process over again.

I throw up less than a mile from my house. When I arrive home, Mom meets me at the door. She hugs me then looks for the engagement ring she had hoped would grace my finger when I returned. She frowns at me.

"Be patient, Mom. It's only a matter of time. It'll happen. Just not like it did for you back in the days of Frankie and Annette."

"You look like hell," she says and wipes the hair from my eyes. "What did you do this weekend?"

"Nothing you wouldn't have approved of, if that's what you mean. I've got a bug or something. I can't seem to shake it."

"Are you sure it's a bug?" she asks.

"What else would it be?" I drag my bags into the house.

"You could be …"

"Mom, please. I'm not pregnant, if that's what you're getting at."

"You never know. You girls these days think … Well, why buy the cow …"

"Mom. Give me a little credit, huh?" I drop the bags in my room and barely make it to the bathroom before the waves of nausea hit again.

*   *   *   *

"I'm going to admit you to the hospital," the doctor says as he finishes examining me.

"What?" I look over at Mom for help.

"You're dehydrated, you've got a fever …"

"Listen to the doctor, Kelly," Mom says.

"But I don't have …" I almost begin to cry. I don't have any insurance.

"You are a very sick young lady," the doctor says. "We need to know what's causing this. Go on over there. I'll look in on you this evening."

Mom takes me by the arm and leads me out of the office. "It's that Asian variety of flu, I'm telling you. It's hard to lick," Mom says. "I saw it on CNN." She pats me on the back and smiles at me. "It's okay. I'll take care of you."

*   *   *   *

The nurse comes into my hospital room. She carries an I-V. "Hun, I've gotta …"

"I'm feeling better, really," I protest. "I don't want a needle in my arm."

"I'm not going to put it in your arm. I'm going to put it in the back of your hand."

"Kelly, really. Stop being such a baby," Mom scolds me. "Listen to the nurse."

"I hate this," I say.

"You've had one of these before, huh?" the nurse asks.

"No."

"It's not so bad," she says.

"Have you ever had one?" I ask her.

"No, but …"

"Then you don't know, do you?" I return.

"Well, no, but I give these all the time and …"

"Kelly, relax," Mom says. "If you'll relax it'll go in much better and won't hurt so much."

"I don't feel dehydrated," I protest as the nurse takes my left hand and begins searching for a vein.

"A little prick …" she says as she inserts the needle into my hand.

I bite my lip. It's not so bad but just the thought of a needle in my hand makes me nauseous. I grab the vomit tray and throw up bile.

*   *   *   *

"Walt? Hey," I say into the phone.

"How are you? Are you better?" he asks.

"Well … I'm in the hospital," I tell him.

"What?"

"They think I've got a bad case of the flu or something. They're giving me antibiotics. I'll be fine."

"Do you want me to come down?"

"No. It's the middle of the week. Maybe on the weekend if you want. It doesn't matter." Actually it does but I can't tell him that.

"This weekend? Oh, well, I guess …" I can hear the disappointment in his voice.

"If you've got other plans …"

"I can cancel. I mean, I was just going to play in the annual father/son golf tournament with Dad out at the club. We're the defending champions, you know. I suppose I could tell him …"

"No. No, you play with your Dad. It's important," I tell him. I feel myself tear up.

"Are you sure? I mean, I'll call you every day," he says. "I do love you, you know."

"I know. I love you, too."

We say goodbye as I dry my sobbing eyes and hang up the phone. Mom returns to my room from her smoking break.

"Walt?" she asks.

"Yeah."

"When's he coming?"

"He's playing in a golf tournament with his father this weekend. He's not coming." I begin to cry.

"You're not married, yet. If you were married he'd be here. If you were engaged even ..." Mom frowns as she sits down in the recliner. "I told you, 'why buy the cow' ..."

"Mom, please. Don't you have some more cigarettes to smoke or something?"

The I-V pump goes off. I'm empty.

*   *   *   *

I don't know why they keep telling me to rest. You can't get rest in a hospital, especially at night. Either the nurses are in every half hour to take my temperature or blood pressure, or my damn I-V pump goes off and they come to reset it. If nobody's in the room, then it's the loneliness that gets to you.

I look over at the twenty-four long stem red roses in a vase that Walt sent me. I suppose he thinks they make up for his absence. Hell, I'd be there if it were him.

*   *   *   *

I've never been so alone as I am at this very moment. The nurses come into my room but I am by myself. All night long I watch the tiny bubbles in the I-V trickle down the plastic tube and into the filter. The clear liquid flows imperceptibly toward my vein.

Mom never left Dad's side.

I am so alone.

*   *   *   *

"Hey, Mrs. Carmichael," Sandra says as she peeps into the room and first notices Mom. "How ya doin', Kelly?"

"Still got a fever," I say.

"Oh, geez, I'm so sorry. You've been here four days already. Wow," she says. "You're not contagious, are you?"

"They didn't say it's the flu. Have you had a flu shot?" I ask her.

"Yeah," Sandra replies.

"Then don't worry about it. Come on in," I say.

She walks in and takes a seat on the end of the bed.

"I saw on one of those talk shows that some of these new infections don't respond to drugs. They say we don't have anything at all to combat them with," Mom tells us.

"Mom, I'm not going to die."

"I didn't say you were," she responds. "I was just making conversation."

"Just because I haven't responded to anything is no reason to call Mike Wallace," I tell her.

"Walt's not coming," Mom tells Sandra.

"Oh, I'm so sorry," Sandra says. "Did he send you the flowers? They're so beautiful."

"Yep. I mean, there's no point in him coming, really. It's not like I'm having some sort of major procedure or anything. Besides, he needs to work."

"He should have come," Mom says. "And he's not working. He's golfing." She pulls out a piece of needle point from her sewing bag, dons her half glasses, and begins to stitch. "That and the fact that Kelly here's a walking udder."

"A what?" Sandra asks.

Mom peers over her half glasses. "Why buy the cow ..."

"Mom, please."

"It's true," Mom says, then returns to her needle work.

"Any idea when you'll blow this joint?" Sandra asks.

"When I can hold down food and water," I reply.

"So maybe by Saturday afternoon you'll be free?" Sandra asks.

"Why?" I ask.

"My brother's having one of his killer parties. You're invited, you know."

"I'd love to go," I say and perk up. "Maybe."

"You're not going anywhere, young lady," Mom says. "You're sick, remember."

"My mom, the warden," I say to Sandra.

*   *   *   *

By Friday night I'm still not better. Sandra calls me up to tell me that she's got it too. I feel really bad. I see no end in site. Maybe Mom should call Mike Wallace.

"Do you think you might eat something?" the nurse asks. "They're serving dinner."

"No. No thanks," I say.

"She doesn't look good tonight," Mom says.

I lay in the bed and stare out the window at nothing.

"We've been here five days and she's still the same as the day we got here. She's still got fever. She still can't eat. You've pumped her up with God knows what. Why isn't she getting any better?" Mom demands.

"Mrs. Carmichael, I know how you feel," the nurse says.

"Do you?" Mom yells at her.

"Mom. Don't ..." I say, weakly.

"Look at her." Mom points to me.

"Let me get Dr. Sloan. I know he's not your doctor but ..." The nurse runs out of the room. I return to my staring.

She comes back within the minute with the doctor and my chart. He flips through the pages then looks up at the nurse.

"This diagnosis ... it's not ..." the doctor looks at me. "Did you say to the admitting nurse you had blood in your stool?"

"Yes," I say.

"Excuse me." The doctor takes the nurse by the arm and leads her out of the room.

Mom and I look at each other and shrug.

Minutes later the nurse returns with a small I-V bag and changes out my medication.

"Be patient, Miss Carmichael. We're going to get you better," she says.

"It's about damn time," Mom says.

*   *   *   *

The next morning my fever has broken. My hair and my gown are soaked with sweat. I'm terribly hungry.

The nurse strolls in to find me trying to change my clothes. Until I removed my gown, I hadn't thought about the I-V tubes being in the way.

"Here, let me help you," she says as she threads the IV bags through the arm of the gown. "You look like you feel better."

"I do," I say. "I'd like to eat something now."

"Well, the doctor wants to do a sigmoidoscopy on you."

"My doctor?"

"No, Dr. Sloan. He's a gastroenterologist," she says.

"Oh."

"After that, then you can eat," she says.

"A sigmoid, huh?" The memories come flooding back to me now.

"Yep. Nothing to it."

*   *   *   *

"Just a little bit more," the doctor says.

"You all say that, don't you?" I ask.

"Excuse me?"

"Nothing." I grab hold of the table, grit my teeth and close my eyes.

"Ulcerative colitis," he says. And it's a pretty nasty case, too."

"That's nice," I tell him.

"It can be treated, though," he says.

"That's a relief."

"I'm going to give you some prednisone and a couple of other drugs."

"Prednisone? What's that?" I ask.

"It's an anti-inflammatory. A real wonder drug."

"Oh. And then I'll be cured?"

"We'll see," he says.

*   *   *   *

I pack my bags as Sandra enters my hospital room. "Hey, you're not sick anymore either," I say to her. "I know you didn't get it from me anyway. Ulcerative colitis. How about that?"

"Where's your Mom?" she asks.

"Getting the car, why?"

"I'm pregnant," she announces.

"Oh, Sandra," I respond. "What are you going to do?"

"Keep it, I think. No, definitely. I want this baby. Hell, I'm nearly forty. There's nobody out there for me."

"Come on, Sandra. Sure there is."

"No, let's be practical. I need this baby," she says.

"Is it …?"

"Yeah. Who else?"

"Are you going to tell him?" I ask her.

"Should I?"

"I mean …" I start.

"I knew what I was doing that night," she interrupts. "If he cared, he'd have called. What's there to tell."

"How about your mother and brother?" I ask her.

"Oh, yeah," Sandra says. "Simple. I'm nearly forty. What the hell can they do to me? I'll tell the truth."

"Good for you," I say.

"I'll tell them I got artificially inseminated at a sperm bank."

CHAPTER 11

▼

HEY WAITER, THERE'S A BAG IN MY SOUP

I have never felt better in my entire life than I do right now. I feel fabulous. And not only that, I look great, too. Size four. I could just die.

I don't care that it's five thirty in the morning and I have nowhere to be. I'm jogging, dammit, and I feel good.

I should have gone to the doctor earlier, I know. So what if I can't go below twenty-five milligrams of prednisone without getting sick. It makes me feel terrific. I'll be off it long before the side effects ever strike.

Four times around the block and I'm barely panting. Next month, I'm definitely moving back to Memphis. Mom's got her shit together. I've got my shit together. It's just time.

"Hey, Mom," I say as I jog past her in the kitchen and head for the refrigerator.

"Feeling better, huh?" she asks. "You know you shouldn't over-do it. It's only been two weeks."

"I'm fine. Size four," I say as I fill a glass with orange juice and gulp it down.

"You haven't seen size four since ..."

"I know. I found an old pair of Levi's in the closet. I know they're left over from high school but they fit," I tell her.

"You laid down on the bed and zipped them up that way, didn't you?"

"Nope," I say. "Got some room to spare."

"No kidding?"

"Can't wait 'til Walt comes here tonight," I say as I suck down the very last sip of juice. "I think I've got this thing licked."

"Not until the doctor says so," Mom says. "No insurance and not taking care of yourself.... why I ought to ..."

"All right Mom. I got the picture."

"You don't even care that this little illness of yours has already set me back over five thousand dollars, do you?" she hollers at me as I walk through the living room.

"Mom, I'm sorry," I say. "I don't have it. I've always been taken care of."

"Yes, I know."

*　　　*　　　*　　　*

I glance with one eye on my watch and the other on the front window as I try to read the catalogue of Memphis State University that Walt sent me in the mail. Nothing looks good to me.

Psychology? Boring. Besides, I'd need a doctorate to really practice.

Economics? Nope. Too much math.

Political Science? Been there. Done that.

Literature? I'd actually have to read the books instead of relying on Cliff's Notes. No thank you.

Nursing? I think back on all the vomit I filled in the little tray. Forget that.

There's nothing in here for me. Walt will have to be satisfied with me just the way I am. Degreeless and directionless. Housewife and mother is not such a bad occupation now that I think about it.

His black Allente pulls into the driveway. I rush out of my room, burst open the front door and rush outside. "Walt!" I call out.

"Hey, baby," he says, surprised to find me so full of energy. "You look great."

"I feel great," I say.

"So you're over this illness thing, huh?" he asks. He retrieves his duffel bag from the back seat.

"Not yet, but soon," I tell him. I escort him toward the front door. "The doctor wants me to stay on some medication for a little while longer but other than that ..."

"God, you look great," he says again as we cross the living room and into the guest bedroom. He gives me a hug and a wonderful passionate kiss. "I've missed you so much," he says.

"So have I."

*   *   *   *

"More mashed potatoes, Walt?" Mom asks him. We sit in the dining room and eat off the good china. We haven't eaten off the good stuff since last Thanksgiving. I don't know why Mom calls these dishes the "the good stuff." She saved up greenstamps for two years to get the set. Walt doesn't even notice or care.

"I'll take some more, please," I say to Mom. She gives me a displeasing look, then passes the bowl. I plump down a large helping of mashed potatoes onto my plate. I catch Walt's eyes look at the mound then back to his own plate. I don't care. I'm hungry.

"Have you given any more thought to what you might major in next semester?" Walt begins. "I mean, you'll need to get your transcripts sent pretty soon."

"I don't know yet. I've been sick. One thing at a time, you know," I say as I take a bite of a biscuit.

"I just don't want you to forget, that's all," he says.

"Is there really a need to go back to school? You should be thinking about settling down and finding something ..." Mom pauses. "... You know, a little more permanent, perhaps," she finishes.

"Kelly's smart. It's a shame to waste those beautiful brains of hers," Walt tells her. "A degree looks good. Makes you more attractive to people."

I don't pay much attention to the conversation. I find the texture of the mashed potato pleasing on my tongue. It fascinates me how wonderful porkchop gravy compliments the flavor of a spud.

"She should have finished her degree a long time ago," Mom counters.

"She's just lacked direction, that's all," Walt says. "It won't happen this time around. I'll see to that."

I shovel more mashed potatoes into my mouth. Right now I can't think about college degrees when I know there's a fabulous chocolate pie in the refrigerator.

*   *   *   *

"I absolutely refuse to corrupt my childhood bed before I'm ...," I protest. "... Well.... not in this room."

"What about my room then?" Walt proposes.

I look through the bathroom and into the guest bedroom. "I carry no emotional baggage over that room."

He grabs me by the arm and pulls me toward the guest room.

"Just be quiet," I warn. "I don't want Mom to hear us."

"God, Kelly, you're practically thirty."

"I know, but I'm still her daughter. She thinks I'm a virgin."

"Oh, please."

"No, really," I say as I slip into the guest bed and caress the sheets. "You know, all these years of living on and off in this house and growing up here I never slept in this bed."

"Slept? You mean made love?"

"No, slept, really. Always in my room. This bed was right here and I never …"

"She does think you're a virgin, doesn't she?"

"Yep."

"I'm going to be your first in here, huh?" He sounds honored.

"Yep."

"Oh God Kelly, give it to me now," he says in a voice too loud for this house.

I put my hand over his mouth to shut him up. "I'm serious. I have to live here. Keep it down, will ya?"

"In a couple of weeks you're moving back with me. Who cares."

"But it's still a couple of weeks," I say. "I love you."

"Me, too." He pulls my gown down past my shoulders. It falls freely onto the frilly guestbed sheets.

*   *   *   *

I wake up to notice daylight streaming through the sheers over the window. I bolt upright and scurry for my pajamas. I hustle back to my bedroom. I barely pull my gown on and slide under the covers when I hear the knock on my door.

"Kelly, are you awake?" Mom calls out.

"I'm awake now."

She opens the door and walks on in. She is dressed and ready for the day. "I thought you might want to cook breakfast this morning. Show Walt you're domestic side."

"Mom, please. He'd be happy with a Pop-Tart, believe me."

"With that attitude it's no wonder you don't have a ring yet."

"We do things different than you did. You always want to overkill. For once take it easy, will you?"

"What's wrong with putting a little icing on the cake? If it gets you married ..."

"Nobody's a housewife anymore. Get a life, Mom," I say. "Quit worrying about me and do something for yourself. We don't want a fancy breakfast. Just put some cereal and those cute little powdered donuts I saw in the pantry out. That's more than enough."

"I don't understand you people," Mom starts. "He doesn't want you to work after you get married yet you've got to have that degree. Prove your worth, huh? Isn't being a wife and a mother enough these days?" Mom demands.

"Some people see it as a disgrace," I say.

"Like your father?"

I examine my nails.

"He never believed in either of one of us, Kelly. Don't screw up your ride this time because I'm not your father ..."

"How do you want your eggs?" I give in.

∗   ∗   ∗   ∗

"I love Chinese food," Sandra says as she peruses the menu of the Oriental Delight, Spivey's local Chinese restaurant. "I could live over there in China. I really could."

"They don't eat this stuff over there like this. It's different," Walt informs her.

"Like how?" Sandra asks.

"They don't eat all this heavy crap," Walt says. "They eat more rice and fish. Not this Kung Pao stuff. I mean, have you ever seen a fat Chinese person before?"

"I don't know," Sandra replies.

"No, you haven't because they don't eat like this," Walt insists.

"I don't care," I say. "Who cares about fat Chinese people. We're here. The food's good. Let's just eat, all right?"

"Besides, we're Americans. What do we know about Chinese food, right?" Sandra asks.

"Not that much apparently," Walt says.

"I'm going to have the beef with oyster sauce. What are ya'll going to have?" I pipe up. You can cut the tension at this table with a ginsu knife. Walt hates my friend.

We all finally order and within minutes our table is covered with mooshoo pork, beef with oyster sauce, kung pao chicken, bowls of hot and sour soup, mounds and mounds of pork fried rice, and a pyramid of egg rolls.

I place my pill box on the table to remind myself to take my medication. Walt rolls his eye at me.

"Damn, Kelly, do you have to take your little pharmacy along with you everywhere?" he scolds.

"I have to take these after dinner. I don't want to forget," I tell him.

"You can't wait until we get home?" Walt asks.

"But we're going to the movie after this. We won't be home until almost midnight. I have to take my medicine now."

"You know it wouldn't hurt you to skip it every once in a while," Walt says.

"If I skip it, I could die," I say.

"Yeah, right," he scoffs. "How much longer are you going to be on that shit anyway?"

"I don't know," I say. "As long it takes, I suppose."

"Kelly really is sick. You should have seen her in the hospital. It was pretty bad," Sandra says in my defense.

"She looks just fine to me," Walt says. "You'll be off that stuff soon, right?" He looks at me not as my boyfriend but more as a parent wanting a child's task completed.

"Soon," I say.

Walt glares at me then turns his attention to Sandra. "There's a lot you can learn from the Chinese people, you know. They also suffer from very few ailments."

I shovel the food into my mouth, oblivious of their conversation. The warm taste of the Kung Pao chicken comforts me and fills up the empty void of alienation which I feel right now.

"You going to eat the rest of that moo shoo pork?" I ask Sandra. I swallow the last of my chicken and scrape my plate clean.

"No, you go right ahead," she says. "And take my egg roll, too. I'm too stuffed for words even." She pushes her plate toward me but Walt intercepts it.

"Ever see a fat Chinese person?" He shakes his head and pushes the plate away from me.

"Fine," I say. "But get a doggie bag, please. I'll be hungry again in a couple of hours."

*   *   *   *

"You've got to get a handle on this and take care of yourself," Walt tells me as he loads his duffel bag into his car. "I need you. And I need you in Memphis. Not here."

"I'm trying," I say. "I eat tons of fiber."

"You eat tons. Period. You look great right now. Better than I've ever seen you. Don't screw up your body. I love it just the way it is." He leans over and gives me a kiss. "Look at me," he says and gently lifts my chin up to his face. "I love you. You're terrific. You've got a lot going for you. Don't let this ... this thing be your downfall. Get a grip on whatever it is and get over it, all right? I need you. I do."

"I'm trying. I really am," I say. "I'm taking the medicine just like the doctor says. I'm doing everything I can. In a couple of months we'll look back on this and laugh. I'll get over this. One way or another, I'll get over it."

"I know you will. I love you," he says and kisses me again.

I try to hold back my tears. "I love you, too."

He gets in his car. I watch him drive down the winding path of our driveway to the street and disappear around the corner. I slowly make my way into the house and through the kitchen. I unconsciously reach for the box of powdered donuts then put them back. I hesitate then take one donut and shove it into my mouth.

I lean against the door of the pantry in sheer satisfaction of that one donut. Then my underwear goes wet.

I run to the bathroom. I remove my jeans and panties. There's a small puddle of blood and mucous clinging to my cotton panties.

"Shit!"

CHAPTER 12

▼

THAT'S NOT SOME OLD BAG, THAT'S ME

I don't know exactly when my life settled into this rut. It just sort of happened. I've been home a whole six months now. Funny but I've held this position longer than any other in my entire life. The position of couch potato. I don't care anymore.

I don't go out. I don't shop. I don't even rent videos. I merely exist. I have no idea when I last talked to Sandra. I sit on the couch all day. I consume whole pots of Kraft Macaroni and Cheese, bags of Doritos, and liters of Diet Coke while I watch the Weather Channel. I sit here for hours, eating and watching the thunderstorms progress across the country. You'd think I was depressed or something. I'm not depressed. I'm fat.

The prednisone has done some crazy things to my body. I've got the signature moon face of a prednisone user with severe bloating from water retention and weight gain. When I walk, I feel like one of Willie Wonka's Umpaloompas. I'm in a size sixteen now. Mom bought me a few knit outfits at Lane Bryant to wear. I look more like an angry and bitter old housewife than I do a young upstart executive.

My doctor has attempted to reduce my dosage and take me off this shit. He's optimistic that I'm getting better. Call me cynical but I believe we'll see a woman Pope before I get off this drug.

Because of all these months of taking the prednisone, I have suffered all of the major side effects. The worst is the hair. I must shave every couple of days. Not my legs. My face. It falls out of my scalp and grows where it's not wanted. I have a mustache, sideburns and hair on my forehead. Waxing and depilatories eat my skin up. Shaving is my only option. God forbid I should kiss a man. I'll give him a bad case of stubble burn.

I remember several years ago when I lived in a dorm with a community bathroom. A girl lived on our hall. Joan Holloway. She was extremely overweight and we would make fun of her all the time. I was only eighteen or nineteen at the time. My friends and I would snicker and lambaste her as she took her shower in the morning. The teasing got so bad, she quit taking her shower at a decent hour and would wait until almost midnight to bathe, when she thought no one was watching.

One night my roommates and I went down to the bathroom to see her. We caught her shaving her facial hair. I couldn't believe any decent woman would or should have to do such a thing as shave her face. I was horrified. I suppose we thought facial hair was contagious. We had her removed from our dorm. I haven't thought about her until recently. Joan Holloway has gotten her revenge and more.

I have hideous stretch marks under my arms from gaining so much weight so fast. They're not even marks. They're more like rips or tears. My stomach and my hips are marked as well. Nothing helps them. I itch like crazy. I don't care if it doesn't look ladylike when I scratch. It brings me relief.

Mom returns from her final night of real estate class at the junior college. She beams with all the enthusiasm and excitement I used to have when I would first start a job. I should be envious. I'm not.

"You passed, huh?" I ask her and mute the sound on the TV.

"Not only did I pass but I made the top grade in the class. Tucker Realty has asked me to associate with their firm," she says. "I'm finally going to have a job." She puts down her book bag and purse. Her permanent scowl is gone. I don't think I've ever seen her this happy before.

"But Mom, you're well fixed. You don't have to go to work if you don't want to," I tell her. "What's the point?"

"I want to work. I know I don't have to. Maybe that's why I want to so much. Now I understand what all the fuss was about."

"I'm happy for you, Mom." I turn my attention back to the television set. The thunderstorms have died down on the radar summary.

"Maybe you should think about finding a job, too," she says. "This sitting around is not healthy for you. You need to exercise, get out, move around. Work might be a welcome change."

"Mom, I've tried finding a career," I say. "See where it got me."

"Then try to get a job. Just a job. Something to get you out of the house for a while. Perhaps down at the dress shop …"

"Oh, right,. The dress shop. The town cow hocking designer chic. That'll really sell some …"

"At least go to the employment agency. You never know."

"Okay Mom. I'll go," I say. I aim the remote at the TV and unmute the sound. Anything to get her off my damn back.

*   *   *   *

"Have you got something in law?" I ask the woman who runs the employment agency. "I'm a paralegal. You know, legal assistant." I take a seat in front of her desk.

"We don't have anything like that," she replies. "Come to think of it, I don't think we've ever had one of those in here before. And we certainly haven't had a request for one."

"So what do you have in the way of office? Legal secretary?"

"Before I start sending you out to any of the offices, you'll have to test first. Typewriter, ten key, the usual."

"I've got ten years of office experience," I tell her. "Doesn't my resume vouch for itself?"

"Well it doesn't tell me how many words per minute you type, now does it?"

"I type around eighty," I say.

"On a typewriter?" she asks.

"No one uses a typewriter anymore," I say.

"Your resume doesn't tell me anything except that you can't stay longer than three months at any given job," she says and points my resume at me. "If you want an office job, you'll have to be tested first."

"All right. I'll take the typing test."

She places a blank sheet of paper into an old blue IBM Selectric, then hands me a page with some writing on it. She dials a kitchen timer to three minutes. "Go," she says.

I place my hands on the unfamiliar keyboard and begin to type. The first four words come out as garbledy goop. My fingers are one letter off. I hit return and start again.

I type as furiously as my fingers will let me. Then I realize that I have a huge black glob at the end of my first line. I have forgotten that I must hit return manually. I manage to finish the first paragraph and three words of the next before the timer goes off.

"Let's see you how did." She takes the paper from the carriage and quickly circles the misspelled words.

"Congratulations," she announces. I perk up. "You've typed fifteen words per minute. I believe that's a new record for this office."

"That's crazy," I protest.

"The test is very accurate," she says. "I'm sorry. I can't place you in an office. You don't know how to type."

This isn't fair. I've typed on a computer for years. I haven't even typed an envelope on a typewriter since Dynasty was last on TV. "That's where all my experience is," I plead. "I've worked high up in corporations and in law firms. I've researched and prepared whole legal briefs for lawyers who did nothing more than read it and sign their name to it. As a matter of fact, one of my appellate briefs I prepared was remanded by the Supreme Court of Mississippi without even one red mark on it. How's that for skill?"

"Test doesn't lie, honey," she says. "Typewriter. Computer. It doesn't matter."

"Then where do you suggest I work?"

"You really want office, huh?" she asks.

"Absolutely," I insist.

"Okay. I'll tell you what. I've got a retired insurance salesman who needs a little office support and companionship a few hours a day. The man's practically an invalid from what I hear. He needs a few little letters typed and some errands run. We'll try you out there. Minimum wage."

"That's it!"

"'Fraid so, honey," She says. "Take it or leave it."

✳   ✳   ✳   ✳

"Mr. Rumph. Mr. Rumph," I call out. I step back off of the front porch and recheck the house numbers. This is the place.

This house at one time was probably quite lovely. It is neglected and in need of paint and love. I peer into the screen door and listen to the television set blare out the theme song to Hogan's Heros. "Mr. Rumph."

"I said come in," a man's voice screams then violently coughs and wheezes.

I open the screen door and slowly make my way into the house. I follow the sound of the television set to the back. The musty old-folks smell is tainted by the stench of infection, uncleanness, cheap liquor, and worse, cheap cigars.

"Hello, Mr. Rumph. I'm Kelly. Kelly Carmichael. The agency sent me."

"'Bout time. Gone three weeks without a girl. So I'm retired. Don't mean I don't still work," he grumbles. He sits in a wheelchair in front of the TV. His tank top is stained with food and who knows what. His fingernails are yellow and longer than mine. Dirt fills the tips. His khaki pants are ripped at the pockets and his fly is unzipped, exposing his soiled light green boxers. His blue chenille houseslippers are matted and ripped. I should leave here now. I should run. I should run as fast as I can. I look back at the door and catch a glimpse of myself in the mirror. I have no where else to go.

"What do you want me to do first?" I ask and look around the bedroom. An oversized metal desk dominates one corner. Large amounts of paper work overwhelm the desk. An old electric typewriter sits proudly in the middle of all of that chaos. It mocks at me.

"Everything," he says. "But first and foremost, run and go get me some bourbon before my wife gets back. And cigars. She won't let me drink, and she refuses to buy me any smokes for fear someone might see her. Here's a twenty. I want the cheapest. Bring me back the change. You are old enough to buy liquor, aren't you?"

"Yes sir, I am, but …"

"Then what are you waiting for? My wife will be home any minute," he says.

I take the money and oblige my new employer. Cheap bourbon and cigars. I really must be in hell. Please God, don't let anyone see me.

The bourbon's easy. Thank God for the convenient drive-through window. The cigars are a different story. They don't have them at the liquor store. Piggly Wiggly it is. I hurry in and rush down the aisle where the tobacco is kept. I retrieve three packs of Tipperillos then nonchalantly make my way toward the cash register.

"Kelly Carmichael. Is that you?" a familiar voice calls out. I turn to see svelte-as-ever Amy Ashbrook. Prom queen, homecoming queen, most beautiful in class. You name the beauty category, she held it. I haven't seen her since our high school graduation. She pushes a cart of trendy salad greens and several liters of Evian my way. Two little children are in tow.

"Amy Ashbrook. Nice to see you," I say.

"Well it's Ashbrook-Allen," she says. "I'm a hyphen now."

"That's nice."

"So how are you doing?" she asks. "I heard you've been sick lately."

"Oh yeah," I say. "I've got some sort of intestinal disorder but the doctor seems optimistic that it'll go away soon," I tell her as I try to hide the cigars from her view. It shouldn't matter. This isn't high school anymore. "I thought you moved away."

"I did but I'm back. Built a house and everything. We've even employed this wonderful decorator from Little Rock to help us furnish it and design the interiors. Julie Elliot recommended her. She's such a wonderful friend. Gave us a great pool man, too."

"A pool, too. Sounds wonderful."

"Oh, it is," Amy continues. "Taylor and I couldn't ask for anything more wonderful."

"You're getting into that cigar craze, too, huh?" Amy asks. She's noticed the Tipperillos.

"For a friend."

"Taylor had a humidor installed in the house. It's just like Arnold Schwartznegger's. We get his cigars from Miami. They don't carry the kind he smokes here."

"I'm sure. Well, it's been nice seeing you, Amy," I say to her.

"You, too," she says.

I turn around and search for a cashier far away from this hell but the only one open is right here. Of course Amy and her children stand behind me.

"Mommy, who's that fat lady you were talking to?" I hear Amy's little girl ask.

"Nobody, sweetheart," she says. "Nobody."

$$*\qquad*\qquad*\qquad*$$

"Look, Kelly. Look. Cards. With my name on them," Mom squeals as she returns home from her first day of work. "I think my picture on them turned out all right, don't you think? It kind of makes me look important."

"They're nice, Mom," I tell her. I aim the remote at the television set and mute the sound.

"And I've got sign plaques with my name on them, too. Look. Olivia Carmichael." Mom caresses the metal nameplate. "They go on top of the for sale sign. My name for everyone to see. How about that?"

"That's great, Mom. It looks good."

"At the office I've got a desk, my own computer, a phone. And look. I've got my own fax number, too," Mom squeals again. "Isn't this wonderful?" "When do you start selling?" I ask her.

"Now. They're going to put an announcement in the paper that I've associated with them. They say that always brings in new clients. And they'll help me out some. Get my name out there."

"I'm happy for you, Mom," I say.

"Say, let's go out to eat or something. Celebrate. My treat, of course."

"I don't really feel up to it, Mom. Maybe tomorrow."

"Oh, well, all right." Mom sounds disappointed. "But you'll come by tomorrow and see my office, won't you?"

"Sure, Mom. Whatever." I lay my head down on the sofa and unmute the television set. I don't want to miss the local forecast.

*　　　*　　　*　　　*

"Skelly, honey," Mr. Rumph calls out. "Can you come here and put some ointment on my planter's wart?"

My fingers stop cold on the Smith Corona.

"I can't seem to get my foot out of this Epsom salt wash either," he complains.

"Your nurse should be here any minute," I tell him. "Why don't you wait for her to help?"

"Oh, I can't ask her to do something as trivial as this. That's not what she gets paid for."

The hair on the back of my neck prickles. I realize that this is precisely the kind of episode which my father was trying to spare me from. Is Ben Carmichael's daughter above this shit? I look at my moon face in the dresser mirror. Probably not today she isn't.

"Come on, girl. Help me get my foot dry. I ain't gonna bite," he whines.

I hesitate then put my hands on his swollen, clammy white skin. I pull his gnarled foot out of the washtub. His yellow twisted toenails are in desperate need of trimming. I pray that he doesn't ask me to trim them.

"Get me that ointment right there, little girl." He points to the nightstand.

I look but there are ten different tubes of ointment there.

"The green tube. The green tube," he yells. "Don't you know anything?"

I pick up the green tube.

"Now rub it in real good," he says.

Before I can even oblige him, the nurse walks in and rescues me.

"Mr. Rumph, trying to get me replaced, I see," the nurse teases. She takes the ointment from my hands and pats me on the shoulders as if I were a little girl. "I'll take it from here, sweetheart."

I step back away from the bed and watch her work, unabashedly. I look at her face. She smiles back at me with what could be perceived as a condescending look but is probably only kindness. Then I remember her from high school. She's only two years older than me. Where the hell does she get off?

Where the hell do I get off?

*   *   *   *

"Walt, please. Let me come up there this weekend. I need to get away," I plead to him over the phone.

"No, no, I'll come there. You need to rest," he tells me.

"I don't need to rest. I need to get away," I tell him. "Besides, since I've been sick, you've been coming here. Don't you want me to come see you for a change?"

"Sure ... but ..."

"Please, Walt. I need this. It would really make me feel better," I say.

"Okay," he says softly.

"Thank you," I say. "I'll see you tomorrow. I love you."

"Yeah. You, too."

I hang up the phone and pop my prednisone tablets into my mouth. I wash them down with a cola. I'm taking sixty milligrams a day. If I go below fifty five I get sick. I don't really think this shit's working but Walt doesn't have to know that yet.

*   *   *   *

"Where are you going?" Mom asks as she passes my room and sees that I am packing.

"To Walt's," I say.

"I thought he was coming down here."

"No. I'm going there. I need a change of scenery. I think it'll do me good."

"This isn't a good idea, Kelly. You're too sick to be ..."

"I don't care. If I don't get away, I'll go nuts. I need to feel normal again. Laying around the house watching the Weather Channel isn't normal."

"What about your job?" she asks.

"Screw the job. I can't return to that ... that man. Nobody can be expected to work for that thing. Fetch my cigars. Get my liquor. Clip my nasty yellow toenails.'"

"Oh, Kelly. It's not like that. It's a secretarial job. You need to work. I can't be expected to foot all of your expenses while you ..."

"Say it, Mom. Whore around."

"That's not what I was going to say."

"I'm trying just as hard as I can to catch this husband for you. Don't screw up my chances," I warn her.

"It just seems to me that running up there and sleeping in his bed will ruin the mystique ..."

"Mom, look at me. There is no mystique anymore." I zip my bag and carry it out the door.

*   *   *   *

I take the elevator to the fifth floor where the Memphis Bar Association is located. Forget feeling like Mary Richards. I just want to feel real again.

"Hi, Debbie," I say to the woman who helped me before.

She looks up from her work and sneers at me as if I've interrupted her. "Can I help you?"

"Yes. I'm Kelly. Kelly Carmichael. Remember me?" I say to her.

She looks puzzled and tilts her head.

"You got me a job at Westward ..."

"Oh, well, I get lots of people jobs," she says as she types in my name into her computer. "Paralegal?"

"That's me."

"And I suppose you want an assignment, huh?" she asks.

"Yes. I'd like to try to find something permanent. Something with a good firm perhaps." I hand her my resume.

She sneers at me again, then looks at my qualifications. "You're resume is sort of weak. You know, you're competing with girls who've got degrees from Vanderbilt and Memphis State. Quite frankly, Shelly, I doubt I can even place you."

"My name's Kelly."

"Oh, sorry. Anyway, I just don't have anything right now. Paralegals like you are a dime a dozen in this city. The marker's saturated. Call back next week. Maybe I can place you in a small office. Perhaps with a public defender. I just don't have anything today. Sorry." She turns her attention back to her work. A young, skinny girl walks in as I head toward the door.

"Allison, honey, I'm so glad you made it in," I hear Debbie squeal as I brush past the girl and open the door. "I've got just the assignment for you."

I let the door slam behind me as I force myself not to cry. I push the button for the elevator and wait. It doesn't come fast enough for me. I run down the hallway toward the staircase and race down it as fast as my hefty body can take me. I try to catch my breath on the sidewalk. The misty rain feels good on my hot moon face. Then my purse slides off my shoulder and hits the pavement with a thunk.

*   *   *   *

"God, Kelly, when are they going to take you off this shit?" Walt asks me as he greets me at the door.

"And it's good to see you, too," I say. I wait for him to take me into his arms. He doesn't. I drop my head and my bags.

Bosco barks at me.

"Hey, Bosco. How ya' doin'?" I ask him and lean down to pet him.

He growls at me.

"Bosco!" Walt yells at the dog. "It's Kelly. Kelly. You remember."

The dog growls at me again.

"Bad Bosco. Bad Bosco," Walt scolds.

The dog retreats to a corner in the living room.

"Oh, Kelly, I'm sorry," He pulls my chin up. "I'm glad to see you. I really am." He finally takes me into his arms and hugs me.

"As soon as I can go without this medicine, I'll return to normal. That's what the doctor says," I tell him.

"And that will be when?" he asks as he picks up my suitcase.

"Soon. Real soon."

"Maybe you should get a second opinion. I mean, geez," he says. He carries my suitcase into the bedroom.

"Perhaps. I'm just so happy to be back." I follow him into the bedroom. "I can't wait to see the city and get some decent food for a change." I'm not going to tell him about my visit to the bar association.

"Oh. You want to go out? I thought maybe we'd stay in this weekend. Maybe I'll cook steaks or order some pizza. I've rented a bunch of movies. I thought you might want to rest."

"I'm not a damn invalid," I protest. "I drove here, didn't I?"

"I didn't mean it that way. I just thought you wouldn't want to go out," he says. "You know."

"I've been hiding myself away at home. I feel the need to get out. Please."

"Sure," he gives in. "We'll go out."

*　　　*　　　*　　　*

I put my new Lane Bryant outfit on. Black knit slacks with a long fuchsia tunic over it. Black is supposed to be slimming but I don't believe them. I still look like an Umpaloompa.

I lean in closer to the bathroom mirror. I look like a werewolf with so much facial hair. I should have taken care of this back home. I pull out my razor and lightly go over my forehead.

"Are you ready?" Walt calls out as he opens the door.

I quickly drop the razor into the sink and brush off the thin hair on my face with my hand. "Coming." I pull my bangs down over my forehead. I turn out the light before I open the door all the way.

"How does this look?" I ask.

"Fine," Walt says. He pulls on a blue and white rugby shirt over his jeans.

"You're not going to dress up?" I ask him as I put on my pearls.

"Why? It's raining outside. Where are we going?"

"Piazano's?" I suggest.

He sighs. "It's so far …" he whines.

"All right. We go casual." I pull off my elastic waisted pants. He stares at my body.

"What?" I ask as I pull on my jeans.

"Nothing."

I put on a T-shirt and an oversize Yale sweatshirt. "There. Is that better?" I put on white socks and my grungy Birkenstocks.

"Sure, whatever," he says.

We drive along Poplar. I feel claustrophobic in his car.

"How about Bennigan's? It's pretty good," he says.

"You don't want to go to Corky's?" I ask him.

"Do you?" He says and whips into the parking lot of Bennigans.

"I guess not," I say.

We walk in and the hostess seats us close to the front.

"Can we have something in the back perhaps," Walt whispers to her.

She looks at me, then to him, and back to me again. "All right," she says and leads us to a dark corner booth close to the kitchen. "Is this secluded enough for you?"

"Great," Walt says. He smiles his approval to her and quickly takes his seat overlooking the whole restaurant before I do. I step back and slide into the seat which faces the wall and the kitchen door. "This is nice."

The hostess hands us the menus. She snickers when she walks off. I stare at him until he raises his menu in front of his face. I pick up my own menu and begin to peruse it.

"Hi. My name's Jack and I'll be your waiter this evening."

I look up from behind the menu to see Jack, my old next door neighbor, placing glasses of water at our table.

"The soup of day is broccoli cream and we have a grilled tuna marinated in teriyaki as our special," he says. "It comes with a side of pasta and steamed veggies. What can I get you folks?" He looks at me as if he recognizes me then looks down at his tablet. He doesn't say anything.

"Yeah, I'll have the Monte Cristo and a beer," Walt says and puts his menu down. He glares at me with impatience. He doesn't order for me.

"I'll have the same except iced tea instead of a beer," I say.

"Appetizers?" Jack asks.

"No, I don't think so," Walt says.

"I wouldn't mind some cheese sticks," I say.

"God, Kelly. You don't need …".

"Kelly?" Jack interrupts Walt. "Kelly Carmichael. Oh my God, it is you," he says. "What the … You look … you look great." I can tell he is carefully searching for the right words so that 'My God, Kelly, you're fatter than a pig' doesn't slip out of his mouth.

"I've got a little illness. I'm taking medicine. Steroids to treat it. That's why I look this way. It'll go away as soon as I'm off the stuff," I explain.

"Oh, Kelly," Jack gives me a hug, then whispers in my ear, "Who's your friend?"

"I'm sorry, Jack. This is Walt McKenzie. He's my boyfriend," I say. "Jack was my next door neighbor down in Jackson."

Walt reluctantly shakes Jack's hand. "Jack. From Jackson," Walt laughs. "Cute."

"I had to get out of there," Jack explains. "Change of scenery. I was lonely down there without you next door."

"Uh, could we get our order, please?" Walt interrupts.

"Oh, shame on me. I forgot I was a waiter for a minute there," Jack says as he hugs me again. "Oh, Kelly, it's so good to see you." He turns and heads through the kitchen door.

"Who the hell was he?" Walt asks.

"He wasn't my boyfriend if that's what you're getting at," I say.

"Well, that's obvious." Walt wipes his hands vigorously with his napkin.

"I can't believe he's here," I say. "He's such a nice guy. He was really good to me when I lived in Jackson."

"You know, on second thought, Corky's sounds pretty good. We can call ahead and get takeout. Doesn't that sound a lot better than a Monte Cristo?"

"But we've already ordered," I protest. "I can't stiff Jack like that."

"Sure we can." Walt rises and practically yanks me out of the seat. He throws a five on the table and pushes me down the aisle toward the front. I turn to see Jack bringing us a plate of cheese sticks and our drinks. He looks bewildered. I turn to wave goodbye to him but Walt ushers me out the door.

*   *   *   *

"What's your deal?" I ask Walt in the car as we pull onto Poplar Boulevard. I suddenly begin to cry uncontrollably.

"I'm sorry. I just couldn't stand to be in there. I don't know," he says.

"You can't stand to be with me," I sob.

"No ..."

"It's true. I look like a Macy's Thanksgiving Day balloon to you, don't I?"

"Oh, Kelly." Walt pulls over into an empty office building parking lot and stops the car. "I'm sorry. I'm not dealing with this very well." He pulls his seatbelt off and hugs me close. "I love you, you know that, don't you?"

"I don't know," I bawl. I wish I could stop crying in front of him but I can't. It feels good to let it go.

"I hate seeing you like this," he says. "You're so unhappy. It's not like it used to be. I don't want you to get hurt. I didn't think you wanted to go out. This is the first time and …"

"It's been so long since I've been out. I feel like a caged bird. I hate it all right now."

"Oh baby. Monday, you go to that doctor and tell him to take you off this shit," he says. "It's doing you more harm than good. Tell him you'll do whatever it takes to get off it. Anything but that drug. Nothing could be worse than that drug. Okay? We're going to get you better and back to yourself. Okay? First thing Monday."

"Okay," I say and dry my eyes.

He starts the car up again.

"First thing Monday, Kelly. First thing."

*   *   *   *

"No, I don't have an appointment. I just need to see the doctor, please," I tell the receptionist at my doctor's office.

"I'm so sorry but he's booked up," she responds.

"I can't wait any longer," I say. "I've got to see him now."

"Are you in pain?" she asks.

"Sort of …" I say.

"Ma'am, I'm sorry but I can't get you in until Thursday if it's not an emergency."

I see the doctor look into the office. He see me and smiles.

"Miss Hall, it's okay. I'll see her now," he says to her. "Come on back, Kelly."

"Thank you," I say and glare at the receptionist. I follow the doctor back to his office.

He sits down and folds his hands together on the desk. "What can I do for you?"

"I want off the prednisone," I state.

"I can't take you off of it right now."

"I'm going to quit cold turkey, then. I want my life back."

"You're just having one of those mood swings," he says. "Give it a day. You'll feel different tomorrow."

"How long will I have to stay on the drugs?" I ask him.

"Off and on, the rest of your life."

My heart sinks.

"You may never get off them completely," he continues. "You just never know."

"The rest of my life? I'm almost thirty. The rest of my life is … is forever. I don't want to stay on this shit for ten more minutes let alone the rest of my life." Tears stream down my face.

"I just can't promise you that you will go into remission next week and not have another episode for years, if ever. I just can't make those kinds of promises. Everybody's different."

"And I can't make it on what ifs anymore. I need real answers. I need to be better or I'm going to…." I stop. "I just need to be better. That's the bottom line. That's it."

"You could have the surgery," he proposes.

"Surgery?"

"Removal of your large intestine. I was trying to save it but … Once it's out, you're cured," he says.

"No more drugs?"

"We'd have to taper you off the prednisone, but … Yeah. No more drugs. No more disease."

"Then take it out. I'll do anything to get me back. Just take it out."

"I'll give you the number of a surgeon in Little Rock. Take a couple of months, though," he says as he scribbles the name and number on a piece of paper. "It'll take you a long time to recover. It's not an easy procedure. An ostomy is not something you wish upon yourself lightly either."

"But I'll be cured and can go on living the life I had before the disease. Right?"

"Absolutely." He writes down the name and number of the doctor and hands it to me.

"Thank you very much." I take the piece of paper from the doctor and kiss it.

CHAPTER 13

▼

THREE BAGS IN
A FOUNTAIN

What do people see when they look at me? I see a nobody with nothing to do. Maybe that will change when I finally marry Walt. I'll be the kind of person Sandra dreams of being: a beautifully dressed, well maintained carpooling Mom in the Junior League with not a care in the world because my wonderful husband will take care of me and treat me like a queen so long as I look good for him and make sure that he has plenty of delicious meatloaf and clean underwear. That's not so bad, is it?

"Sandra!" I yell through her screen door. I can hear her mute the television. She waddles to the door.

"Kelly, oh my God, is that you?"

"Yeah, it's me," I say as she opens the screen door and stares at me. "Go ahead, look at me. Everyone else does. If I was smart, I'd run away to the carnival. Then people wouldn't stare so damn much."

"Get in here, girl." Sandra waddles toward the couch.

"Look at you," I say, "You're almost ready to ..."

She stops me. "Don't even say it. My brother says it enough. Pop. I swear, if I hear it one more time ..."

"Oh Sandra," I say. "We haven't even given you a shower yet. I feel really bad."

"Don't. Jeff's wife has given me tons of things. A baby bed, strollers, the works. She's had her tubes tied. She doesn't need the stuff anymore. And Momma's bought me a few things too," Sandra says. "I'm trying hard not to make this an issue. Thank God for empire waisted dresses. You know, I don't think anyone at work has even noticed."

"I haven't heard anyone talk but then again I don't get around much anymore. Look how long it's been since I've seen you."

"I don't care. You know that," she says. "But as for my family, well, I'm sticking to my story."

"Maybe it's all for the best."

"Let's face it," Sandra says. "I'm never going to find a husband."

"Did you even try to contact him?" I ask.

"No. And I don't want to. Who am I kidding? I knew what I was doing that night."

"God, Sandra. You can't take it back now."

"I'm forty years old without any prospects for a husband. What else am I supposed to do?"

"You're braver than I am," I say.

"Well, we do what we have to do," she shrugs. "Say, you want to come over to my brother's house tomorrow. He's cooking steaks."

"I'd love to but look at me."

"Kelly, it's just my family. My brother's married, my mother's widowed. Who are you expecting to be there? It's steak."

"All right, I'll come," I say. "Just so long as I'm not mistaken for the cow."

"Please, enough with the cow jokes," Sandra protests. "Jeff is threatening to throw me on the rotisserie and slather me down with barbecue sauce. At least yours is water weight and will go away when you get off the drugs. The baby will weigh what? Six, seven pounds. How am I going to get this shit off?"

"What do you think they invented the thighmaster for?

*   *   *   *

Mom and I sit in the surgeon's office in Little Rock. We listen to the Muzak and patiently wait for any name to be called. No one else is there and the two receptionists do not look especially busy.

"Nice office. Clean, unpretentious. I think he's actually good," Mom comments.

"You can't tell by the office how good he is. And there's no one else in here. What if he's a quack?" I ask.

"Then why would your doctor have recommended him?"

"I don't know," I say. "Why did I spend a week in the hospital before the doctor discovered what I had? Mom, maybe I'm making a huge mistake."

"Miss Carmichael," a nurse calls my name.

"Too late," Mom says. We follow the nurse down a short hallway and into a modestly appointed office. It's adorned with pictures of his family and, of course, his credentials.

"Hello, I'm Dr. Borden," he says as he extends his freckled hand for us to shake. "I see you want an illeostomy."

"I just want to get better. If that's what it takes to get me back to normal, then that's what I want," I say as Mom and I sit in the leather chairs across from his desk.

"I've reviewed your charts and I'd say you'd do well with this type of procedure," the doctor tells me.

"She'll have a colostomy, right?" Mom asks. "Later, she can have that reversed if she gets better, huh?"

"No. Removal of the colon is permanent. It's an illeostomy. We fashion it from the end of the small intestine which will protrude from your right side, an inch or two from your belly button. You'll wear an appliance, a wafer and a bag. It can never be reversed," he explains.

"A bag?" I ask.

"Or you can have a J-pouch procedure where we fashion a sort of sack in the rectum area," he says. "We'll do one surgery first and give you an illeostomy. Then we'll form the pouch. About eight weeks later you'll come back and we'll attach the intestine to the pouch after it's had a chance to heal. If your sphincter muscle holds, you'll do well."

"And if it doesn't ..."

"Well, then you stand the risk of leaking, having an accident. Sometimes you get what's called pouchitis, an inflammation in the pouch and we'll have to treat you for it. We never really know how a person will do with the J-pouch until we do it. It's more of a vanity thing, really. Some people don't like the idea of a bag."

"So how's the bag?" I ask.

"Pretty easy, really. It's a bag. You dump it when it's full, change it when it's dirty, and go about your business," he explains. "Oh sure it has it's fall backs, but all in all it's one surgery and hardly any of the problems. Low maintenance," he says. "After a couple of years, you'll hardly notice it at all."

"And I can lead a normal life with no limitations?" I ask him.

"I've got one patient who parachutes and scubadives. I've got another one who's an avid cyclist and runner. Another who's a golf pro out at one of the country clubs here," he says. "No, not too many limits, I'd say. Can't eat nuts or raisins. I'd stay away from too much popcorn."

"Sounds great. And no more medicine?" I ask.

"Once you're weaned off the prednisone, you're on your own."

"How much will this procedure cost," Mom asks, "and how long will the recovery take?"

"About fifty thousand dollars and eight weeks," he says. "And I've got an opening in two weeks, on October twenty first."

"That's your birthday, Kelly," Mom says.

"Yes. Yes, it is," I reply. "I want that bag thing. That's what I want for my birthday."

*   *   *   *

"And I suppose you want me to pay for this fifty-thousand dollar operation, huh?" Mom asks me in the elevator when we leave the doctor's office.

"You want me to marry Walt, don't you?" I ask her as the door opens to the ground floor lobby.

Mom smiles wryly.

*   *   *   *

"Sandra, I thought you said this was family. I don't recognize half these people," I tell her as we walk up the driveway to her brother's house and observe the full blown party.

"They're just some of Jeff's hunting buddies and their wives," Sandra says. "Except for that guy over there. I don't think he's married." Sandra points to an average height olive skinned man with a receding hairline and a five o'clock shadow.

"Who's he?" I ask.

"I have no idea. Hey, Jeff," Sandra calls out to her brother as we approach him. "Who's that guy over there? I've never seen him before."

"He's too young for you," Jeff replies. "He's thirty one."

"Give me a break, Jeff."

"Nick Giavanni. He's a member of my hunting camp. Hey, Nick," Jeff calls out.

Nick turns and approaches. He sips a beer and walks with an unusual sort of confidence most Southern men do not possess. If you put a fedora and a suit on the guy, he'd look like Mafia.

"Hey, Jeff," he says.

"Nick, I'd like to introduce you to my sister Sandra and her friend Kelly."

"Hi," I say.

"Hello," he says. "It's very nice to meet you."

"You're not from around here, are you?" I ask.

"What gave it away?" he asks and scratches his chin. "I was trying really hard to blend."

"Hell, Nick, you look like the spokesman for Ragu spaghetti sauce," Jeff tells him.

"Could it be that I'm Italian?"

"Don't let this guy fool you," Jeff says. "He may look Italian but deep down inside he's definitely one us. Just a pure dee Arkansas redneck."

"You do kind of walk like a gangster," Sandra says. "Are you in the Mafia?"

"Not exactly, although I do have an Uncle Guido. Honest to God."

"You do walk with an attitude," I say.

He leans over to my ear. "Is that bad?"

"No, no. It's very good," I say. "You walk like you're well adjusted. Happy."

"And I thought it was because my legs are too short for my body," he replies.

"So you're good friends with my brother, huh?" Sandra asks as Jeff walks back to his barbecue grill.

"Somewhat. He fixed me up with his receptionist, Karen. She's here somewhere."

"Shamu? She's here?" Sandra squeals.

"You call her that too, huh?" Nick asks Sandra.

"Are ya'll making fun of big girls?" I ask him. I look down at the oversized clothing which I hide in.

"Oh no, Kelly. It's not because she's a big girl, really," Sandra explains. "That's not it at all. It's because she seems to accentuate her features by wearing tight fitted black spandex leggings with a short tight black cardigan over a tight white T-shirt. All the time. It makes her look like a killer whale," Sandra says. "I'm sorry, Nick."

"Don't apologize. I'm not dating her," he says. "She just bugged the heck out of Jeff to fix her up with me. I thought I was being nice to take her out on one date. Emphasis on the one," Nick explains. "Now she's stalking me. I can't get rid of her. I've got to do something."

"Do you have another girlfriend?" Sandra asks him.

"No," he says. "That's the problem, isn't it?"

"If you had another girlfriend or at least the appearance of one, she'd probably leave you alone," I suggest.

"That's not a bad idea," Nick says and smiles. "I tell you, I can't even go anywhere without her following me. She's making my life hell."

"Hush, here she comes," Sandra says and nods her head in the direction of Shamu, dressed in her signature tight black and white.

"Are you single, Kelly?" he asks me.

"Yes, but I'm sort of ..."

"Be a sport and just play along, okay?" Nick asks me. "I'm desperate here."

"Sure," I say. "But ..."

"Hey, Shamu!" Nick calls out to her. "Watch this!"

Nick grabs me by the shoulders, dips me suddenly, and places his lips against mine. He forces my mouth open. Gently and slowly he penetrates past my teeth and onto my tongue. And I forget what I am. I give in and allow the sensation to travel down to my toes. I kiss him back. He presses his hand hard to the back of my head and probes my mouth with his tongue. Then tenderly he withdraws, releases his hold, and pulls me upright, into reality.

Nick winks at me, then shrugs at Shamu. She thrusts her overloaded plate of barbecue at Jeff and storms off the patio and into the house.

"Thanks, Kelly," Nick says. He shakes my hand as if we've just concluded a business matter. "I hope I didn't offend you."

"No. My pleasure." I feel my face turn red but I smile at him.

He cocks an eyebrow. "I'm going to get another beer. Would you two like one?"

"Sure," Sandra says.

Nick turns and walks away.

I hear the sound of tires spinning on the driveway.

"Oh my God, Kelly," Sandra says and nudges me with her elbow. "I'm sure you're glad Walt wasn't here to see that one," Sandra whispers in my ear.

"Absolutely."

*   *   *   *

"About that kiss ..." Nick begins.

"You don't have to apologize," I say.

"You don't even know me," he says.

"So what do you do, Nick," I ask him as we take a seat on the glider under the large live oak tree in Jeff's back yard.

"Why is that the first thing people ask you when you first meet someone?" Nick comes back.

"I'm sorry," I apologize. I know I've hit a nerve. Perhaps he's been laid off work and can't get a job. This could be sad.

"Don't get me wrong," he continues, "but wouldn't it be nice to get to know someone for who he is, not what he does?"

"I suppose."

"If everyone judged a book by its cover, a lot of wonderful literature would have gone unread. And that would have been a terrible shame," he says.

"You're right."

"So what's your favorite thing in the whole wide world to do?" he asks me.

"Right now, it's eat," I say with a laugh. "I'm not really a fat person."

"You're not fat," he says.

"I'm taking this medicine, see," I tell him.

"Prednisone," he says.

"How did you know?"

"I can see it on your face," he tells me.

"It's awful." I put my hands up to my face to hide it. "Want to see what I really look like?"

"No. I already know what you really look like," he says.

"Oh."

"Can I call on you sometime?" he asks.

"Well, I'm sort of ..."

"... seeing someone, huh?" he says.

"You're really sweet and all, honest. But I ..."

"That's okay," he says. "Thanks for the kiss, though." He stands up. "It's nice to meet you, Kelly."

*   *   *   *

"He's got to be some kind of guy to stand by you through gut surgery," Mimi says as she smashes out her cigarette and shifts positions in her recliner. A bird lands on the feeder by the window. It flings sunflower shells against the screen.

"Oh, he is," Mom says. "Best thing that's ever come along for Kelly. He's ready to get on with his life and take a bride. I'm just so excited that Kelly's the one he's chosen. What a wonderful life they're going to have together."

"I haven't even been proposed to yet. There's no ring on my finger." I flash Mom my left hand.

"A technicality, that's all," she says. "If you'd quit giving him the milk for free, you'd have had a carat and half sitting on your finger right now."

"Oh, Mom, please," I say.

"What if this Walt doesn't want her after all this mess?" Mimi asks. "You're body ain't exactly going to be a work by Van Gogh. More like a Picasso when it's all said and done."

"Oh, come on, Mimi," I say. "How bad can it be?"

"Remember your father's …"

"Mimi, I don't have cancer."

"Walt's not going to leave her. He's the one who's insisting that she get on with her life and do this," Mom says as she lights a cigarette. "I mean look how miserable she is."

"I'm miserable, Mimi."

"And you should see how Walt dotes on her all the time," Mom says.

"Well, ordinarily I would, but some people forget I exist and don't bring their new beaus over for even a five minute introduction," Mimi says with contempt.

"I'm sorry, Mimi. There's never enough time. We just get wrapped up in our lives …"

"I forget, you two women have careers. No time for Mimi."

"Not me. I quit my job at the Rumph's," I say.

Mimi shakes her head. "You, my dear, weren't ever meant for working. You were meant for marriage but you wouldn't listen to us. Only to your father. Marriage might actually be the only profession you're probably good at," she says. "You sure do like being taken care of, don't you?"

I sit on the couch and do not answer her. I try to think about Walt but Nick's kiss comes to mind instead. I shiver.

"I hope Walt keeps," she continues. "I don't think anyone else will have you after you get cut open like you're gonna. But we'll see. Hell, if you're really going to get married, I guess I can give you this damn thing now." Mimi rises from her chair and motions for us to follow her into the hallway. She opens the closet, sifts through some old blankets and sheets and pulls out a beautiful double wedding ring quilt. "I made it when you turned sixteen. You may need to wash it. It's got a lot of dust on it." She holds it out for me to take. "I hope you and Walt enjoy it."

Mom stands behind me and pats her approval on my shoulder. It's the first time I've genuinely felt accepted by her.

"It's beautiful," I say and caress the soft patches of calico.

"Well, take the damn thing," she yells and thrusts it to my chest. The dust particles fly into the air. I take the quilt and sneeze.

"I always believed you were allergic to marriage," Mimi says.

*   *   *   *

"The surgery's next Friday, but I go in on Thursday," I tell Walt over the phone. "Can you be there?"

"Of course I can be there. Why wouldn't I?"

"I know you're working hard," I tell him. "There won't be much happening on Thursday when I check in. I'll probably just lie around and watch TV and try to relax. I'll need you more on Friday, I'm sure."

"I'm there for you, Babe," he says. "I'm always there for you. Don't you know that?"

"I know." I bite the nail on my thumb. "For seven, I suppose. I wish I could see you sooner than that. For some quality time together, you know," I tell him.

"I know. But after the surgery and all, well ... we'll be mar ... we can ... We'll be together real soon. I promise. I love you, you know," he says.

"I do love you, too."

"Friday, Friday," he repeats. "Friday? Your birthday's Friday, isn't it?"

"Oh, yeah, I guess it is," I say. "I don't care. I want this to be over so I can get on with my life."

"The doctor did say you'd be normal, right?" he asks.

"Oh, absolutely. No limitations. Well, if you call not eating peanuts or raisins limitations."

"What's this thing, the uh, what do you call it?"

"Bag? It's a bag, I guess. The doctor said I'd hardly notice it. Normal life."

"What about ... um ... having ... I mean ... Can you ever get or have ...?" he beats around the bush.

"Pregnant? Is that what you mean?"

"Yeah. Pregnant. Can you? Can you have children?" he inquires.

"Not a problem. Like I said ..."

"Normal life?"

"Normal life."

*   *   *   *

"I'm telling you, this is my absolutely last meal for a long time. Tomorrow I begin a liquid diet for the surgery. I have to be completely cleaned out," I tell Sandra as we sit down at our booth at the White House.

"Then we'll consider this day to be your birthday," Sandra says as she picks up the menu. "Sky's the limit."

"All right," I reply.

"I'm taking off work Friday to be there, Kelly. Seven, huh?"

"No, Sandra, you'll do no such thing. It's surgery. Besides, it's a four hour procedure. You're better off at work. If something happens to me, well, then Mom will call you. It's not like I've got cancer. It's nothing. Piece of cake."

"Are you sure?" she leans over and asks.

"I'm sure. Piece of cake."

"Ooo, piece of cake sounds good," Sandra says.

"When's your due date?" I ask her.

"This Sunday," she says.

"Then you don't need to be up at the hospital. Or maybe you do? You'd be right there …" I say with a laugh.

"I'll come see you Sunday, then. Nobody has their first on time," she says.

"How about a Super Duper?" I ask her.

"Sounds great. Two Super Dupers and a basket of chips for the big girls!" Sandra says.

We order our burritos. When they come Sandra attacks her like this is her last meal. I suddenly don't feel so good. So much for my final feast.

"You usually eat yours and half of mine. Not the other way around," she says. "What's wrong?"

"I don't know," I reply. "I guess I'm just nervous. I feel sort of crampy."

"You fixin to start?" she asks as she shoves a bite of burrito into her mouth.

"No, I've got a couple of weeks yet, almost three. I'm just nervous, I suppose. It is major surgery, after all."

"You're braver than I am, Kelly."

I sit at the table and watch Sandra devour her burrito and half of mine, too. I feel hot, heavy even. My palms sweat and I feel the blood slowly drain from my face. "You ready to go?" I ask her. "I don't feel so good."

"Sure," she says and scrapes the last bit of burrito and sauce from her plate as I signal for our ticket. "But you've got to make a birthday wish in the fountain. You just have to."

"Okay. It's on the way to the car. This I can do. I'll just fling a penny out of the window as we drive by. How's that?" I say.

"Now come on. You have to do it right." Sandra grabs me by the arm as she leaves the cash on the table. It's your birthday. You've gotta do this."

"It's not my birthday, yet."

"So we'll pretend." She waddles out of the White House with me waddling behind her. I've never been so big in all my life. I'm outgrowing my size sixteen Lane Bryant wear. But soon there will be no more prednisone. And I'll have Walt. I'll have a nice comfortable life. He'll treat me nice. That's what I'll wish for. No more prednisone and for Walt.

Sandra hands me a penny as we approach the large town square fountain. "Make it a good one," she says.

"Oh, I will." I close my eyes and hold the penny. No more ...

"Bitch, you got some nerve!" I hear someone scream from behind me. I open my eyes and turn my head just in time to see Shamu jump me. She sends us both into the fountain. I fall hard on my butt and the wind gets knocked out of me. She pulls at my hair and it hurts.

"You stay away from him," she screams.

I feel myself lose total control and my wet underwear and Lane Bryant stretch pants get even wetter with slime. I look down to see the water I am sitting in begin to turn a dark crimson brown.

"Oooo, what the hell kind of period do you have?" She side steps the blood.

I look up at Sandra who stands in the water over me. "Oh my God, Kelly," she says.

"Get out of my way," I hear a familiar voice say as he pushes Shamu out of the way. It's Nick.

"I don't feel so good," I say as I feel the world slowly growing dimmer and smaller as I try to faint.

Nick picks me up out of the water. I try hard not to pass out.

"I'm too heavy for you," I tell him.

"Nonsense. You weigh a hundred and eighteen pounds, right?" Nick says.

"I did, didn't I?" I ask. "How do you know?"

"Saw it on your driver's license," he says as he makes his way toward a silver domestic pickup truck.

"Hey! Where are you going? What about me?" Shamu yells from the fountain.

"I don't care about you," Nick shouts at her as he places me in his truck.

"How am I going to get home!" she screams. "I'm all wet!"

"Take a cab," Nick replies and he slides in beside me with Sandra holding me upright on the other side.

"I didn't get to make my wish," I tell them. I open my hand. The penny is still there.

"So you'll do it later. After your surgery," Sandra says. "Right now you're going to the hospital."

"But my wish ..." I stare at the penny.

"Jeff told me about the surgery," Nick says to Sandra as he starts the truck's engine. "I hope she's going to be all right."

"She will be," Sandra tells him.

We back out of the parking lot and drive past the fountain. Shamu still stands in the middle of it. I slump toward Nick's shoulders. He takes my head and rests it on his arm.

"Hang in there, Kelly," he says. "You're going to be just fine. I'm going to see to that."

I feel the penny slide from my hand. I watch it hit the floorboard and disappear.

CHAPTER 14

▼

THE BAG MENAGERIE

Daddy always said that vengeance is its own reward. I've never thought of myself as a vindictive person and I certainly don't view my mother as vindictive either. Hell, you could beat Mom over the head with a baseball bat and she'd practically thank you. All in all the Carmichael women are not doors. We are the mats.

"Miss Carmichael, you're here for an illeostomy, right?" the clerk says to me as I stand before the admissions desk to the hospital up in Little Rock.

"Yes. That's right. Illeostomy. That's me," I reply. My hands and voice shake.

"It's going to be three to four hours before they have your room ready. Maybe you've got some shopping to do or something," the clerk tells us.

I look at Mom. She shrugs. "I don't much feel like shopping," she says.

"Then let's just stay here and wait, all right? My nerves are all shot to hell," I say.

"I know," Mom says. "Mine, too. I'm just so glad they didn't make us wait after your fountain fiasco. What were you thinking, Kelly?"

"Mom, please. It wasn't like that was intentional or anything. Nothing happened."

She frowns at me and then wanders around the waiting room. I pull my suitcase over to a seat, plop down, and flip through the magazines on the side table. I don't feel like reading *Diet Today*.

I watch Mom saunter around the lobby. She pauses at each picture of the board of directors and reads their names, one by one, until she makes her way to the phone booth on the left side of the lobby. She sits down in the booth and peruses the directory.

After ten minutes in the booth, Mom says, "Get your things. We're going to take a ride."

"Okay," I say. "Where to?"

"Just out," she says as she takes my bag in her hand.

We drive to West Little Rock, past the restaurants and trendy shops. We finally turn onto a street in a pretentious neighborhood.

"Do you have any idea where we're going?" I ask her. "Maybe," is all she says. "Mom, please. This isn't like you. You hate secrets."

"I know."

"Do you have some sort of surprise for me?" I ask. "After all it is my birthday tomorrow."

"No. No birthday surprise. You're surgery's enough birthday for one year," she says. She drives the car into a complex of posh condominiums.

"You have an old friend here or something?" I ask her. She reduces her speed and scrutinizes each address.

"No, not really," she says.

"Then ..."

She stops the car. A white BMW is parked in front of a two-story townhouse. The car's personalized license plate reads 'Elinor T.'

"Oh my God, Mom. This is the woman, isn't it?"

"Yep. That's the one," she says.

"What are you going to do?" I ask her.

"Nothing. I just wanted to see where she lived."

"You should do something," I say. "Go steal her license plate," I beg.

"No, I couldn't," she says and blushes.

"Fine. Don't do anything. Let's just get out of here before she sees us. I hate this, Mom. I really do. It's sick." I begin to tear up but I don't cry.

She wheels the car around, speeds out of the complex and drives down the road a few blocks. She turns quickly into the parking lot of a convenience store.

"What are you doing, now?" I ask.

"Just stay in here. I'll be right back," she reassures me. A minute later she returns with a bag in hand. She places it on the seat and I look into it. There's a carton of eggs inside.

"What the hell do you need eggs for, Mom. I'm going into the hospital for cryin' out ... oh my God!"

"Yep." She giggles like a schoolgirl. "I figure we're due."

"Oh my God, Mom. Oh my God."

She drives back to the condo's parking lot and rolls down the front windows of the Cadillac. She opens the carton of eggs. One by one she flings them at the BMW and the front door of the Elinor T's townhouse.

I pull myself halfway through the passenger side window and fling the eggs over the car at the townhouse. Then the front door opens. It's Elinor T. I hold the egg in my hand and stare at the girl in my sights. She's not much older than I am. More what I used to look like if only I had had some money back then. I'd almost swear we were sisters, she looks so familiar to me. Then I remember.

"What the hell … Hey!" she yells at us. Mom peels out.

I let the last egg fly out of my hand as the car jerks and lunges forward. The egg hits Elinor squarely on the head. As we round the corner of the complex, I watch Elinor wipe egg from her face.

*   *   *   *

When we return to the hospital, my room is still not ready. We venture to the cafeteria to pass some more time.

I am amazed at the selection of items in the cafeteria for a liquid diet. I choose an oriental chicken broth, Seven-up, and orange Jell-O. This looks so much better than the bouillon cubes and water I've been consuming at home.

Mom chooses the chef's salad and an extra packet of spicy French dressing, no doubt bolstered by her sudden sense of adventure.

We sit and eat in silence until a group of doctors approach and occupy the table next to us.

"Sit up straight," she says.

"Why? I'm comfortable."

"They're doctors," she says between her teeth.

"So. I've got Walt."

"You never know when you might need a back-up."

"Mom, who's going to pick me?" I ask her. "I look like a Weeble. Weebles wobble but they don't fall down, remember?" I sing softly.

"He's looking at you," she says and nods in the men's direction.

I halfway turn to see. They are looking at me. Then they turn away.

"Classic prednisone moon face," one instructs the others. "See the indications …"

I swivel back around and look at Mom.

"They're talking about you, aren't they?" She smiles and happily chomps a radish.

"Yes, Mom. Yes, they are."

*   *   *   *

We follow the nurse to the G. I. wing of the hospital. She informs me that I will be spending the next ten days or so here.

"Dr. Borden likes to keep all of his patients together," the nurse says. "It's kind of like a gastroenterology zoo around here." She laughs.

"And I'm going to be an exhibit, huh?"

"I guess you could say that," she says.

We walk into a room where a young woman puffs on a cigarette.

"Now Ethel, you know this is a non-smoking hospital. We'll have none of that here," the nurse scolds.

"If I can't smoke, I'll go mad, I tell you. Mad, mad, mad," Ethel snaps.

The nurse takes away her pack of Marlboros. "Ethel, this is your new room-mate. Her name is Kelly."

"Screw you, bitch," Ethel says to me in a low, almost sadistic tone.

The nurse turns to us and shrugs. "I'm sorry."

"Look, my daughter can't stay in this room," Mom whispers to the nurse.

"But there aren't any other rooms available. Not for a couple of days," the nurse protests.

"I ordered a private room for her. I paid the difference in cash at the front desk. Just like we were instructed. We were promised a private room," Mom insists.

"And you'll get one when one comes available. Until then …"

"If you don't get her a private room right now, I will go to Edwin Applegate myself. I trust he is still the administrator of this facility?"

"Oh yes, ma'am. He's still in charge," the nurse says.

"Good. I've been meaning to look him up while I was here. He's an old college buddy of my husband's," Mom says. She smiles big and examines her nails. "In fact, he was a member of our wedding party."

I stare with awe at my mom's new found assertiveness. Before Daddy's death she not only would have put up with the room but she would also have bought Ethel her smokes. And then she would have complained only to me.

"Give me ten minutes, ma'am. I think I know where I can get your daughter a private room," the nurse says and scurries down the hall.

"I'll bet you do," Mom says.

We take my bag from the room and sit down in a small corner waiting area.

"I'm impressed with you," I tell her. "Really, I am. Do you honestly know the administrator?"

"Heck, no," she says. "I saw the name under his picture in the lobby downstairs. It was worth a shot."

"Damn, Mom. You're all right."

*   *   *   *

I try to make myself comfortable in the hospital bed but I'm nervous. Nurses come in and out of the room, take my blood pressure and temperature, and make me fill out silly forms.

"Did you finish the bottle of Rosie's that the doctor instructed you to drink last night?" a nurse asks me. Rosie's is a laxative designed to clean out your system.

"I drank about half the bottle before I threw up. I can't stand the taste of it," I explain. "It's nasty."

"We've got to start cleaning you out. I'll be right back."

I've been banking on a couple of enemas for that. I can't drink that shit.

Mom relaxes in the extra bed. I watch as she dozes off. She looks peaceful, not worried at all.

The nurse emerges from the corridor not five minutes later with a gallon jug. She plops the container onto the bedside table. "You've got to drink the whole thing," she says as she places a small plastic cup beside it.

"What? A glass? What is that stuff?"

"It's Go-Litely. And no. The whole gallon."

My eyes get really big. "I can't drink all that!" I protest.

"You have to. Get busy," she taps the top of the bottle, smiles, and exits the room.

"Thanks, Nurse Ratchet," I call out to her.

The nurse giggles.

I stare at the jug. It gets larger and larger the longer I stare at it.

Mom stirs. "What's that?" she asks as she sits up.

"Go-Litely. I have to drink it. All of it."

"Oh, your father had to drink that stuff," she tells me.

"And did he drink all of it?"

"Almost all of it, I think," she says.

"Oh." I open the top and pour the clear liquid into the cup. I stare at it some more. "Bottoms up," I say. I take a large gulp of the substance thinking it's like water. It isn't. It's an awful lime-aid like mess that makes me gag as I try to choke it down. "Oh, God."

"It's to clean you out," Mom says.

"There's not much in me to clean out," I say. I look at the cup again and take another sip. I choke on it and spit it back into the cup.

The nurse pokes her head through the doorway. "Finished yet?" she asks then looks at the bottle and frowns.

"I can't," I whine.

"You have to. No way around it," the nurse says. "As a matter of fact, I just gave a ninety something year old woman a gallon of it. She drank it down like it was mother's milk."

"Then give her the rest of mine," I offer.

I take a sip of the mess again and swallow. It comes back up again. I hold my mouth and rush to the bathroom and throw up.

*   *   *   *

"My, aren't these lovely," the nurse says as she brings me a dozen red roses.

I try to hold in the first enema. "Uh, huh," is all I can manage to say.

The nurse pulls the card from the stick. "May I," she asks.

"Uh, huh," I say again.

"That's my girl. Love, Walt," she reads. "Oh, isn't that sweet?"

"Uh, huh. Can I go, now? Please!"

"Give it just a couple of more minutes, hon." She snoops around my bedside table. "You haven't drunk the Rosie's or Go-Litely. You have to be cleaned out, you know."

"Uh, huh."

"Must be nice to have a boyfriend," the nurse says. She sits on the bed. The subtle movement makes me want to let the enema go.

"Uh, huh."

"He's rich," Mom tells her.

"Figures," she says. "All the good ones are taken." She looks at me long and deliberately, like I stole her boyfriend and this is my punishment.

I shoot her a pained look.

"Oh, all right. Go."

I rush to the bathroom. I barely place my butt on the seat before it all comes out.

I walk back into the room, relieved and somewhat refreshed. Maybe now I can relax.

The nurse is gone. I look over at my roses. Six enemas stand next to them.

*   *   *   *

The nurse peers into the commode. "You look clean."

"I can't do this anymore," I bawl.

"Oh honey, I know it hurts. If you had only drunk the Go-Litely …"

The thought of the substance makes me heave. I bend over the toilet and throw up nothing.

"You go relax for a while, hon. I don't think anything else is going to come out of you tonight," the nurse tells me. "We'll start an I-V on you and get you prepped for in the morning, okay? Go on. Go to bed." She gently pushes me as if I'm a little girl.

I sit on the bed and stare at the phone. He hasn't called. I just knew he'd call. With Mom on a smoke break I decide to phone him.

I dial the number and it rings. I let it ring ten or twelve times. I hang up when the nurse's assistant enters the room. She carries a small plastic tray.

"You having the illeostomy tomorrow?" she asks me.

"Yes."

"I've gotta shave you. Get you ready for the surgery."

I pull my gown up and look at my belly. "There's not much hair down there. It's all on my face."

"Your pubic hair. I've gotta get that," she states.

"Oh."

She sits in the chair and unwraps the razor from the kit. She pushes my gown up and my panties down. She begins to shave me.

I turn my head away from the assistant and stare at the phone. I cry. The wall clock reads ten after twelve.

Happy birthday to me.

*   *   *   *

I open my eyes. A nurse tiptoes into the room.

"Miss Carmichael?" she asks.

"Yes."

"I hate to wake you but there's a young man at the nurses' station. He says he's just got to see you."

"Send him in," I say. "Wait." I open the tray table and pull up the mirror. I try to smooth out my hair. I can't see well in the semi-darkness. "Okay."

The nurse exits the room. She returns a few seconds later with Walt.

"Hey, Baby," he says. He quickly crosses the room to my bedside. Mom doesn't wake.

"How'd you get up here?" I ask.

"I just came through the emergency room and made my way around until I found you," he says.

We embrace and kiss. Walt gives me a small stuffed Teddy Bear with a big red bow.

"It's so cute," I say. I set it down on the tray table.

"You okay with everything?" he asks.

"I guess. I'm not chickening out if that's what you mean."

"I don't want you to. If this is the only way to get over this, then you've got to do it," he says.

Mom awakens. "Oh, my. Walt!"

"Hi, Mrs. Carmichael. How are you?"

"Good. Oh, I'm so glad you're here."

"Nothing could keep me away," he says. He hugs me and kisses me again. I feel like everything's going to be just fine. It's all worth it now. This is the reason.

*   *   *   *

I turn the television to The Weather Channel. Before I go into surgery, I at least want to know what the weather is going to be like. Walt sits next to me and holds my hand.

"The Weather Channel! What's with you and the damn weather. You're always watching that," Walt says. "You're stuck inside. Who cares about the weather. Let me have that remote." He takes the remote from my hand. "Here, let's watch a game or something."

I turn to look at him. He finds a sports show on ESPN and becomes totally engrossed in the commentary.

At least he's here.

*   *   *   *

"Miss Carmichael," I hear a nurse say to me. I slowly wake up. "I'm going to give you a little something to make you relax before we take you down to surgery."

"Okay," I say. I sit up in the bed.

The nurse gives me a shot in the I-V, then leaves the room. Mom is up and dressed. Her makeup is impeccable.

"Well, here I go," I say to her.

"Yep. Here you go," she says.

The room begins to spin slightly. I slide down under the covers to sleep but the orderlies wake me and adjust the bed. Then they slowly wheel me down the hall and toward the elevator. I'm flying.

*   *   *   *

The room is cold. The only sound is the tinkling of stainless steel against steel. I look to my left. The anesthesiologist hovers over me. I look to my right. The instruments line the table along the wall. Big instruments. Huge instruments. I see a saw and a rib spreader. Oh my God, I've made a terrible mistake here.

I look up at the anesthesiologist. He injects the tube with something.

"Count back from ten," he says.

No, no, no, no. I don't want to do this now. I've changed my mind, I scream to no one but myself. But the darkness and comfort of uncaring envelope me.

*   *   *   *

Clouds. Clouds of pillows. Soft, billowy, steel blue clouds cradle me.

"Turn over, Sweetie," a tender voice says. "You're doing just fine."

I roll over and embrace the clouds.

*   *   *   *

"Babe? … Baby?" I hear Walt's voice. I try to move but I can't. I feel my face. There's a tube running through my nose. There are tubes and lines running all over me. I see a red tube which runs down into my arm. Blood. "You're doing good. They said you're doing just fine. You're home free," he says.

"It's out?"

"Yeah baby, it's out." He brushes my hair away from my eyes. "You're going to be just fine."

He dotes on me like a devoted husband. I feel secure.

"Where's Mom?" I ask.

"She's staying in my hotel room. She needed a break." he says.

"What time is it?"

"About seven thirty," he says.

"At night?"

"Yeah. At night. You've had a long day. Rest." He leans in his chair and turns the television set on. I drift off to sleep.

✳   ✳   ✳   ✳

"It hurts. It hurts," I whine. Tears stream down my cheeks.

"What hurts, baby?" Walt asks. He leans over me.

"My back. It hurts so bad. Where's the egg crate they promised. That soft foamy stuff. Where is it?" I ask him. My back is on fire and the pain is intense. I try to switch positions. I can't. It makes it worse.

"I'll go check with the nurse. Just take it easy," he says.

"Okay," I sob.

He returns to the room a few minutes later. He shakes his head. "They say it'll be an hour or so. They've got to order it."

"What time is it?"

"About nine fifteen. In the morning," he says.

"It hurts so bad," I tell him.

"They'll fix it. I promise."

✳   ✳   ✳   ✳

I watch the clock. At ten fifteen no one has come to relieve my pain. "Where the hell is that egg crate," I scream. "God, it hurts."

"I'll check," he says and leaves the room.

He comes back with a nurse.

"We've ordered the egg crate, Miss Carmichael. It'll be here soon," the nurse says. "You say you're in pain?" She leans over me.

"My back. It hurts," I explain to her. "I can't stand it. Help me. I can't stand it any longer." Tears drip on my cheeks.

"Your morphine pump is working just fine. Go ahead and push the button, Miss Carmichael. That'll relieve the pain," she says and leaves the room.

I push the button. Nothing. "If I only had that egg crate, I'd feel so much better," I tell Walt. "Please go check on it. Please, Walt. Please. It hurts so bad."

"Okay but …"

He comes back in. "They don't know when it'll come. And they say you shouldn't be in any pain. That everything's working just fine."

"CAN'T THEY SEE I'M HURTING."

*   *   *   *

At one thirty I bawl. "Can't you stop this pain, Walt, please. Can't you get me the egg crate. I need the egg crate," I beg him. I push the button to the morphine pump but nothing happens.

"I'll go again but she's not going to do anything," he says.

He returns with the nurse. "Miss Carmichael, I'm telling you, you can't possibly be in any pain."

"It hurts. It hurts so bad," I scream and cry.

"I'll get pain management," she says. "But everything's working just fine."

"Get me an egg crate!" I yell. "It hurts."

"She wouldn't be doing this if it didn't hurt," Walt assures the nurse.

"She can't possibly be in any pain."

*   *   *   *

At two fifteen a blonde headed man pushes me up from the mattress and looks at my back. "The epidural is working just fine," he says. "There's no problem here. Everything's working just fine. She's getting plenty of pain medication."

"It hurts," I whimper. "Doesn't anyone believe me. It hurts. Oh God, it hurts!" I push the morphine pump. Nothing.

"It's working fine," he says and shrugs. "I don't know what more I can do for her. It's working just fine." He shrugs again and leaves the room. I look at Walt. He stands helpless beside my bed. "What else can I say? I've tried to tell them," he says in defeat. He leans over me. "I've done all that I can do. What more do you want from me?"

I take his shirt in my hand and yank it. "GET THE GODDAMN EGG CRATE!"

He quickly runs from the room. When he returns, three nurses follow him with a pastel green egg crate mattress. They remove me from the bed. I sit in the chair like a rag doll. They quickly place the egg crate on the bed and make it up again. They put me back in bed. Exhausted, I fall asleep.

*   *   *   *

"Hey, Sweetheart," Mom says.

I look around the room. Walt is gone.

"Where's? …"

"Went to get something to eat. He'll be back later," she assures me. "How are you feeling?" She strokes my hair.

"Fine. I feel fine. Why?"

"No pain?" she asks.

"No. I feel tired. Really tired," I say.

Mom sits on the other bed and retrieves her needle work from it from her sewing bag. The nurse comes in.

"Miss Carmichael, time to check your pouch," she says. "And I think we can take your tube out, too."

"Sure," I say.

She places a towel on my chest and tells me to blow out of my nose. She pulls the tube out. It feels like removing uncomfortable shoes. Relief.

She removes the bedcovers and opens my gown to reveal the bandages and a bag on my stomach. She opens the bag and empties it's foul smelling contents into a bowl. Then she cleans the bag with a turkey baster and some water. She closes it up with a clip.

"That's it?" I ask.

"Yep, that's it," she says. "Let's take a look at your incision." She carefully removes the bandages. A series of staples run a couple of inches from below my bra line almost all the way down to my privates. The scar is nasty and hideous. My stomach churns. I feel faint. I look away toward the door. There is Walt. His mouth is open and his eyes are wide with amazement.

"Honey," I say.

"Oh God, Kelly."

"Walt, it's okay. It doesn't hurt," I reassure him.

"I can't do this. I just can't. I'm sorry," he says and shakes his head. "I'm sorry Kelly." He backs up, out of the room and into the hallway.

"Walt. It's okay. It's not that bad. Walt?"

Mom looks up from her needle work, at me then at him.

"Oh my God," he says. He grabs his stomach and gags.

As he backs up again, he bumps into Nick and smashes the bouquet of flowers in his hand. Walt turns and runs. Nick stands in the doorway.

"Walt!" I scream. The tears flow from my eyes. Mom rushes past Nick and down the hall.

"Did I come at a bad time?" Nick asks as I weep uncontrollably. He peers over the nurses shoulder. She seems perplexed. "Nice scar," Nick says.

I wail louder as Nick brushes the crushed flower petals from his shirt. They fall to the floor like snowflakes.

CHAPTER 15

▼

A Bag Ain't Nothin' but a Place to Keep Your Shit

Welcome to the Dart Comfort-Fit 9000 Stoma Support System, designed for optimal comfort and control. First, find the exact size of the stoma by measuring the diameter with the templates provided.

Second, remove the Dart Comfort-Fit 9000 wafer from its container and center the template around the small opening. Trace the cutout onto it.

I remove the template from the box and place it over my two-week-old stoma. I stare at the staples which keep my insides and guts from falling out onto the Berber carpet.

"God."

I touch the moist, pink small intestine which protrudes out of the right side of my belly, the stoma. I place the template over the stoma. The hole is too big for it. I take three or four measurements with the template before I find the right size. I place the seven-eighths inch cutout onto the back of the wafer as instructed and trace the shape with a ballpoint pen. I glance at my neglected nails and nervously cut the opening with my cuticle scissors.

Third, remove the Handy-Prep Skin Wipe from its sterile packaging and swab the area around the stoma. This will provide a protective barrier between you and any intestinal discharge which might penetrate the appliance.

I gently swab the area around the hideous protrusion which is supposed to be my salvation. I wince at the stinging sensation of the alcohol in the wipe's solution. I discover that there is no feeling whatsoever between the stoma and my scar.

"I guess I won't be needing my bikini anymore." I shake my head and stare at my reflection in contempt.

"Why, God? Why?" I ask.

Fourth, apply a thin bead of Dart Stoma Paste approximately one half inch away from and around the opening of the wafer.

I pick up the tube of paste, open it, and squeeze an awkward bead of the mixture around the cutout as if it were caulk. The tube sputters and sprays paste inside the opening and all over the marble counter top of the lavatory.

"Oh, for the love of ..." I try to wipe the stuff up with my fingers but the sticky concoction smears all over everything like tacky glue. Tears of anger and despair form in my eyes.

"Dammit."

Fifth, attach the wafer around the stoma and apply light pressure to perfect adhesion.

I follow the instructions but the wafer barely sticks to my skin. It slowly curls up and out at the corners. I press harder on the wafer but it continues to curl up. I grab some bandage tape and anchor the wafer to my skin. I smile at my handy work and ingenuity.

I look at the commode and the basket of Cosmopolitans and Vogues beside it. I realize I will never again sit on the toilet and read.

I press harder on the wafer for added precaution. The paste oozes out around the stoma. I instinctively reach for a Kleenex and dab at it but the tissue sticks to the paste. In disgust, I pick out the fragments of the tissue from around the stoma.

I sigh in despair.

Sixth, the Exclusive Dart Comfort-Fit 9000 Resealable Pouch, with its patented Zip-Tech closure, fits securely around the plastic flange on the wafer. Simply snap the two together and you're ready to go!

Before I can place the bag onto the wafer, the stoma spews out a foul brown substance the consistency of thick gravy and spits out undigested English peas. The discharge splats on my bare feet, then splatters onto the carpet.

"Oh, shit."

*　　　*　　　*　　　*

"Mimi! The phone, Mimi. Get the phone," I holler to my grandmother who snoozes in the chair. She doesn't hear me. I slowly roll my aching body off of the couch and onto the floor. I carefully ease my way upright or as close I can to upright. I walk like a ninety year old man.

"I'm coming, I'm coming," I say as I hold my stomach with my hand to prevent my guts from falling out. My butt burns with each step. The phone quits ringing by the time I reach it. I check the caller I-D. It's not Walt. It will never be Walt.

I dial Mom's number at the office. "Yes, may I speak to Olivia Carmichael, please?" I ask the receptionist.

"This is Olivia," Mom says. She sounds so professional, so independent.

"Hi, Mom. You called?"

"Oh yeah. I did. How are you doing?"

"Fine. I'm tired from getting the phone but I'm fine," I say.

"Why didn't Mimi answer it?"

"Because she's sleeping and left the cordless phone on its station," I complain. "Did you want something? I can't stand here forever. This is tiring."

"No. Not really, except to tell you I'm going to be a little late. I'm showing houses until after five. I'll bring something home for dinner, all right?"

"Sure. Mashed potatoes. I only want mashed potatoes,"

"That's it?"

"A Coke perhaps."

"All right, then. I'll see you around six, Sweetie. I love you and take care," she says.

"Yeah," is my only reply. I hang up the phone in the kitchen and make my way toward Mom's room for the cordless. I sit on her bed and try to catch my breath. Then I lay down for a minute to rest. The doorbell rings.

"Mimi, will you get that!" I call out.

I wait for a response but the doorbell rings again. Slowly I roll off the bed and scoot my way to the front door. Mimi snores.

I open the door to reveal Sandra and her newborn.

"Shouldn't you be at home resting with the baby?" I ask her.

"Why? We needed to get out. See the sites," she responds.

"See the freak with the bag …" I say.

"Kelly," she scolds and makes her way in.

"So what's her name?" I ask as I inch my way down to the couch.

"Sara Jane," she says. The baby coos.

"Nice," I say.

Mimi awakens and rises up. "Oh Sandra, it's you," she says and reaches for her cigarettes.

Sandra frowns her disapproval at Mimi.

"Mimi, do you mind. She's got a baby here," I tell her.

"What? Like one lousy cigarette's going to stunt the child's growth," Mimi complains. "Hell, I smoked through the pregnancy of both Olivia and Phil. They turned out all right. Sort of. Hell, they're probably better than most 'cause I did smoke. Toughened them up, so to speak."

"Mimi, please ..." I plead.

"It isn't healthy for her," Sandra adds.

"Ah, hell. What's this world coming to? I de-clare," she says and stomps off through the kitchen and out onto the patio. "It's damn chilly out here," she yells. "An old woman could surely catch her death of cold on a day like today." She lights her cigarette and slams the sliding glass door.

"You're doing all right?" Sandra asks me again.

"As can be expected of someone like me," I say.

"You want to hold the baby?"

"No. I'm weak. I might drop her," I say. "She's pretty. She looks like you."

Sandra blushes. "You think?"

"Sure," I lie. The baby doesn't look like anyone in particular. It just looks like a baby. I can't remember what Dan looked like.

"So how long did the doctor say it'll take for you to be back to normal?" she asks.

"What's normal?"

"No. I mean, when will you be able to get around, go to the White House Grill, do the things you used to do?"

"I don't know. Whenever," I reply.

"So what are you going to do when you recover? Go back to Memphis? Try to work things out with Walt?"

I scoff. "I'm not going back there. Let's face it, I'm ruined. I'm a nothing. He doesn't want me. Nobody does. I'm thirty years old and I'm all used up."

"Kelly, this isn't like you. You'll change your mind when you feel better. You're just in pain. It's the painkillers talking. You'll feel different in a couple of weeks. You'll be back to normal then."

"I shit in a bag, Sandra. You call that normal?"

"What was your other alternative?"

"I made a mistake." I throw my hands up in the hair. The effort is painful. My abdomen and my head throb.

"When you recover and lose the weight, Walt will see what he missed and come back to you," Sandra says. "I think he'll stand by you. I really do."

"Like Dan has stood by you?"

"That wasn't his decision. It was mine."

"Whatever." I fall back on the couch. "Look, I'm feeling real weak and tired. Perhaps we can continue this visit another time. The doctor said I really didn't need visitors anyway."

Sandra rises and the baby cries. "That's all right," she says to her. "She's hungry and I need to get home and feed her." She rocks the baby as she makes her way to the door.

"If you don't mind letting yourself out," I say.

"No. I don't mind," Sandra whispers. "I understand."

"Good to see you, Sandra."

"Yeah. You, too," she says and lets herself out. I can hear the baby wail from behind the closed door.

Mimi comes in when she sees Sandra leave. "Proud mama showing off the illegitimate, huh?" she asks as she lights another cigarette with her last. "Not in my day." Mimi sits in a chair. "All men are scum, you know that? Yep. You're better off without them, Kelly. Yes, you are. You don't know how damn lucky you are."

I turn the television set onto the Weather Channel.

*   *   *   *

"Get up," I hear Mom say. She hovers over me in the bed. She nudges me. I wince from practice, not pain.

"Why? I don't have anywhere to be?" I say.

"Four months is long enough. Get up and find a job, an activity, something. Run the vacuum, for crying out loud. I don't care. I'm just not going to have you sleeping the day away while I work my fingers to the bone."

"I hurt. I'm not ready yet," I whine.

"And you won't be until you get up off your butt and get out there."

"What time is it?" I ask.

"One o'clock," she says. "I've got to go back to the office. Do something useful with the afternoon for once."

"There's nothing for me to do. It's pointless."

"Get up." She shoves me this time.

"Ow ... don't."

"This is your last day. Find a life and get on with it," she says as she crosses toward my door. She wears the houndstooth suit I bought for Dad's funeral. "That Italian guy sent you flowers again. Nick whatsit."

"He's stalking me."

"He's concerned about you," she insists.

"He likes girls with scars."

"He likes you, Kelly. I don't see Walt's name on any flowers. I don't even see Walt."

"That's because Walt's a real human being, Momma. Scars are repulsive," I say.

"I don't think it was the scar, Kelly."

"What's that supposed to mean?"

"Nevermind," she says. "Nick seems like a nice guy."

"Jeffery Dahmer was a nice guy, too. What are you going to say when I come home in a body bag?"

Mom leaves the room. "The last day, Kelly. This shit's got to go." I hear her heels click as she walks across the kitchen floor. She slams the door.

I slowly roll out of bed. My abdomen has healed but my rear end is sore, raw, and sweaty. I waddle to the living room and flip on the television. The local forecast says clear and cold, a typical winter day. Not much is happening on the national weather scene either. Dull and boring.

I walk into the kitchen. Peach roses this week. Last week he sent me hot pink ones. I know that the colors of roses are supposed to signify something. Do peach roses mean Uncle Guido's in town?

I pour myself a bowl of Lucky charms and sit down to read the want ads. 'Girl Friday, receptionist, motel housekeeper, over the road trucker. Now there's a career I've yet to try. Trucker. Oh, wouldn't Dad be proud?

The phone rings as I circle a want ad for 'Assemble parts at home. Lots of $$$.' "Hello," I answer.

"Kelly. Hi. It's me, again," the voice says. "It's me, Nick. How are you doing?"

"As good as can be expected."

"Oh. So whatcha doin' these days?" he asks.

Just what I've got time for. Small talk from a stalker.

"Not much. The usual."

"Well then, since you're not doing much, let's do something. Tonight. How about the White House Grill?"

"Tonight?"

"Sure. Why not? It's Friday. The weekend. It's a date night. People do still date around here, don't they?"

"I suppose. You know, I'm still recovering. Maybe we should …"

"I'll pick you up at seven thirty," he says. Before I can turn him down, he hangs up.

Seven-thirty. Maybe I'll be lucky and a big meteor will hit earth and we'll all die. A lot can happen in six hours.

*   *   *   *

No such luck. I stand before my bathroom mirror at seven-twenty five. I've dropped down to a size twelve. I have no clothes that fit me. The Lane Bryant's are too big. My original clothing is too small.

I settle for some oversized jeans and a big sweatshirt. What do I care. I'm not out to impress anyone, least of all a stalker.

I lift my sweatshirt up and caress the healing scar. I feel the bumps which the staples made. My ostomy gurgles. Something's wrong with a guy who would want to go out with a girl like me.

"Where are you going?" Mom asks. She pauses at my door.

"To get a life. Isn't that what you want me to do?"

"You and Sandra going out?" she asks.

"No, Mom. She's got her own life. And a baby," I reply.

"Kelly, will you please snap out of this."

"Mom, you should be happy for me. I've finally found something I'm good at. Lying around."

"For the love of …" she begins but the doorbell cuts her off. "Who are you going out with?"

"A guy, Mom."

"Who? Do I know him?"

"He's some biker dude I've been seeing while you've been at work. We're going to get married and have lots of children, give them names like Axel and Greasemonkey."

Mom frowns at me, then proceeds to the living room. She checks her hair in the mirror before she opens the door.

"Hello, Mrs. Carmichael. I'm Nick Giovanni," he says.

"Oh. Hello," Mom says. She looks at me as I walk toward her. She has a puzzled look on her face.

He's dressed casually in khakis and a sweater. "These are for you," he says to Mom. He hands her a bouquet of flowers.

"Thank you," Mom says. She takes them in her hand and sniffs them. "Kelly, Nick's here." She steps back and whispers in my ear, "You're going to wear that? He seems like a really nice boy. Go change your clothes."

"Mom, please," I say. "Hi."

"You look great, Kelly," he tells me. "You're really looking good."

"I suppose. These things take time," I say.

"So, are you ready?" he asks, clasping his hands together.

"Sure. Might as well," I say.

"You two have fun," Mom says and winks at me. "I like this guy. He's so cute," she whispers in my ear.

"Bunnies are cute, Mom. Stalkers aren't," I whisper back.

*   *   *   *

"This isn't the way to the White House Grill," I tell him. He turns his pickup down a side road on the opposite end of town.

"I know," he says with a smile. "Change of plans. I've got a nice surprise set up."

"You can't get away with it, you know. Eventually they'll catch up to you," I say.

"Huh?"

"I won't say anything. Just take me back now," I tell him. I slide myself closer to the door.

"That's my house over there," he says. He points toward a white frame two story farmhouse, well lit, surrounded by a white picket fence. He keeps on driving past. "You like it?"

"It's nice," I say. It could be anyone's. I have no idea where we are. I've just had major surgery which I've almost recovered from. Why couldn't I have gone then, not like this? For once in my life, I'm downright scared to death.

He turns off the highway and down a dark, bumpy road. The pickup truck bounces us along for a couple of hundred feet. The headlights illuminate a large greenhouse. He turns off the engine but leaves the lights on. The glare from the plastic greenhouse bounces back into my eyes. It's almost blinding.

He turns the headlights off, gets out of the car and comes around to my side. I'm still buckled in the seat. "Well, come on," he says and extends his hand out for me to take.

I look at him with all the fear that's inside of me. I shake my head.

"Kelly, come on. This is going to be great," he says and touches my elbow. I cringe.

"Oh, God," he says. "You think I'm a stalker or something."

My eyes tear up.

"Oh, no. No. No. God, am I an idiot," he says and slaps himself on the forehead. "No. You think … This is the Collins' greenhouse. We're just down the street from my house. They're my neighbors."

"It's dark. I don't really know you. I didn't know," I tell him. He unbuckles my seatbelt and gives me a hug.

"Come on. I have a surprise for you," he says. He takes me by the hand and leads me into the dark greenhouse. I wipe my eyes as he flips on the light.

There in the middle of the greenhouse is the most elaborate picnic feast I've ever seen, right down to the red-checkered tablecloth on the sandy floor. Two wine glasses mark our places. A bottle of Chianti, a bowl of fruit, and a wheel of aged cheese complete the feast. He turns on a portable stereo. Italian music oozes from the speakers.

He lights several candles as I take my seat. Then he turns out the lights. The shadows of the ferns and bougainvillea dance to the music in the shimmering candlelight.

"Oh my God. This is the sweetest thing anyone's ever done for me," I say. "This is so beautiful."

"I'm glad you like it," he says.

"Why would you do something like this for me?" I ask him.

"Why wouldn't I?"

I take the glass of wine he offers me. He is quite handsome in the candlelight. "I'm sorry I didn't believe in your intentions," I say. "Just with all the flowers and phone calls and everything, I couldn't believe that anyone would be interested in someone like me. Except maybe …"

"… a stalker?"

I laugh at my foolishness. "So you're not a stalker."

"Almost. I'm an attorney."

I choke on the wine. "An attorney? You must be new here. I've never heard of you before."

"Been here six months. I set up a satellite office down here from a firm I'm a partner in up in Little Rock. Kirkland, Giovanni and Brown. Guess who I am?"

I laugh. "Brown?"

"You tease." He laughs, too. "I do a lot of disability cases, social security, workman's comp … I wanted to get out of the city. This was a good opportunity to spread out our client base. So I took it. I like it here." He hands me a cracker with some cheese on it.

"I used to be a paralegal," I tell him.

"No way. I like you even more," he says. "Wait. Used to be? I've been trying to hire a paralegal for months," he says. "What do you do now?"

"Nothing. Nobody is interested in someone like me," I tell him and take the cracker.

"What do you mean someone like you?" he asks.

"Look at me. I'm a mess," I tell him. "I couldn't even get hired by you."

"Did you send me a resume? They haven't sent me anyone."

"Like I said, I'm a mess. Don't worry about it. I'm used to it." I feel myself start to cry.

"Hey, now. It's okay," he says and hands me his napkin to dab my eyes. "I don't think you're a mess. Not at all."

"You should open your eyes, then," I tell him.

"I wish you could see what I see," he says.

"What's that? An umpaloompa? A Shamu? Moby Dick?"

"Stop that. I really like you, Kelly. I really do. I'd like to get to know you if you'd just let me."

"I'm sorry. I'm just not really ready for all this," I tell him. "I don't even know you very well. And you don't know me, either. Not the real me."

"Real you? I see a very brave, very beautiful person who is afraid to let herself be herself. Afraid to let go and be free."

"I'm not afraid of letting myself go," I protest. "I'm just discriminating, that's all. I let myself go from time to time."

"Is that why you kissed me back that afternoon?"

"For your information, you forced yourself on me," I tell him.

"But you didn't put up a fight. Why?"

"I don't know," I say.

"Sure you do? Why?"

I suddenly blush. "I felt safe. I felt wanted. A little sexy, even. And I felt impulsive. Like I was doing something wild and forbidden. It felt good."

"But you didn't know me then," he says.

"Touché'."

"I'd really like to get to know you," he says. "I mean that." He leans over to kiss me. I look at him and remember Walt. I pull away.

"I come on pretty strong, I know," he says and sits back down. "I'm sorry." "You've got nothing to be sorry about. I'm the one who should apologize," I say. "I'm vulnerable right now, that's all. Can you understand that?" I fondle my wine glass.

"Sure. I can respect that," he says. "That's why I like you. You're not as impulsive as I am.

I take a sip of the wine. I wish I was right now.

CHAPTER 16

▼

MY FAIR BAG LADY

When I was growing up my mom used to tell me that marriage is a lot like pizza. Even when it's bad, it's still pretty good. She used to say the same thing about sex. Come to think of it, I never remember her eating that much pizza.

Sandra, on the other hand, eats lots of pizza. Unfortunately, it's the frozen kind. Brands come and go with her. The flavor is synthetic and although the outside is warm, the center is always cold.

My pizza has almost always been the original parlor type. It's intensely flavorful, rich and fulfilling. And there are so many flavors to choose from. The problem with the parlor type is that it never sticks to the box. At least Mom's pizza stuck to the box.

"Well is he rich?" Mom asks again.

"Why is it so important to you?" I retort. I reach for a cookie across the table as Mom pours more coffee into my cup.

"I want you to be happy," she says.

"Mom, if you and Daddy had had more money, he'd have still been a heel. Probably even worse than he was. You'd only have more stuff. That's all."

"He is rich. My brother says he's loaded," Sandra says. "And he's an attorney. A very good one at that."

"An attorney," Mom says with a smile. "You should work for him."

"Yeah, right. No one in this town even wants to hire me. I'm surprised he even wants to date me," I lament.

"He's got the hots for you. So Jeff tells me, anyway," Sandra says. "And he's an attorney."

"You know, it doesn't matter anymore what he does. He's just a guy. A very nice guy. Can't ya'll leave it at that?"

"You're going to marry him." Sandra says. "I just know it."

"I am not," I reply.

"Wedding! Ha!" Mimi shouts. "How about the wedding cake in the form of a big giant pizza? And all the groomsmen carry Tommy guns and smoke stogies and …"

"Mimi, please," I protest. "I'm tired, it's late … and I'm not getting married to him."

"He's I-talian, ain't he?" she says and reaches for her pack of cigarettes. Sandra coughs in protest.

"Ah, the little one. I remember. 'Fraid some growth might get stunted, I know," she says and carries herself and her pack outside. "You're gonna marry him," she shouts from behind the sliding glass door. "Little I-talians running around. Guido, Paulie, Mussolini."

"Mimi, please!" I shout back to her. "I'm not marrying him."

"Not yet, anyway," Sandra says as she rocks her child back and forth.

"Nick's nice and all. At least he seems to be," Mom says. "But Walt … I just wish Walt was …" She pauses.

"Wish Walt was … what?" I ask.

"He was such a nice boy. He treated you like a queen," she finishes. "He just got scared is all. Maybe you should try it again with him."

"Face it, Mom. He's never coming back," I say.

"Before you get involved with this Nick boy I just wish maybe you'd find yourself again. You know, get your college degree, make a life for yourself for once," Mom says.

"Excuse me? I don't get this, Mom. Six months ago you couldn't wait for me to get married and out of the house. Now you want me to wait? I don't understand. Since when did you start siding with Daddy."

"You need to figure out who you are. I never got a chance to do that," Mom explains. "Now that I'm working, I'm just finding out that there's a lot more to me than toilet brushes and dirty laundry. I think you're on the rebound. Besides, all Nick's seen is …" She stops.

"Go ahead, Mom, say it. All he's seen is a what? A fat ugly girl with a hideous scar. What if this is all there is, Mom? I don't know what he sees in me. I'm thirty years old. I'm tired of running away from myself."

She hangs her head, shakes it, then rises up again. "It just seems to me that you're getting involved with this boy for all the wrong reasons. You're still recovering. You're dependent. You can't support yourself and you're latching on to the first boy who will take you away from home."

"Isn't that what you did, Mom?"

"Well, no, there were other boys," she says.

"You were barely eighteen. Eighteen, Mom, and Daddy was a freshman in college and you had just graduated high school."

"We had known each other all of our lives," she protests.

"And that made it better? Mom, you couldn't wait to get out of the house. I've been in and out of the house more times than I dare to count. If it's so bad, then why the hell do I keep coming back? I've been failing my whole life on other people's suggestions. Let me at least fail on my own, okay?" I plead. "At least Nick sees me. I don't even see me anymore."

Sandra's child begins to wail. "She's learning early," Sandra says. "Yes, sweetheart," she says to the little one. "Men will do this to you. Because they're scum."

"Then why do you all keep coming back for more?" Mimi asks as she takes her seat at the table again. "You don't see me crappin' in my own bed, do you?"

"Not all of us have a pension or a hefty insurance policy to fall back on?" I say.

"Is that all you even date for?" Mimi asks. "You're a smart girl, Kel. You don't need some dumb man to look after you. Learn from Sandra's example. Men are only good for one thing. Lousin' up your life."

"My life's not bad. I wanted this child," Sandra protests. "Men aren't scum for everybody. Just for me."

"It's like I always said about marriage. It's a lot like pizza ..."

"Mom, please," I protest.

"Kelly's got that I-talian pizza part down then," Mimi says.

I wish he was the real thing, I think to myself. I'm so damn tired of sampling flavors.

*   *   *   *

I look into the mirror. I don't get what Nick sees in me. I only see what Walt doesn't, the shell of what used to be a relatively attractive girl who used to fit into a size six. Now I'm thankful that tens fit. And as for this scar ... Geez, even I'm repulsed by it. A damn bag. I'm a bag lady, now. A helpless, homeless bag lady.

I sit on the edge of the bed at seven-thirty, on a Friday night. I could have had a date with Nick. I need some time to think.

So here I am. Alone. I turn the television set on and automatically turn it onto The Weather Channel. It's sixty-three and partly cloudy in Memphis, Tennessee. It's eighty-four and clear in Phoenix. No major weather systems to entertain me with tonight. Bob is not on location and nobody cares about the weather in Europe. Not even me.

As I turn the channel to something more interesting, the doorbell rings.

"Can you get that, Kelly?," Mom shouts from the kitchen. "I'm baking cookies right now."

"Sure," I answer back. I toss the remote on the bed. "I don't know why you're baking those things. Nobody's going to eat them. It's just the two of us," I say to Mom as I cross to the front door and flick on the porch light.

"You never know who'll drop by," Mom shouts back.

"Expecting the vacuum cleaner salesman, huh?" I joke as I look into the peephole. It's just Walt. Just Walt. Walt …

I reach for the doorknob, and it registers in my brain who is actually standing on the porch. My heart beats faster. The doorbell rings again.

"Kelly, answer the door," Mom calls out.

"Mom!" I yell between my teeth and open the door.

"Hi, Kelly," Walt says. He offers me a bouquet of wrapped pink roses, my favorite. "How are you doing?"

"I'm doing very well, thank you," I say. I take the bouquet, and then step away from him.

"You look good," he says.

"You, too."

"I missed you," he admits.

"I, uh, I …"

"You can tell me to go. I'm the worst heel in the world. I know," he says. "But I was stupid. And wrong. And I miss you."

I start to cry. "I miss you, too," I say. He takes me into his arms and hugs me close.

"Can I come in?" he finally asks.

"Oh my gosh. Yes. Come in," I tell him. I sniff the roses. They smell divine even if they are slightly wilted.

"Hi, Mrs. Carmichael," Walt says. "I thought I smelled your cookies at the door."

"Oatmeal raisin. Your favorite," she says.

*   *   *   *

"Kelly. Kelly," Walt says as he taps on my bedroom door and opens it a little bit. "Can I come in?" he whispers.

"Sure," I say. He looks so good. Better, actually. I think he's been working out a little. The hurt which he caused me has faded away with his touch.

"You look really good," he says to me as he caresses my arm and my hand. "You really are beautiful, Kel. You always have been. It took a lot of courage for you to go through that illness and surgery like you did, and I was a real son-of-a-bitch to you."

"It's okay. It's over," I tell him.

"No. I gotta say it," he insists. "I was so wrong. I've missed you terribly all these months. I sat there in the living room with Bosco and I knew I needed you."

"I knew there had to be a reason for the cookies. Since Dad died, she doesn't cook like she used to. Funny. She's become a lot like me."

"That's not so bad, is it?"

"I don't know. I guess not," I answer him. "It's just that I would have thought you had them lining up at the door."

"What do you mean?"

"Dates," I say and jokingly slap him on the side. "You've got all those girls in Memphis to choose from. Why would you possibly choose me?"

"Because I love you, Kelly," he says. He gets down on his knees and takes my hands into his. "I didn't realize how much I missed your sense of humor, your touch, your smell, your laugh, your intellect until I didn't have it anymore. I want to take care of you. I want to love you. I want to spend the rest of my life with you." He lets go of my hands and reaches into his jean pocket. "I want you to marry me." He pulls a gold ring from his pocket. On top of the band sits at least a one-carat diamond surrounded by a swirl of baggettes. It's absolutely the most beautiful ring I've ever seen. "Kelly, will you be my wife?"

He places the ring on my finger. Oh my God. He wants me to be his wife. *He wants me to be his wife.*

*   *   *   *

I don't care that it's my childhood bed. I don't care that my mother is a living room and hall away from me. I know that she would approve with a band of gold around my finger. I don't care about anything right now. I'm engaged and about to make love to my fiancé. Fiancé.

He slowly unbuttons my shirt and I unbutton his. He removes his jeans and I pull my drawstring cargo pants off. He gently lays me down on the bed and kisses me deeply. It's been so long since I felt like a real woman, sexy and passionate. I completely give myself to him and relax as he removes my bra. He even touches my scar. He smiles at me, kisses me and caresses my breasts. I remove my full cut cotton "grandma" panties. My bag is close to empty. It sloshes and falls between my legs. It's a part of me now. I try not to think about how it looks or sounds. It sounds normal to me.

Walt's hand moves down my stomach. It suddenly stops at the bag. He pulls his hand back. I take his hand and put it back. He hesitates. "Don't you need to remove that or something? Put it away for a while."

"I can't. It's a part of me," I tell him and continue to kiss him. "Just flick it out of the way."

He pulls back from me. "Just move it so I can …"

I look down at the bag between my legs. "You do it."

"No. That's okay. I might hurt you or something."

"You can't hurt me. It's only a plastic bag," I tell him. "Go ahead."

"I can't."

"Sure you can. Just take it and move it to the side. It's not that hard," I say.

He reaches for the bag, touches it, then puts his hands on my shoulders. "You do it."

I pull away from him. I take hold of the bag and squeeze it. I fondle it in front of him. He turns away. "It's a part of me, Walt. I could have had the other operation and not had this thing sticking out of my stomach but I didn't. I chose the bag. It didn't seem like it would be as much trouble. Maybe that was the wrong decision. Maybe I should have gone for the reconnect. But I didn't. I chose the bag. Now I have to live with that decision. If you love me, you have to love the bag, too. You have to touch it. You have to move it away. If you can't do that, then you don't want me."

He looks at the bag again then looks away. "You've just got to give me a little time to get used to it. That's all," he says. "It's … it's … different than what I expected. You know … It's not you. I just need some time, I guess."

"Sure. I understand," I lie.

He kisses me on the forehead and retreats toward the guest room. "I really do love you," he says, his eyes intent on my face.

I realize I'm completely naked, except for the ring on my finger. I pull the sheet up around me. "I know you do."

He closes the door behind him.

*   *   *   *

I wake up bright and early the next morning. I shower and put on the nicest outfit I can. For the first time in a long time I feel as though I look more like myself. More like the Kelly that Walt fell in love with. The package looks almost the same. Almost. I feel determined to show him what he'll be missing.

I leave the comfort of my room and there in the kitchen are Mom and Walt. She seems so happy. She laughs. He laughs. I don't want to spoil the moment.

They see me anyway.

"Come sit down," Mom says. "I'm making scrambled eggs."

I take a seat at the table across from Walt. Mom eagerly picks up the coffee pot to fill Walt's cup and brings me one. I take the mug from her hand. Then I realize I'm still wearing the engagement ring. I feel it tighten around my finger.

"Is that what I think that is?" she asks with a smile. "Oh, my. See, Kelly. Love is blind. You can't shut it out," she says. "I'm so happy." She gives me a hug but I don't return it. I simply stare at Walt and he returns the look.

"Funny. Love wasn't blind last night," I say.

"Kelly, please. Don't start right now," he says.

"Start what?" Mom asks. "When are we setting the date?"

"I told you I need some time," he tells me.

"I gave you all those months. Not one word. Then all of a sudden you want to marry me. Then you need some time again."

"When your Mom called me and said you'd healed, I thought she meant it."

"What are talking about? Mom? What's he talking about?"

"I don't know," she says. She turns and begins to crack eggs into a bowl. "So I called him. You're wearing his ring now. Everything's wonderful. Let's have some eggs."

"I thought you'd be the old you," Walt says. "Now you're just ..."

"What? Some old bag?" I ask him.

"You know what I mean."

"No, Walt. I don't know what you mean?"

"What do you mean?" Mom chimes in. "You're supposed to be happy. Engagements are supposed to be happy."

"You expect me to waltz in and make love to you last night like everything's wonderful. I'm sorry. Until you do something with the bag, I can't handle it."

Suddenly an egg hits Walt on the side of the face. I didn't throw it.

"What the …"

"That bag is there for you," Mom begins. "She did that for you. She went through bloody hell for you. What do you mean you can't handle the bag?" Mom demands.

"You threw an egg at me," he says and wipes the yolk and shell from his face.

She throws another one at him. "And I did it again."

"Jesus," he shouts.

"I thought you were something special. Someone wonderful who would take care of my daughter. I'm sorry I called you."

"I'm sorry, too," he says. "This is a nice shirt."

Mom hurls the whole carton at him.

I pull the ring from my finger. It scrapes my knuckle as it slowly slides off. I take his hand in mine, turn his palm up and place the ring in his egg-filled hand.

*   *   *   *

Nick's truck rides rough over the old brick street of downtown Spivey. We pass his law office in the old post office, then round the corner and park by the fountain. The water sparkles and shimmers at night.

I reach down to pick up my purse and spot a shiny penny on the floorboard. I pick it up and examine it. It's my birthday penny!

"You should make a wish in the fountain, huh?" Nick asks.

"Yeah, I will," I say and smile at him. We walk over to the fountain. Nick pulls a coin from his jean pocket. He rolls it around in his fingers, closes his eyes, then flicks it into the water.

"What did you wish for?" I ask.

"Now you know I can't tell you that," he replies.

I hold the shiny penny tightly in my hand. I think hard about what I want to wish for as if this were the last wish I will ever have again. I place the coin between my fingers, close my eyes tightly and fling the penny into the fountain. It makes a tiny splash and quickly sinks to the bottom to become intermingled with all the other coins in the fountain.

"So what did you wish for?" Nick prods me. "Something big ticket, huh? Like a car or the sweepstakes?"

"No," I reply. "For the first time in my life, no. I didn't."

"I hope you didn't waste it," Nick warns. "Wishes come true, you know."

"I know."

He takes me by the hand as we walk toward the Whitehouse on our date. He smiles at me. It makes me feel warm and wonderful.

I look up at the stars and the moon in the cloudless sky. I take in a deep breath. The air is still and the temperature is just right. A perfect night. Just like the Weather Channel said it would be.

"Come on. What'd ya wish for?" he prods me.

"I can't tell you. All I can tell you is that I wished for someone else's wish to come true."

"And do you think it will?"

I remember Daddy's wish for me. To be happy. I smile up at him. "It's in the bag."

The End

About the Author

Photo credit: Rob Blackmon

Tracy Lea Carnes received her ileostomy on October 1, 1993, the day after her 30th birthday, after a long battle with ulcerative colitis. She stays active by cycling, hiking, scuba diving, sailing, playing golf, playing rugby, rollerblading, and has recently even learned the flying trapeze. She resides in Shreveport, Louisiana with her beloved cat, Spot.

A portion of the proceeds from this novel go to support the United Ostomy Associations of America (UOAA) 30+ Network. (thirtyplusnetwork.org.)

978-0-595-47744-9
0-595-47744-5